An Evening at the Beach

James Ward

COOL MILLENNIUM BOOKS

4

This is a work of fiction. All names, characters, and events are the product of the author's imagination, or used fictitiously. All resemblance to actual events, places, events or persons, living or dead, is entirely coincidental.

First published in 2012.
This edition 2021.

A CIP catalogue record for this book is available from the British Library.

ISBN: 978-1-913851-52-1

This novel was produced in the UK and uses British-English language conventions ('authorise' instead of 'authorize', 'The government are' instead of 'the government is', etc.)

To my wife

Abraham said, "I pray thee not to be angry, O Lord, if I speak just once more: suppose ten men can be found there?" God said, "For the sake of the ten I will not destroy it."
Genesis 18.32

Contents

DOG HOSTELLING

When Marge finally decided to reveal her best ever idea, she was leaning against the doorframe in her pyjamas, holding a cigarette between her fingers, and the ashtray beneath it. Mike wore his boxers and a T-shirt with 'I am most definitely not with her' on. He scratched his right ear, sipped his tea and doubled his newspaper back on itself so he could get a closer look at the actress emerging from the courtroom. On the table stood a toast rack, a plate with two buttery knives and a bowl with milk at the bottom and a cornflake on the rim.

"You know the other day," she said, "when we were talking about starting a business, and you said, 'I'd like to open a betting shop where Josie's used to be', and I said, 'No, why don't we get a bank loan and make Josie's a flower shop', and you were like, 'There's already a flower shop in the village', and we started to try and think of what had never been done so we could do it before anyone else, and maybe patent our idea, but then we couldn't think of anything?"

Mike folded the page and held it up. "Look at her. That's Lindsay Lohan. Look at her."

"Well, I've thought of something." She came and sat opposite him. She put the ashtray down, sucked her cigarette then stubbed it out. "We could open a dog hostel."

"A what?"

"A dog hostel."

"What? Like a place for stray dogs?"

She whooped with delight, clapped and turned her whole body to the door. *"Hear that, Johnny? He just said, 'A place for stray dogs'! Parp the bloody horn, Johnny!"*

Two loud honks came from the dining room. Mike stood up and bowed to the right and left and sat down again. He unfolded the paper, turned the page and read about an armed robbery. Marge went to the fridge where the scoreboard was. Beneath 'Week beg.

7

3/4', their names were in two columns. Three strokes under Marge's and two under Mike's. Marge added another under Mike's. "Fourteen hours left."

"Even Stevens now," he said.

"I meant, you know like in a youth hostel, you've got all these houses in different parts of the country, and young people and sometimes older – any age, really: whatever time of life – go and stay at one for a night or so, then they walk on to another and so on until they've done about ten in a fortnight, then they go home and that was their holiday?"

"I know what a youth hostel is."

"Well, you know how people with dogs sometimes find it hard to get anywhere to stay because people don't like dogs?"

"Don't they let dogs in youth hostels, then?"

"I wouldn't have thought so. What if they savage someone?"

He shrugged.

"Anyway, it is, isn't it?" she said. "It's hard to get somewhere when you've got a dog. Look at when Beezer was alive. We couldn't even *go* on holiday that year."

"Yeah, but that was bloody Rhodes. That's abroad."

"You know what I mean, though. And there's the doings. No one wants dog doings."

"So what are you saying? We should buy like ten or twelve houses in different parts of the country and dogs would come and stay in each for a night, then they'd walk to another, then they'd walk to another until they'd done all whatever number, then someone, their owner, would come and pick them up and give us some money?"

"We'd take the money in advance."

"What if the dogs got lost?"

"They wouldn't come on their *own*, Mike! God help us! – Johnny! *Johnny!*"

"*What?*" came a voice from the living room.

"*Your dad's just said, 'What if the dogs got lost?', like as if they'd come on their own!*"

There was a roar of laughter from the living room and two parps of a horn.

"That doesn't count," said Mike.

"No, the owners would bring their dogs with them, and we'd have six rooms, say, with bunk beds in, but they wouldn't be normal bunk beds. What they'd be is like each compartment, where you put your sleeping bag, would have a door on, and the owner would sleep in there with their dog, and they'd close the door at night to stop the dog getting out and fighting with other dogs, and inside each compartment, we'd have a little light and a buzzer-thing, and in the morning, one by one, we'd switch on the lights and sound the buzzers and that would tell each owner the coast was clear for the next ten minutes, till we woke the next owner up that is, and that they could come out with their dog and get dressed and showered and there'd be no risk of their dog getting in a fight."

"Doesn't give them much of a window though, does it?"

"What? Anyone can get dressed and showered in ten minutes. I can."

"Marjorie Burns, you bloody can *not!*"

"I bloody can."

"Oho, so you're the world record holder? Because you'd have to be to get out of bed and get in the shower and get dressed in ten minutes. Anyway, you're a woman. You don't have to shave."

"Even if I did, and I'm not saying I don't, I wouldn't shave if I was on holiday, would I?"

"Yeah, okay. What if there's a fire and someone can't get the door to their bunk bed compartment-thing open?"

"Now you're just making up problems."

"That's not a made up one."

She donned her making-fun-of-Mike face and an affectedly whiny voice. "'What if a spaceship comes and all the dogs are beamed aboard and their owners are killed by green jelly things with ray-guns?'"

"Yeah, but that couldn't happen," he replied, unfazed, "but there actually could be a fire. The fire inspector's definitely going to come round and inspect the place – places – before we open them, and the first thing he's going to say is, 'What if there's a fire and someone's trapped in their bunk bed compartment?'"

"What if it's a she?"

"What?"

"The fire inspector. You said 'he'. It could be a she."

"I didn't. I said, 'they'."

"I'll say, 'One thing you haven't noticed about these bunk bed compartment doors, Mrs Inspector, is that they're fire doors.'"

"They're going to look fairly stupid then. The fire inspector, I mean."

"Yeah."

"What if - "

"Oh, bloody hell! What if, what if, what if!"

"I'm only trying to - "

"Yeah, but you can't just keep picking at the *details*, Mike! Pick, pick, pick. Those are *details.* Are we going to make the bunk bed doors out of pine or plywood? Are we going to get the showers from B&Q or Homebase? Are we going to give the guests ten minutes to get showered or twelve? Bloody hell, Mike. It's no wonder we're so poor when you're always like this!"

"Yeah, well one of us - "

She stood up wielding another cigarette. "Shut *up*, Mike! I've heard enough from you today. I'm only trying to help. Help the family. Guess what? I don't really *want* to open a dog hostel if the truth be known. I never thought when I was young, 'I know what I'll do when I'm older: I'll open a dog hostel'. Nobody in my class did. I'm doing it for *us*."

"I'm just trying to - "

"You're bloody lucky you're married to me, Michael Burns, that's all I'll say. I shouldn't think any other wives sit at home thinking of businesses to run. *You* bloody think of one if you're so bloody clever. Go on! You think of one. And it better not be a bloody betting shop, because we've been through that."

The noise of the television came from the living room. A studio audience booed then cheered. A car went by outside. Mike swept the toast crumbs into a pile and wet his index finger and put it in them and licked them off. When they were all gone he put his elbow on the table and settled his nose into his fist. He sighed. Marge picked up the paper.

"Where's Lindsay Lohan?" she said.

"Don't know. Somewhere in the front."

He put one of his bare feet on top of the other. He took his left fist from under his nose and put his right one there. There was another cheer from the living room, then a boo, then another boo, then a cheer.

"Sorry," he said.

"I wish I had a daughter like Lindsay Lohan."

"Maybe we could get a van."

"What?"

"With the dog hostel. It's just the owners, like because they're on holiday, they might not want to walk their dogs thirteen or fourteen miles to the next one. We could get a van and take their dogs there for them, and the owners could walk there and have a little mini-holiday away from their dogs."

"Oh, forget about the dog hostel. It was just an idea."

"No, it was a good idea."

"No, it wasn't. You know very well it wasn't."

"No, it was. It was a good idea."

"No, it wasn't."

"Call Johnny in," he said. "Let's ask Johnny. *Johnny, come in here!*"

"Don't call Johnny in. Leave him be."

Johnny was twenty-five with a beard and a ponytail. He wore furry monster slippers. He appeared at the kitchen door in his dressing gown carrying a plate. "What?" he said.

"Has your mum told you about the dog hostelling idea?" Mike asked.

"Yeah."

"What did you think?"

"Okay. I think you should call it dogging."

"*Johnny!*" Marge said. She turned to Mike for support. "I don't think that's very funny."

"It's crude," Mike said.

Johnny put his plate in the sink and left. They heard him run upstairs.

"I think we've upset him," Marge said.

"Yeah, but that was completely uncalled for."

"He means well. He was only joking."

"But even so. God help us."

Marge stubbed her cigarette out halfway through and put it on the side for later. "Ring his mobile. Tell him I'm making some Angel Delight and putting it in the fridge for him."

Mike reached for his mobile and dialled and waited. "Your mum's making some Angel Delight and putting it in the fridge," he said.

There was a pause as Johnny responded loudly.

Mike looked at Marge. "What flavour, he wants to know."

"Butterscotch," Marge said.

"Butterscotch … Yeah, bye. He says he'll be down in about an hour."

"Would you like to see the logo I drew?"

"What logo?" he said.

She shrugged bashfully. "For the dog hostels."

"Well … yeah. Please."

"I did it the other night when we got in from The Grey Lady."

"What, on Thursday? You were rat-arsed."

"How could I have drawn *this*, then?" She reached to the unit and picked up a copy of *Hello!* She flicked through it until she came to a piece of A4 lined paper she'd inserted for safe-keeping. It showed a dog's head with a long muzzle and a circular nose, grinning. "Da-dah! Not bad, eh?"

"What sort is it?"

"A Dachshund. Just its head."

"What, a sausage dog?"

"Yeah."

"Has Johnny seen it?"

"He said it was cool. It needs a bit of colour."

As she reached to take it back, she knocked the cornflakes bowl off the table. It hit the floor and smashed.

They looked at it and at each other.

A cheer came from the TV in the living room, then a boo. Marge put her logo back in *Hello!* and closed it. For a moment they thought they might never mention dog hostelling again.

But in the distance a pack of hounds set up barking. Marge and Mike withdrew into thought. Neither could remember anything similar before, not that many dogs all at once. Their eyes met significantly and each knew what the other was thinking.

A sign.

TWO ROOMS AT THE ELITE

The first question people always ask is, why was Colonel Albright at The Elite at all? Everyone else had stopped going there years ago. More or less perched on a clifftop, *obviously* it was only a matter of time before it plummeted into the sea. Their second question is, why didn't the local council compel the owner to put up the shutters long before what happened, happened?

Well, let's begin with the colonel. I think he'd been a regular guest for so long that he'd stopped noticing how precarious the place was becoming. But I also believe he was one of those people whose habitual reaction to danger is to scoff. To stop coming to The Elite just because he might end up sliding into the Atlantic one day (accompanied by ten tons of rubble), probably struck him as the acme of cowardice.

On the plus side, it was close to his favourite golf course, and the guaranteed absence of other guests meant complete peace and quiet. Above all, it meant that the owner, Rosa Stein - a tall, straight-backed woman with dyed black hair, in a neat bun, and sharp eyes - would be completely devoted to him for the duration of his usual fortnight. He and she were almost certainly a little in love, in the infinitely subtle, incorporeal way old people sometimes are: love as a kind of recognition of the real imminence of death, and the sad fragility of all life on Earth. Occasionally, she invited him to her Friday evening meal, then he knew to cancel whatever else he'd planned. It meant she felt particularly lonely. She never spoke of herself, though, even after the Kiddush wine. He knew she'd once been a refugee from the Nazis, but apart from that, nothing.

As for the second question - why the council didn't close it - you'd probably need to begin with some knowledge of Rosa herself. She'd been through a lot in her long life, and forcibly evicting her now – even for her own safety - could easily become a PR disaster. Yes, clearly, something would have to be done about her at some stage, but all the experts agreed that The Elite's particular section of cliff had at least another five years' stability left in it.

And in some ways, she was an isolated problem: everyone else in the vicinity had long since retreated inland; nowadays, the next dwelling of any kind was two hundred metres away. Finally, she was old. Brutal though it sounds, I genuinely believe some members of the council hoped she would die before they had to bite the bullet and get her out. Five years might just do it.

In any case, one morning in mid-August, Colonel Albright was sitting alone in the lounge at the front of the hotel with his *Telegraph* and a packet of Dolly Mixtures when he heard what he thought was a Harrier jet fly by. He muttered his knee-jerk grumble about the bloody RAF and turned to the financial pages.

Over the next twenty minutes, the room became progressively colder. He got irritably to his feet and went to the radiator.

No problem there…

But then he noticed something else. The clock ticked sonorously on the mantelpiece but it was no longer the only sound in the room. A gale seemed to be blowing up outside. He went to the window and peered along the northern cliff edge but he could detect no visible signs of a wind: the oat grass beyond the garden wasn't even leaning; the seagulls rested languidly on the sky as if it was a pillow.

Mrs Stein was out shopping, so there was no point calling her. He opened the door to the corridor and found himself looking at … nothing.

Which he then realised was the *sky* and the *sea*. The rear corridor didn't exist anymore.

So, that had been no Harrier jet.

For a moment, he was frightened. Then he remembered, he was British: it didn't do to panic. If the rest of the hotel was going to collapse, so be it, but he'd looked death in the eye many times before now, and he'd long since outlived his allotted threescore years and ten.

But then he remembered something else. The missing bit of the hotel had his new golf clubs in.

No point in crying over spilt milk, though. He found his shoes, pulled on his sports jacket and walked outside. The sun shone, though it was cold for the time of year. From the side on, the hotel looked as if it had been sliced almost exactly in half. Going by what he could make out, the TV room had gone, the two back bedrooms, the storage cupboards and the 'pantry'. That still left the two front bedrooms - his and Rosa's - the lounge, and the kitchen.

Which was academic, really, apart from what was in there to be saved.

He walked in a quarter circle to the front of the building. From here, The Elite looked entirely intact, as if nothing whatsoever had happened. Amazing really, and slightly disturbing. Like a bad dream.

As far as he could tell, no one was coming to investigate. Presumably, no one farther inland could see anything had occurred. Most people never ventured too far away from their own homes anyway.

He hoped no one had been down on the rocks at the time of the collapse. But no: the tide was in.

And he and Rosa were unharmed. All in all, it could have been an awful lot worse.

Rosa Stein was in town buying challah loaves. When she returned, two hours later, she found the colonel standing alone on her lawn with his hands in his pockets. Their eyes met. He wet his index finger and smoothed his moustache - a nervous habit he'd been in since his first stay twenty years ago.

"What's the matter?" she asked.

He took her to the side of the building. Her mouth fell open. She dropped her shopping bags and sat on the grass as if she couldn't trust her legs to keep her upright.

He got down next to her and put his arm round her. They stayed that way for thirty minutes, not speaking, then she burst into tears.

"It could have been worse," he said.

She went straight from crying to laughing. She wiped her eyes roughly. "I've just had a thought. Your new golf clubs."

He gave a dismissive grimace. "Pah!"

"The tide will have gone out by now. We should go and look for them."

"They're only golf clubs! I've got others, and even if I hadn't - "

"I need to do something mechanical. Just indulge me, please."

"You're in shock."

"Aren't *you?*"

He stopped and turned to face her. He let out a flute of air. "Actually, yes."

They made their way down to the beach by means of an overgrown footpath, thrusting the nettles, gorse and brambles aside with switches snapped from an elder tree. A skylark sang overhead. The sun was warmer lower down. A nice day for a catastrophe, he thought. It should have been driving rain, pounding waves.

Half an hour later, they stood on a patch of shingle looking into a rock pool. To all appearances, the golf clubs had vanished.

"You'd think they'd just sink and stay put," he said.

"The tide's very strong. People underestimate it."

He looked up at where the back of the hotel used to be. "Quite."

She wiped her eyes again. They re-focussed on the search. The rocks were slippery with sea lettuce, and the bigger pool surfaces were ruffled by the breeze, making them difficult to see into. A herring gull hovered noiselessly overhead.

"Should we be looking for anything else besides?" he asked. "Wasn't there anything of yours in that part of the hotel?"

She shrugged. "A few photographs. Memorabilia. My late husband's things, a few of them. Nothing I'm expecting to find."

"Good God, Rosa. And we're hunting for bloody *golf clubs?*" He saw immediately he'd blundered into too-personal territory, so he clicked his tongue and changed the subject. "You must have known this might happen, mustn't you?"

"Someday, maybe. Not today. Didn't you?"

"I, er, realised it was a possibility."

"So why did you keep coming back?"

"You put excellent food on the table punctually, you exterminate dust and creases without mercy. And we've had some jolly good times."

She raised her eyebrows. "Really."

"The time your kitchen nearly caught fire and I had to re-paint the wall before the safety inspector came? That day we watched an entire oak fall into the sea five hundred yards upshore? That oil spillage, rescuing those cormorants - "

She scoffed and cut him off. "Happy days, yes."

"What will you do now?"

"Probably live in the remains until the council re-house me."

"'The remains'? You mean, in the front half of the hotel?"

"For the time being. There are still stairs."

"What about gas and electricity?"

"I'll call the supplier in the morning. I can be very persuasive."

He stood arms akimbo, and his eyebrows came together, locking his gaze on her. "Look, this might not be the right time to bring it up, but ..."

"Go on."

"I booked for two weeks. This is only my second day."

She waved her hand. "I'll give you a full refund, minus the deposit."

"I wasn't - "

She laughed manically. "What am I saying? You're the best customer I ever had. What do I need your money for? You can have it *all* back."

"I don't want a refund."

"Then I fail to understand. Please come to the point."

"What I was going to say is, is it okay to see out the rest of the fortnight? My room's intact, and you'll still be cooking, presumably, if only for yourself."

She craned her neck forward as if to put her ears within better hearing. "You want to *stay?*"

"If it's not too much trouble."

She put her head on her shoulder and looked at him as if he was insane. Then something seemed to rise in her and she flooded with light.

The sun went behind a cloud and it rained for two hours. They trooped back the way they'd come and spent the next three hours raising the drawbridge. She filled the emergency generator in the alcove with diesel and hauled a portable stove and an ice-box upstairs. He boarded the windows so the panels couldn't be removed from outside, then went hurriedly into town and bought enough canned food, bottled water and digestives to last them a year. They locked the front door and fastened its five bolts. He had no idea why it had all become so serious so quickly until suddenly she caressed the wallpaper with trembling fingers and looked around herself and whispered, "I couldn't leave you". Then everything fell into place for him. She was one of those people who identified so strongly with her own dwelling that, over the years, it had become part of her. History, biography and masonry, all tied up in one inseparable package.

His room had a chair, TV, washbasin, bed and a dresser. Hers – identical in outlay – stood across the landing. A west-facing window gave a view of the heath, the distant hills and, on a clear day, the sunset. The far wall was cracked from top to bottom and, as far as either of them knew, rested on the cliff-edge with centimetres to spare. The floorboards were spongier than before and the wind whistled through the eaves as it hadn't when he'd arrived. In between their two rooms, the stairs led down to the bolted exit, and the living room where the carpets were now sodden. All the ceilings dripped. After six hours it was like living in the belly of a ghost.

Two days later, the world finally woke up to them. They were eating baked beans on buttered bread when the police pulled up in two cars and a van. Colonel Albright sat on the chair and Rosa sat on the edge of the bed, which sagged slightly. They could hear the ocean, but they couldn't see it.

They heard a helicopter roar overhead. They both experienced a frisson of fear, the sort of thing inhabitants of besieged cities must once have felt when their enemies unveiled a line of cannons.

They went to the window. It was midday. The sun glistened on the dry grass and four policemen marched towards them.

"What do you want?" she called.

They stopped. They wore yellow waistcoats over their uniforms. One of them pushed his hat back and grinned. "Isn't it a bit obvious? Are you injured, love? We're going to come in and get you, that all right? How long have you been there?"

The second one muttered something inaudible. He put his sleeve to his mouth to conceal a snigger.

"Nothing to worry about," the first went on. "We'll have you outside in no time. Just don't move till we say, that's all."

"The front door's locked," she said, "and you don't have my permission to enter."

"What?"

"You can't force us to leave," she went on. "We're staying."

He laughed again, nervously this time. "The whole bloody place could collapse any minute. How many of you are there?"

Colonel Albright leaned out of the window. "Just two."

The policeman shook his head. The smile dropped from his face and he turned to his colleagues. "Bloody, *bloody* hell. Fantastic."

"Don't get any ideas about battering the door down," Rosa continued. "You'll knock us into oblivion. And don't try to cut your way in. We won't go without a struggle and that'll make for a topple too. Or we'll have heart attacks, we're both in our eighties."

The policeman spread his hands. He did a quarter-turn of exasperation, then turned back to face Rosa. "What the hell do you want then?"

"To be left alone," she snapped. She slammed the casement.

She and the colonel watched the policeman turn his back and get his radio out. All four officers began to saunter away. Colonel Albright sighed.

"You don't have to stay here," she said tetchily.

He interlaced his fingers and spoke without looking at her. "What are we holding out for?"

"I don't know," she said. "Nothing."

A megaphone squeaked. *"This is the police."*

"We must be holding out for something. What are our demands?"

"Like I said," she replied, "I honestly hadn't thought about it."

"It's conventional to ask for *something*. You refuse to budge until they accede to your demands."

"I know."

"So? What sort of a new house do you want?"

"I don't want a new house," she replied.

"For your own safety, we must insist that you leave the building immediately."

The colonel leaned back. "It would have to be a council house, of course, given that you're technically destitute. But there must be better and worse areas."

19

"I've just said: I don't want a new house."

"Your bargaining power remains good only so long as we can stay here."

"I know."

"We're tempting providence."

"You are in grave danger. Repeat …"

She stacked their plates. "Like I said, you don't have to stay here."

"It's you I'm thinking about. I'm tip-top."

Her eyes filled with water and she put the plates down. "I - I don't want to leave it while one brick remains standing on another. That's all I know."

They sat in silence for a few moments. "Irrational, but not incomprehensible," he said at last.

"And very risky. I think you should go."

"If you do not leave the building of your own free will, we will be forced to take measures to compel you to do so. Repeat: you are in grave danger. If you do not leave now …"

"Even if I wanted to go," he said, "which I don't, I'd have to open the front door. And that would be the end of you here too."

"Ah." She nodded. "Yes."

"Nevertheless, I must admit, I'm anxious."

"I'll know when it's time to go," she said. "I won't let us die. I'll know."

He leaned forward indulgently. "How?"

"Because – because I – I realise this is going to sound insane – I know this house."

He chuckled and pressed her hands between his. "Let's hope so. Well, I won't leave you, Rosa, whatever."

"I found my photos," she said quietly. She placed a thick envelope on the table and coloured. "I've – I've brought them over to show you. If … you're interested?"

He beamed. "I'd rather hoped we'd swap life-stories someday. Fire away then."

She took out a picture and passed it. "This is me when I was a girl."

"Very pretty. Gosh."

"Nineteen forty-three. That's my mother and father and that's my brother. We'd just arrived in Palestine."

He smiled. "I was in North Africa in forty-three. Eighth Army."

The police cordoned off the area around the house while they took counsel. Two hours later, tents arrived to the south of the perimeter, occupied by well-wishers, voyeurs and a folk band. To the north, ten caravans and two lorry loads of recording equipment became the media village. Every evening at six and ten, the colonel and Rosa Stein sat side-by-side and watched a new episode of themselves on the fuzzy TV powered by the generator.

On Friday evening, however, matters came to a head. The Met Office issued a severe weather warning for the northwest coast. Gale force winds were due to hit the mainland at eleven and the consensus was that The Elite couldn't outlast the buffeting. The Home Secretary called an emergency session of the Civil Contingencies Committee. BBC News 24 broadcast live updates every twenty minutes. Congregations said prayers.

"I feel terrible about the fuss we're causing," Rosa said, getting up and switching off the TV. She sat down and ran her hands through her hair. "But it'll be over soon."

"One way or another. Takes me back to the war, actually. Never knew whether today might be your last look at the sky."

"It's too late to turn back now. We'll be okay. Trust me."

He smiled weakly. She took a pair of challah loaves from a bag and lit two candles which she stood on the dressing table. She covered the bread with a cloth and poured two glasses of wine and switched off the light. She said the Friday evening prayers standing up, and they ate and drank without speaking. Then she left him, to go to her room.

As he lay in bed, unable to sleep, he realised he was no longer just anxious, but actually scared. He could hear the wind building in power, the sea swelling. The floorboards creaked of their own accord. He'd left the curtains open, hoping to look at the stars, like he had in the army. But there was such a glare from the floodlights on the heath that the sky was invisible.

Was she mentally unbalanced? Perhaps. He'd read books where people came to identify with their homes – and vice-versa. The House of Usher, Hill House, Macondo. The way she kept stroking the walls and mumbling when she thought he wasn't looking. Not that it mattered. He'd vowed not to leave her and he meant it. Which probably meant that, sometime tonight, they were going to die.

On the plus side, it would be quick. A two-hundred-foot drop followed by ten tons of debris, they wouldn't know anything. The anticipation was worst.

Suddenly, the glare outside disappeared. He saw Ursa Major and he knew he was dreaming. He was a boy and it was sunrise. He was standing six miles back from the cliff edge in the middle of an impossibly long field. He began to run towards the sea, and as he ran, he got older and older, and the day raced. When he reached the place where The Elite stood, it was vacant: no building at all, just grass. It was sunset now, he was eighty-something and, without stopping, he threw himself off the ledge. He expected to plummet, but he flew. He felt euphoric.

He heard a knock at his bedroom door. He sat up. The door opened. Rosa stood in her dressing gown, holding one of her Shabbat candles. She looked imperious.

"Time to get dressed," she said. "It's finished."

He blinked hard and pretended to bide his time, as if it was a matter of indifference. "Where's my jacket?"

"Never mind, we haven't time."

He slipped his brogues onto his bare feet. "Ladies first."

She didn't move. They stood looking at each other for a minute, the candlelight accentuating every wrinkle and liver spot. "Remember the other day," she said softly. "You said I might be able to get a council house?"

"You can depend on it."

Her voice cracked. "Would you come and visit me there?"

He nodded and kissed her cheek. So she really liked him, after all. If he died now, it probably didn't matter.

Anyway, if they made it, he might even be able to persuade her to come and live near him. By some miracle, the future was ajar – just slightly – in a way he'd long thought it would never be again.

"Hold my hand, Colonel Albright."

They walked calmly downstairs. Her candle looked like a tiny, bobbing fairy. Outside, he could hear the storm, waves pounding the cliff like they were enraged. She removed the bolts and flung the door open. They stepped into the gale and a blinding light.

Behind them, the earth shuddered. They sensed The Elite falling to its knees and vanishing downwards into the void. Yet all they could see and hear were people advancing in numbers with emotional yells.

Suddenly they were being wrapped in blankets, umbrellas were being held over them, arms were embracing them. Someone in the distance let off a firework and the sky filled with a starburst. Rosa Stein clutched the colonel and wept.

"Tell them you want a mansion," he whispered in her ear.

BECAUSE YOU'RE SPECIAL

Moira and Audrey watched surreptitiously from the *Amunoso* stall as a middle-aged woman slipped greetings cards into her shopping bag. Theirs was one of six glass battleships displaying branded perfumes, creams and other gift ideas, lit from beneath, and manned by women in uniforms of skirt-suits, silk scarves, court shoes and heavy make-up. Except for those serving customers, they were all looking the same way.

Clive, the store detective, leaned by the escalator, disguised in a jumper, chinos and loafers. He pretended to examine a Father's Day card, but he was rapt too.

Moira adjusted her tights through her skirt. "Poor thing. Trapped as a bird in a box. Look at her."

"No one could want that many greetings cards. She'd have to sell them on."

"It's not about that, Audrey. It's about the sensation of stealing. I did Psychology."

"Really? When?"

"Five years ago now. Sixth form."

Moira was tall with blonde hair and blue eyes. Audrey was short with black hair and brown eyes. They prided themselves on being able to cater to all ranges of customers.

"I wonder if she knows Clive's watching her," Audrey said.

"Probably. They often do."

"I wonder when he'll make his move."

"He has to wait till she's left. Technically, she hasn't stolen anything yet."

"She might put it all back for all we know."

"Exactly. She might even go to one of the tills and buy it."

"I don't think so."

"Nor me."

"Poor thing."

"Mm."

The woman grabbed a clutch of birthday cards and thrust them into her bag. She was about forty, with small hands poking out of her overcoat. Her firm mouth and level eyes suggested she knew what she was doing, but the heaviness of her brows and jowls intimated too much loss and worry to care. She stepped back and examined a christening card. Then put it in her bag.

Sheila from *Chanson* next door sidled up and nodded in her direction. "Gloria says, watch that." Then she scuttled away.

"Unbelievable," Moira said, as she watched her go.

Audrey nodded. Gloria and Sheila hadn't an ounce of compassion. All they cared about were sales.

"I don't get it," Audrey said. "If Clive knows she's shoplifting, and he can't stop her till she's out of the shop, why can't he just go up to her now? Why can't he just tell her he knows what she's doing, and please could she put it all back?"

"I'd never really thought about it like that. Maybe he's got to get a certain number of 'kills' under his belt to justify the store employing him."

"But ... but that's awful."

"That's why some of them – store detectives, I mean – plant stuff on customers. The customer walks out of the store, not knowing. Then the store detective grabs them, and gets a pat on the back from the manager. So they say. I don't know."

"I might go up and tell her," Audrey said.

"Don't!"

"Why not?"

"You'll lose your job!"

"They can't sack me for that."

"Oh, really?" Moira said. "What union are you in, then?"

"Union? No union."

Moira smiled. "Audrey, we're just a pair of drones as far as the management's concerned. They can sack us for anything they want, whenever they like. Anyway, it might be for her own good."

"Pardon?"

"She obviously wants to be caught. Look at her."

She had moved over to Footwear. She picked up a T-bar sandal, slipped it into her bag and went to a pair of pixie boots.

"The chutzpah," Moira said.

"It's heartbreaking. No one in their right mind does that. She must have gone wrong somewhere. Something must have happened to her."

"It's not our problem. Sorry, it isn't. How long do you expect to work at Haight and Johnson, Audrey? If it's any real length of time, you're going to see lots of shoplifters. You can't intervene with all of them. We're here to sell perfume."

"I can't bear just standing here, watching Clive getting ready to pounce."

Moira chuckled. "Most women in this store would give their eye teeth to stand and watch Clive. Some of them, all day long. Look at Gloria: her tongue's hanging out. And Stella – look at Stella. Incidentally, he fancies you, you know. Did you know that? Clive? That ought to cheer you up."

"Well, it doesn't."

Audrey had never noticed before: she and Moira were quite different. Moira could distance herself from this sort of thing. Clive too, presumably. No, she didn't fancy Clive at all. Why would she? With his slavering mouth, intent on a professional conquest. No, she wouldn't want to kiss that or go anywhere near it.

"Don't be too hard on Clive," Moira said. "He's being watched too."

"You mean, by Gloria and Stella?"

"By the in-store cameras, silly. He's being videoed just as much as she is. If he meant to go and tell her to put it all back, he probably should have done so at the start. If he does it at this point, Mr Thompson is going to be like, 'Why did you wait so long, Clive?' Don't you see? She's passed the point of no return now, as far as he's concerned. If he - oh my God, she's coming over!"

Moira raced behind the counter and looked at her own shoes.

Audrey hesitated and stood her ground. *Offer her one of the free samples.* Yes, yes, good idea. Then, while she was diverted, she could... take her bag? ... and put it behind the counter? – yes, while she wasn't looking! – And Moira could take out all the stolen items, yes! Then they'd have to get her out of the store. Somehow. Or – tell her she'd been spotted. Implore her to put the things back, to –

"Excuse me, Madam," she said. "Would you like a free sample?"

The woman looked at her as if there was a thick pane of glass between them. Her eyes were glazed. She smelt of alcohol. She smiled, but didn't stop.

Audrey cleared her throat. Maybe raise her voice, just a notch? *"Excuse me, would you like a ..."*

The woman passed. Their eyes met and Audrey disintegrated. Despite the woman's smile, the only thing there was misery and despair.

She'd missed her only chance. She should have spoken much louder, used her arms, interposed her body -

Moira shimmied back into existence. *"What the hell were you doing?* We don't want her stopping *here.* Did you *smell* her?"

"I was just trying to help!"

"For God's sake, just *mind your own business!"*

The woman turned right and back to Greetings Cards. She put more birthday cards in her bag. She wiped her nose with her index finger, then rubbed her eyes.

"Look," Moira said, "be sensible about this. What's the worst that can happen? She's a genuine saddo, anyone can see that. Clive's going to grab her; she's in no state to run or struggle. Then he'll get a commendation, or whatever it is store detectives get when they nab someone. And she'll get away with a caution probably, then she'll probably get counselling or some sort of therapy. If we help her get away, we're not necessarily doing her a favour. She won't get *any* help then. She'll be on her own. We've agreed she's an attention seeker. Just let her have the attention."

Common sense. But somehow it made it even more horrible. An indictment of the woman for submitting, the world for standing back, the store for its voyeurism. Audrey flushed. She wanted to take her scarf off and sit down with a glass of water.

The woman drifted back to the shoe section. She stumbled and fell down with a slap. An elderly couple sharing a wicker basket came to help her. They fussed over her, talked to her, set her going again and walked away shaking their heads.

Store detectives were coming down from other floors now. There was John, the barrel-chested ex-Royal Scots Guardsman from Homeware, Darren, the part-time fitness instructor with the moustache from Leisure and Sports, Eric from Electricals, and Chris from Children's. They acknowledged each other with nods. Eric grinned and rubbed his hands together. A thrill ran through the shop assistants and transmitted itself to the customers. They all stopped and turned to watch what was left of the performance. The woman showed no awareness. She put the other T-bar sandal in her bag.

Audrey remembered something she'd seen on television years ago that had made her queasy. The strange thing was she wasn't normally squeamish, and – even odder – it was *Walking with Dinosaurs*, which wasn't even real.

It was about a herd of cow-like creatures. They just ambled around all the time, minding their own business. One day, one of them got wounded and the others abandoned it. A group of big lizards had been following, looking to attack. They circled the cow-thing, sniping at it when they knew it was beyond recovery. What was so disturbing was that this was supposedly the dawn of a new age. The gentle, bumbling cows were about to become extinct; the Earth was passing to the lizards.

The shoplifter raised her head and made a lurch for the exit. She was barely across the threshold when Clive clapped her shoulder. The other store detectives rushed up as if to decide a contest. She dropped to the floor with another slap. She yelped and sobbed and swore.

Clive and John hauled her upright and marched her back inside and through the 'Staff Only' door with her feet paddling. Her cries grew more and more muffled then died out. Eric picked up her bag and dangled it on his index finger as if it would demean him to carry it properly. His smile looked as if it had been taped there. He winked at Audrey.

Most people were laughing. Gloria and Sheila were applauding, their eyes and mouths gaping. A few people pretended they hadn't seen. Others – Moira among them – looked angry or disappointed.

"I have to go outside," Audrey said.

She charged through Greetings Cards and edged past two customers to get to the pedestrian precinct. Getting a glimpse outside, she went down on her haunches next to the marble doorway. As she snatched at her scarf and pulled it off, her mind whirled. The street was filled with velociraptors and the air with pterodactyls.

ON THE EVERLASTING OPENNESS OF THE FUTURE

It's difficult to say exactly how it felt. One minute I was sitting in my armchair in my flat in Kensington, the next I was somewhere quite different – on a padded recliner in a bare room, surrounded by ten British army officers and a single civilian. I didn't speak. I was too fazed. But I was aware of a collective gasp.

One of the officers approached me diffidently. "Would you – you're - "

"Could you tell us your name?" another said.

I rose fumblingly to my feet. "Er - what's going on? Where am I?"

The civilian thrust a syringe into my arm. "This is only a mild sedative, Sir, it won't knock you out. Just sit back. You'll probably be in shock for a while."

I stood still for a moment, then I guess it must have taken effect. I sat down.

"What … year is this?" the first army officer said. "Please?"

"Two thousand and ten," I said.

There was a ponderous silence. "That's … two-oh-one-oh?"

I nodded.

Someone handed him a microphone. He beamed. "We've done it. We've bloody done it!"

Everyone in the room burst into applause. I didn't know what they'd 'done'. Teleportation of some kind; it had to be. Given the sedative, maybe it wasn't so odd that I was okay with it.

"The Prime Minister's on the line, Colonel," someone said.

The colonel was still shaking hands with everyone. He broke off. "Put him on speaker, Kevin. We all deserve to hear this."

The next moment, a statesman-like voice: "I won't keep you long, Ross. I know how pleased you must feel, and I'm sure you want to get back to work asap. I simply want to extend my hearty congratulations. This is a massive step towards securing the long-term future of mankind."

More ecstatic applause. I was taken away to be debriefed.

Over the next two hours, I found out about them, as well as vice-versa. This wasn't 2010 anymore, it was 1976. The Cold War was at its height, and these chaps were in the forefront. The question was, what could I tell them about the future – their future, my past? Forewarned was forearmed. That was why they'd abducted me.

I told them what I could. I teach History in a secondary school, so they'd got lucky. I described President Gorbachev's arrival in power in Russia in 1980, the rise of Solidarity in Poland, the tearing down of the Berlin Wall, the trial and execution of Ceaușescu in Romania, Gorbachev's replacement by Boris Yeltsin, the breakaway of the former Soviet Republics. They looked incredulous, but they mm-hmm-ed and took reams of notes.

Eventually, one of them gave me a pat on the shoulder. "Well, I think we've gone as far as we can with this. You're free to go now."

"Go where?"

"It's going to be a long process of readjustment for you. But don't worry. We don't intend for you to cope alone."

"You mean you're not sending me back to 2010?"

He smiled. "Sadly, we haven't developed the technology for that yet. Besides, what would we be sending you back to? Your coming here has undoubtedly altered it beyond recognition."

It was a scary thought. Over the next few hours, I kept looking to see if I was disappearing – I mean, literally. What if I'd altered the future to such an extent that I'd died sometime before 2010, or been killed? But then in that case, I could never have come back in the first place …

None of it made any sense at all. Added to which, there was a strong possibility I was going to become depressed. I was born in 1960, you see, and obviously now, most of the rest of my life was going to be spent reviewing things I'd already seen – or hadn't, to the extent that my coming back had changed them. It would be another thirty-four years till I was back in 2010 again.

My 'rehabilitation' took the form of lodging for a while with a 'normal couple', the Taylors, in a well-to-do suburb in Hertfordshire. Eric Taylor was a defence analyst and somehow connected to my arrival. Joan didn't have an official job, although she was on lots of committees.

The plan was for me to go into teaching in a local secondary school again. I'd take a while readjusting to the primitive teaching methods – chalk and talk, mainly – but at least Ofsted had yet to be invented.

The evening after my arrival, the Taylors and I sat down to dinner together, the first of many such, I assumed. It was January the eighth. I'd always been a bit of a rock and roll fan, and, well, by six-thirty, all other conversation had fizzled out.

"It's Elvis's birthday today," I said. "Bet neither of you knew that."

Tom looked at me. "'Elvis'?"

"Presley. You know, 'Heartbreak Hotel', 'Hound Dog', 'Jailhouse Rock'?"

He and Joan looked blank.

I shrugged. "So you're not fans. What about the Beatles? Everyone likes the Beatles."

Joan put her knife and fork down. "Oh my goodness, you're a *Beatles* fan?"

"I wouldn't say 'fan'. They're okay."

"I – I've never met another Beatles fan," she said. "I saw them in concert in 1963, just before they split up. I've got all their records."

"I quite like their early stuff," I said. "But for me they started to go off with *Sergeant Pepper*. I never understood *The White Album*, or *Abbey Road* - "

I could see the disappointment in her face. "I think you must be thinking of some other band. The Beatles only released two albums."

"It was not taking off in America that did for them," Eric said, going to his bookshelf. "No British band's ever cracked the US. Apparently, one of them – Paul McIntyre, I think he's called – lives round here somewhere."

"Paul *McCartney*," Joan said. "He's a dentist."

"You would know, dear," Eric replied, winking at me. He went to the bookshelf and took down *Everyman's Encyclopaedia* Volume 5, and flicked ponderously through it. "Ah yes, here we are. I thought the name rang a bell."

He passed it to me.

Elvis Aaron Presley. Rock and roll singer whose innovative technique was a major influence on modern musical styles. Along with Buddy Holly and Richie Valens, Presley was killed in a plane crash near Clear Lake, Iowa on February 3, 1959 (see separate entry).

I pretended to take this in my stride and flicked through the encyclopaedia as if to admire its comprehensiveness. I was shaking. John F Kennedy was still alive. The Second World War hadn't ended till 1951. There were no entries for Israel or Hiroshima or Vietnam. The Beatles had split up early in 1964.

Joan left the room with the plates. I heard her running the tap.

Eric leaned over to me confidentially and lowered his voice. "I hope you won't mind, but I've been asked by the chaps in Intelligence to tap you for a little bit more information. The fact is … well, you kept mentioning the, er… Berlin 'wall'? It would help awfully if you could be a little bit more specific. You see, there are just so *many* walls in a city that size."

THE LADY WITH THE DOG

Since Chloe's parents ran a hotel, it was probably a scientific law that they should row occasionally. She sat at the kitchen table, still dressed in her school uniform and trying to answer the five 'Big Challenge' questions on page 12 of *Key Stage 3 Biology*, doing her best to ignore the rising voices. She ran both hands through her curly yellow hair, put her Biro down where she could retrieve it and scanned the cross-section of a flowering plant on page 13. 'The sepal' – what was a *sepal?*

"Well, *somebody* had to tell her!" Frank said, taking up position in the middle of the kitchen. His wife stood slumped against the Formica units, facing him with folded arms.

Frank was forty-nine, thin, with a purplish nose, jowls that seemed to pinch his face and big hairy hands. Except for an untidy horseshoe of hair starting at the nape of his neck, he was bald. His wife was as tall as him, but stouter, with dyed-blonde hair that seemed to peter out at her shoulders. She rarely lost her temper, but when she did, she put both her hands to her head and pushed her temples in with her fingertips. She unfolded her arms and switched to doing that now.

"Given that you've absolutely *no* people-skills," she said, "I think it might have been a good idea to consult *me* first. At least I could have broached the matter diplomatically!"

"What's there to be tactful about? She's breaking the rules."

"She's an *old woman!*"

"I wasn't going to patronise her, Connie."

"Oh no, you certainly wouldn't do *that*."

He flopped down on the chair next to his daughter's and stretched his legs out beneath the table. "I'll tell you why I didn't consult you first. Because you'd have let her stay." He looked for something to fidget with. He flicked a glance at the sepal. "You'd have found some excuse," he added.

34

"I certainly wouldn't have rushed in with all guns blazing," Connie replied.

"You'd have let her stay."

"It wouldn't have killed us."

He grimaced and slapped the table. "Yep, knew it."

"You humiliated her. She was in tears when she left the dining room."

"Repeat: she was breaking the *rules*. I wasn't going to patronise her. Rules are rules are rules are rules are rules."

Normally the two pans chuffing on the cooker, the extractor fan and the noise of the jukebox from the bar on the floor above would have been inaudible. But during this kind of row those were exactly the sorts of things that came into the foreground, as if to fuss over what was going on. The off-white walls with the framed food hygiene certificates, the tiled floor, the brash metallic fridge-freezer and the wooden table in the middle of the room all became similarly less shy and somehow more present-at-hand. Frank picked up the latest copy of *Hotelier* and flicked through it. He seemed to have caught from Chloe the notion that studied indifference was the key to progress. He stopped at a feature called, 'We test the market's top chest freezers'.

"What *happened* with the 'old woman'?" Chloe asked quietly, shutting her textbook. She knew from experience she had to keep her parents talking if they weren't to become entrenched. "What 'old woman'?"

Connie stirred the lamb stew, scraping the beginning of the burn off the bottom of the pan. "You just do your homework, there's a good girl."

"There was a dog in her room," Frank said.

"I said, *let her get on with her homework!*"

"What sort was it?"

"Fox terrier, I think. I'm not an expert."

"Frank, I'm warning you …"

He sighed. "I'm not being unreasonable."

"What would you have done, Mum?" Chloe asked.

Connie sighed irritably. "If you must know, I'd have waited a while. I'd have gone to Maria and said, 'When you made up the bed this morning, did you notice anything strange?' I mean, fair enough if she'd said, 'Yes, I found evidence of a dog in there'. But then I'd have said, 'Well, why didn't you tell us earlier?' Which is just the point. She *would* have told us if she'd found anything. The fact that she didn't means she didn't. And I think if Mrs Whatever-her-name-is can keep a dog that quiet, good luck to her. She's old. We can afford to turn a *bit* of a blind eye, just once in a while. It does us no harm at all; probably the opposite."

"Assuming Maria even made up the room *properly*," Frank replied.

"Why on earth wouldn't she?"

"Oh, come on. She's not the world's greatest maid. She gets tearful whenever she's criticised."

"She's homesick for Poland. She misses her mother."

"She might not even *know* the 'no dogs' rule for all we know."

"Yes. And that's precisely why *I* would have asked her."

He'd been outmanoeuvred. His eyebrows descended like shutters and he humph-ed.

"How did you find *out* about the dog, Dad?" Chloe asked.

"I heard it barking, so I used the master key to go in," he replied. "While Mrs What's-her-name was downstairs at dinner." He put his magazine down. He laughed. "Now I'm in the doghouse myself!"

Chloe forced herself to chuckle. In response, Frank started laughing at the fact that he'd made his daughter laugh. Connie turned round and her expression softened.

"*What* did he just say?" she asked her daughter, a laugh all ready to appear on her face.

"I said, *I'm in the doghouse!*" Frank gasped.

Suddenly, Connie was laughing too. None of the three thought it funny. Each was laughing at the other two. The notion of anyone at all finding humour in 'I'm in the doghouse' was tragic, thus hilarious, so a truly great find.

Half an hour later, Connie and Frank were sitting holding hands across the table. In between them were two glasses, a half empty bottle of wine, and two dirty plates, stacked. They had decided to let Richard, their manager, take over for the night. Chloe had gone to the cinema with three of her friends.

"What are we going to do about the lady with the dog?" Connie said indolently.

"You're right. She's not hurting anyone. We can turn a blind eye, I suppose. Just this once."

"I'll go up and see her in a minute, poor thing. I can't get over the thought of her in tears when she left the dining room."

"Hey, we had a good time with Chloe tonight, eh?" he laughed. *"Eh?* It was just like old times!" He slapped the table.

"Before she became a ... dread word ... *teenager."*

There was a long pause in which the silence seemed to come alive like a creature. Suddenly, Connie's expression darkened. "Frank?" she said.

"What?"

"We need to talk."

His innards swerved to avoid a sheer drop. Those words never heralded 'It's time to throw a party' or 'I've just won a holiday in Ibiza' or 'I'd like to rub your back'. "What is it?" he said.

She hesitated. "She hasn't gone to the cinema."

"Pardon?"

"Chloe. She said she was going to the cinema. She wasn't."

"Well – I – well, what? - where is she?"

"I don't know. She goes ... *off* with her friends. I don't know where to." She wiped a sudden tear and sniffed. She reached inside her sleeve for a hankie. "I think we're ... losing her. I've been thinking it for a while. Sometimes I can't get to sleep for - "

"Hang on, hang on, deep breath. Now let it out ... Now, let's not jump to conclusions. I mean – I don't understand. Where *is* she if she isn't at the cinema?"

"I don't know! I've just said!"

He broke into a nervous smile. "Come on, she's probably just hanging round on a street corner – 'chilling', or whatever it's called, like a normal teenager. They all 'chill'. It's nothing to worry about, is it?"

"We *don't know* what she's doing! That's the whole point! That's what I'm *saying!"*

"Have you tried ringing her?"

"Of course I have! She's got it turned off!"

"Okay, let's try to be rational. Let's just go back a bit ... Okay. How do you know she's not at the cinema? I mean: *know*."

"Because she hasn't any money. And she would have taken her glasses. And – and I just *do*."

Frank drew an involuntary mouthful of air and pursed his lips. If he continued to probe, that would look like he was questioning her intuition (not a good idea); but his silence would be taken as endorsing it (also unwise).

"I think this wine's slightly corked," he said eventually.

Connie scraped her chair back and went to lean against the units, resuming her argument-position of earlier. She grabbed the end of her hair, twisted it with both hands, bit her lip then released it. "We've got to do something."

"What do you suggest?"

"Something's got to give. Frank, I know you're going to think this is radical, but I've costed it. Just let me speak for a moment. With the money we got from my parents' house and a small loan, I think we can reach a solution. We might even end up better off than we were."

"I'm listening ..." His tone was already dubious. He hoped it wouldn't be dog-hostelling. He'd read about that somewhere.

"It's Chloe we're talking about here, Frank. Our daughter."

"Yes, yes, I got that bit. Go ahead."

She folded her arms, then re-folded them the wrong way and finally dropped them. "Okay, I suggest we put Richard in charge of the hotel for a few years and go and live in the countryside. I suggest we buy a dog, maybe two – Frank, you saw how her face lit up when you said the lady upstairs had a fox terrier! She's *always* wanted a dog! We're talking about her formative years now. If we're not *here* for her ... Put it another way. It was different a few years ago, when her grandparents were alive. She misses them something rotten. So that's another big hole in her life. And if they were here, they'd help us look after her but - "

"So maybe we do need to make a *bit* more time for her ..."

"A *bit* more time? Hel-*lo?* Take a look at us! We're working all the hours God sends! I mean, when was the last time we even watched telly? Let alone read the newspapers? All you read is bloody *Hotelier*, and all *I* read is lists of accounts. Anything might have happened out there for all we know. The country might have been hit by a nuclear bomb!"

"That's a bit of an exaggeration."

"Not much of one. Anyway, I'm not finished yet. Next, I think we should take her out of school and educate her at home. We wouldn't have to sell up: with Richard in charge, we could easily afford to keep the hotel on until she goes to university. Like I said, I've costed it! With the money we got from my parents' house ... sorry, I've said that bit already. We can come back here: the hotel, I mean. When she's older. I - "

"But can't you see? That won't work! That's not me being awkward. She's got friends here, she loves St Leonard's Academy's and she's doing really well there. We can't take her off to the middle of nowhere. She wouldn't stand for it."

Connie wrung her hands and looked at the ceiling like she always did when the discussion wrong-turned. "So what do *you* suggest?" she asked.

"I don't know. Maybe we should ask her to bring her friends home. They might be quite nice. We can hope, can't we?"

"What if they turn out to be ... 'the wrong crowd'?"

"We'll just have to cross that bridge - "

Suddenly there was a loud, rapid knocking at the kitchen door. They both started. Connie rolled her eyes and let out a stream of air through clenched teeth. Frank stood up unhurriedly and opened the door.

It was Maria. Her eyes were wet and sticky, her shoulders hunched; she held her hands towards her face and she shuddered. She didn't wait to be asked in; she strode over to the kitchen table, rested her knuckles on its surface, and almost retched a sob.

"What on earth's the matter?" Connie asked, her tone midway between irritation and panic.

"I have done a terrible thing! And now I am thinking it cannot be undone!"

"Sit down," Frank said, suddenly filled with a conviction of how ridiculous the hotel trade was, anyway. She'd probably dropped bleach on the fitted carpet or something.

"What is it, dear?" Connie said. She put her arm round the maid's shoulder.

Maria was about twenty-seven with skin so white it was difficult to see where her calico blouse ended and her neck and wrists began. She was nearly six feet tall in her pumps. She sat down.

"Aren't you supposed to be off duty?" Frank asked her.

"I know! I know!"

"I'll get you some tea," Connie said, kneeling down next to her. "She's in shock, Frank. Get her some tea. Strong, with plenty of sugar. What is it, dear? Come on. We all make mistakes. *It's nothing to do with Chloe, is it?"* she suddenly shot out.

Maria shook her head vigorously.

Connie made eye-contact with her husband and put her hand discreetly to her heart. "Well, we'll put it to rights. You'll see. No matter what it is."

"It is – it is – *the lady with the dog!"* Maria managed to get out.

"Er, you *knew* about the dog?" Frank said.

Connie waved him off. "What about the lady with the dog?"

"She is the lady off the news!" Maria said.

"What do you mean?"

"The lady off the *news!"* Maria repeated, as if the words were so momentous she had to repeat them to make sure she'd actually said them.

"Bloody dogs," Frank grumbled. Not knowing what was on the news made both of them look incompetent, he knew that. "They're always up to something ... chewing the furniture ..."

Suddenly, running footsteps approached the open door. Three unknown teenagers – a boy and two girls - burst into the kitchen and came to a sudden halt. Maria and Connie yelped, scrambled to their feet and backed, clutching each other, to the far side of the kitchen. Frank threw open the cutlery drawer, grabbed a carving knife and interposed himself between the intruders and the two women.

The boy was dressed in a pale hoodie, washed-out jeans and trainers; he had a wide mouth and black, gelled hair. The girls looked like twins: plump and small with identical snub noses. One was dressed in a puffa coat which almost swamped her; the other wore a pink T-shirt with 'Babe' on. All three were breathless; for some reason they looked mortified.

"We don't keep any money in - " Frank's throat constricted. He swallowed, raised the knife and started again. *"We don't keep any money in here!"*

But at the appearance of the weapon, the teenagers retreated to the far end of the kitchen. "We – we don't want your money!" the boy said.

"Martin?" Maria said.

Frank looked at Maria. Maria looked fixedly at the boy, as if she couldn't believe her eyes. The boy blushed.

"Martin goes to my church!" Maria told her employer.

"Chloe sent us!" the boy went on. "She asked us to give you a message!"

"Chloe sent them!" Connie yelled. "Put the knife *away*, Frank! *Chloe* sent them! Oh my God! Sorry! *We're so sorry! Put the knife DOWN, Frank!"*

Frank dropped the knife as if it was red hot.

"She said to tell you the lady with the dog's the lady off the news," Martin said. He swallowed. His eyes swept the room, looking for a reaction.

Silence.

"And you mustn't let anyone know," he went on. "We worked it out tonight when she told us. We all rushed straight back here."

"We all know that!" Maria said, getting upset again. "We all know it *already!"*

"But don't tell anyone else," the Babe girl insisted, coming out from behind Martin.

"What's anyone talking about?" Frank said weakly.

"Where is Chloe?" Connie demanded.

"Upstairs with the dog woman, I think," Martin said. "Giving her the kiss of life, I think."

There was a stunned pause. Connie dashed out of the kitchen, followed by Maria, followed by the twins. Martin and Frank stood dazed.

"Er, sorry about the kitchen knife," Frank said at last. "You're a friend of Chloe's, yeah?"

"Don't you think we should go with them?" Martin replied.

"In a minute. I just need you to – please? – just bring me up to speed on the lady with the dog? I mean" - he swallowed - "I just haven't seen the news for a while, and - "

Martin smiled. "You mean you haven't *heard* about the terrier woman? It's only, like, National Sensation of the Year! You haven't even *heard* about it? Sorry, rude. Sheesh."

"Maybe you could just summarise it for me quickly," Frank said. "Before I go upstairs. I should probably be upstairs with my daughter."

Martin cleared his throat. "Sure, yeah, sorry, okay, okay, let me think." He put his hands on top of his head and interlaced his fingers. "She's called Martha Blogg, seventy-five, spinster, no family. She used to live on her own in - Cromer, I think it was, in Norfolk – with her dog, 'Bustup'. Anyway, about six months ago, a burglar got into her house. Big man, violent. Meant to bash her face in and get her stuff. To cut a long story short, Bustup tore his face so badly he had to have surgery. He escaped – just - but the police caught up with him a week later. He got six months. But in a separate court case, brought by I-don't-know-who under the Dangerous Dogs Act, the judge ordered Bustup to be put down; 'destroyed' as they sometimes call it. Anyhow, Miss Blogg got in her Morris Minor and strapped her little dog into the passenger seat and they've been on the run ever since. She's a real hero. The police found the Morris Minor abandoned in a ditch about a week ago. God knows how she ended up here."

Frank went pale and wiped his face. He remembered, as if in a nightmare, telling 'Miss Blogg' he knew about her dog so she'd have to leave, and how she'd welled up. And now - ?

"You – you said Chloe was giving her the … the kiss of life?" he said.

"She'd decided to end it all. Poisoned the terrier as well. Chloe made her throw up. I saved the dog, or I hope I did. Room's a bit of a mess. Not very good publicity for the hotel if they do die, of course."

"Bloody hell. Bloody, bloody hell."

He ran upstairs and entered the room to find the old woman sitting on the edge of the bed, head hanging, hair in disarray. She gave no sign of registering his arrival. Maria sat on one side of her, and Chloe on the other. Chloe had a cup of something and was getting Ms Blogg to sip from it.

Frank found himself unable to meet his daughter's eyes. Several things flashed through his mind at once: how proud he was that she'd given someone the kiss of life; how grown-up she looked; Connie's words 'We're losing her'; how she'd supposedly lied about going to the cinema; how he needed to make more time for her -

The twins were tossing a pillow to each other while Bustup jumped in the air and tried to catch it. Judging by the feathers on the carpet, he'd already been successful several times. Connie stood to one side, dispassionately surveying the whole scene.

"A word outside, Frank," she said.

As he followed her, it struck him for the second time that evening just how unfunny 'I'm in the doghouse' was. With this difference: there could be no remedying the situation now, given how badly he'd treated Ms Blogg.

"I couldn't have known," he said, once they were in the corridor.

"She's coming to live with us, Frank," Connie replied.

"Er, *what?*"

"Chloe asked her, and she said yes."

"But that doesn't - "

"And I've agreed. I know it's mad, but I had a kind of epiphany. Right here, about five minutes ago. Everything became very clear for the first time in a long while."

"It's not very clear to *me*."

"We're going to tell the neighbours and our friends she's my aunt – if they ask. No one else is to know any different. You won't be able to appreciate this yet, but it may be the answer to all our prayers. You'll see."

Er, no, he wouldn't. She was old. She might need caring for twenty-four-seven soon. And she had a dog. Dogs chewed furniture. This one might even attack the guests. By way of clearing his mind, he tried to focus on something trivial: the wallpaper. It was a peach paisley design, peeling near the dado rail.

"Her friends are quite nice," he said. "Martin even goes to church. It's not like we need someone to keep Chloe from going astray. You were worrying about nothing. Think about what you're saying."

"Watch my lips, Frank. *Chloe asked her, and she said yes.* It's not like we haven't enough room. And how often do you get the chance to be your daughter's hero anymore?"

He nodded, hoping to look sage. He noticed the door on number twelve needed re-hanging. Low priority, that one, though – 2015, at the earliest.

God, what a disaster. Sod the door. Talk about how the mighty are fallen. He was as redundant as a dodo. All in twenty-four short hours, since the incident of the bloody lady with the bloody dog. What a bloody awful bloody catastrophe.

*

Two women at opposite ends of their lives sat huddled together on Blackpool beach, the collars of their overcoats turned up against the cold. Purple clouds hung above the horizon, pinned against a red so concentrated it seemed to come from some deeper level where the purest colours were separated for display. The younger woman was home from university for the day. She loved being here, everything about it.

Downwind towards the ocean, silhouetted against the sands, a lone couple walked their dog. The man threw a stick. In half an hour, they would rendezvous on the seafront with their daughter's friends – all twenty or thirty of them - and go out for a meal somewhere pet-friendly. Charlie was old now, in dog years nearly as old as Great Aunt Tilda. He didn't like being left out.

But nowadays, no one was.

THE QUEEN OF THE FENS

It was an outrage. Two slices of beef each, three potatoes and a sprout - that was the lot. There was space in between for a Yorkshire Pudding. But they'd run out of those as well.

Amanda and Rodney sat alone in the restaurant section of the pub, moping. His blazer, open-necked shirt and cravat were the sort of thing her father wore, because he'd gathered she was unusually attached to her father. She wore a blue print dress reaching from her neck to her pumps. Four men sat ten metres aside at the bar, murmuring, while the log fire shimmered in the horse brasses. It was dark outside.

"Do you think they'll make us pay the full price?" Amanda said.

"They shouldn't."

"Maybe they're going bankrupt or something."

He scowled. "That's not our problem. They're ruining your birthday."

"I don't mind that much. It's only my nineteenth."

"It's still special, Amanda. To me, it is."

"It's not like I'm eighteen or twenty-one."

"I wonder if we should complain."

"They'd probably shout us down. Or make out we're being awkward, and threaten to call the police."

He shrugged. "People think you can be intimidated when you're young. They assume you don't know anything."

"I suppose. They think all we care about is parties and having a blast."

"Like that 'Tempeste de Serrault', on TV. The so-called Queen of Paris."

She spluttered into her orangeade. "But I love that advert!"

"She's not even French. Karen Gough's her real name."

"It's such a lovely idea, though. Admit it. *Amunoso: Because You're Special.*"

"Skipping along the Champs-Élysées at four am, in your underwear, making taxis veer onto the pavement, where they're clambered over by children in fairy costumes: that's not my idea of the Queen of Paris."

She sighed. "I hope I die before I get old."

"Maybe we should just walk out without paying."

"What? Why would we - "

"Ssh! Keep your voice down!"

"Why?" she said.

"Why what?"

"Why would we want to walk out *without paying?*"

"Because, look at the way they're treating us."

"Point taken, but - "

"We booked this. It wasn't like we just turned up and said, 'Have you got a spare table?' Even if we had, they could have said, 'Yes, we have got a spare table, although we've almost run out of food'. But no, they accepted the booking and served us pretty much zilch. And now they're acting like there's nothing wrong."

"I like that word, 'zilch'."

"Let's stand up for ourselves. Let's stand up for all young people."

She scoffed. "*The Fox and Hounds* is in the middle of the Fens, Rodney. What if we get lost?"

"That's exactly what they're counting on. They think they can serve us up two half-empty plates and we'll just sit here because we've no alternative."

"It is wrong of them, I admit. It - "

"What they don't realise," he went on, "is that our greatest weakness is our greatest strength. We're young. We're edgy. We're going to walk out of here without giving them a penny, and believe in ourselves. Yes, we might sink into a bog and never be seen again, but it's a risk we're willing to take because - because we're fully alive!"

She dipped her eyes and swapped the salt and pepper pots round. "I'm too scared to do that."

"I know how you feel, but sometimes you've got to stand up for what's right."

"Look, we've only been going out for a fortnight, and I really like you, Rodney ..."

"I like you too. A lot."

"But I think you asking me out was a mistake."

"What? How *could* it be?"

"Because you don't really know me."

"But what I do know, I like."

"I'm really quite boring, that's all. I listen to Chris de Burgh and Ronan Keating and I want to be Queen of Paris. I only read Chick-Lit, and only then if it doesn't have too much swearing and sex in it, and I know in advance it's got a happy ending. I don't like alcohol much, so I only ever have a sip of Chardonnay at Christmas and New Year, and I pour the rest away. I'm probably going to vote Conservative at the next election because my parents do, and I love them. They're coming to get us at eleven. What are they going to think if we're not here?"

"I wouldn't say Chris de Burgh and Ronan Keating are boring. If you like it, fine, that's my motto."

"I think we should wait for Daddy. We won't have to pay anything when he hears what they've given us. *They'll* probably end up having to pay *us*."

"I wasn't going to say anything, Amanda, because I didn't want to spoil your birthday, but I think I might be in love with you."

She gasped. "But - "

"In fact, I am."

"How on earth would *that* spoil my birthday?"

"Because it's just too heavy. I thought I'd merely sing Happy Birthday to you and maybe kiss you, if you'll let me, but then leave the I-love-you announcement till next week, so you didn't think I'd only said it because it was your 'special day'."

"Oh, wow, what, *really?*"

"Yes," he said.

"And so, if I sink into a marsh, you'll try to save me? Alternatively, I could ring Daddy and tell him we've decided to get a taxi. We could actually get one. If we're going to go without paying, we don't have to walk. I could ring from the toilets. I've got my mobile."

"We'd have to walk a bit first."

"Why?"

"Because if we ring for a taxi," he said, "how are we going to know when it's got here? It's dark. We can't keep looking out of the window. The landlord will get suspicious. And what if the driver comes into the pub to get us and he meets him?"

"What if he does?"

"We'll have to pay for the meal, or there might be a fight. And if we pay, we might not be able to afford the taxi. Then there'll be more violence."

"Maybe I should just ring Daddy from the toilets."

"No, look, Amanda, please don't ring Dad – I mean, your father. *I* want to look after you. Me. I love you. Give me a chance?"

She bit her lip. Her eyes blazed. She swapped the salt and pepper pots again and took a bite of her beef. "Okay."

"I'm going to count to three, then we're just going to walk out, yes?"

"Agreed, yes. Golly."

"Do it casually. Just walk to the exit as if we're just going outside for a minute, or you're going to the Ladies and I'm going to the Gents, and we've just experienced the urge at exactly the same time. Yes?"

"All right."

"Don't put your knife and fork together. It's got to look like we're coming back."

"Do you think they'll come after us?"

"I doubt it."

"What about that dog of theirs? The one we saw earlier?"

"Let's not think about it. Are you ready?"

"All right."

"One … two … three."

They pushed their chairs back, joined hands and walked to the exit. As they passed the men at the bar, they blushed. The men looked quizzical.

Amanda's mouth popped open. "It's, er, okay. We're just going to the toilet together."

"It's – it's her birthday," Rodney blurted out.

Outside, they began to run. A mist fell, hiding them. The pub receded into the gloom. They waited till they were sure no one had followed, then they slowed and turned to each other and laughed nervously. They'd done it.

But the mist deepened and the stars disappeared and they lost all sense of direction. Suddenly they couldn't get a signal on their mobiles, and on all sides, it was grassy and drizzly and black and silent.

After an hour and a half apparently marking time, their hair and clothes were soaked and their hands and feet were numb. Somewhere in the distance a bird squawked like something from the Jurassic age. Amanda began to cry.

"I'm f-f-freezing. I th-think I'm going to die."

"This is all my fault, Amanda. I've let you down."

"Don't be s-silly."

"Yes, I have."

"N-no, no, you haven't. Don't say that."

"It was meant to be a nice birthday meal, but instead I led you to a slow death from exposure on the Fens. You can't let a person down more than that."

"It's f-fine."

"It isn't. It's the epitome of disappointment."

Suddenly they felt something hard underfoot.

"It's a road," Rodney said.

"I love you, Rodney. I'll r-r-remember you in Heaven. What did you say?"

"Oh my God! Here comes a car!"

She clapped her hands over her mouth and more tears spurted out. "Oh my God, we're s-saved!"

"I love you, Amanda. Remember that, whatever happens. Stay here."

He knew he was taking his life in his hands but since his credibility was in tatters it probably didn't matter if he got squashed. It might even be for the best. He ran into the road and began to holler, wave and jump. He was caught in a pair of headlights. The vehicle pulled to a sharp halt.

It wasn't a car, it was a *Hobgoblin* lorry. The driver – a middle-aged man with a goatee and blond hair - wound his window down and leaned out, grinning. "Guess you'll be wanting a lift?"

"Oh, yes," Rodney said. "Yes, please."

"Hop in." The man laughed. "Never like to see a guy die on the Fens. It upsets me."

Amanda appeared from the mist.

"I've got a girlfriend," Rodney said.

"All aboard then. Guy, gal: don't like to see either meet a miserable end. I'm only going to *The Fox and Hounds*, mind you. After that, you can probably ring for a taxi."

When they walked back into the pub, their dinners were exactly as they'd left them. The men at the bar averted their eyes as they entered. Someone said, "They're out". Someone else rushed to the toilet.

They sat down at the table, with their plates in front of them. Amanda put more salt on her potato. They ate what remained of their meals without looking at each other.

The landlord arrived, a stout man with a shirt button missing over his stomach and a tea towel draped over his left arm. He beamed. "Enjoy that?"

They kept their eyes on the table and nodded. No one seemed to have noticed that they were soaked through. Or perhaps they were being very tactful.

"Want another helping?" the landlord said.

They nodded.

"Good. We've got plenty. And, er, Miss?"

"Yes?"

"Your father rang while you were out."

Amanda looked up. "Daddy?"

"It's all right," the landlord said. "I didn't tell him where you were. I told him John was giving you a tour of the old stables out in the yard. But, er …"

He opened his mouth wider for a new sentence to come out. But then he turned and went back into the kitchen.

He returned with a birthday cake with nineteen candles on. The men at the bar began to sing 'Happy Birthday'. Rodney joined in. Amanda blew out the candles.

"Your father sent it over," the landlord said.

"Good old Daddy," Amanda croaked.

Rodney blushed. Tears of humiliation came into his eyes. The cake was a good eighteen inches in diameter and iced with scenes from fairy tales. The detail was so minute, and accompanied by such extravagant effects, it might have come courtesy of Peter Carl Fabergé. In the centre it said, 'Happy nineteenth to our wonderful daughter with love and kisses from Daddy and Mummy'.

The landlord cut it and gave them both a slice.

"Give everyone at the bar a slice too, please," Amanda said.

Rodney ate his as if it was marinated in vinegar and it was all he deserved. The landlord carried the remainder to the bar where it was greeted with an appreciative roar. He returned with a pint of *Hobgoblin* and a large glass of red wine.

"This is from Thomas," he said. "Beer for the gentleman, wine for the lady. Drink up. You're only nineteen once."

They waved a thank you to the men at the bar. Thomas nodded, picked up his pint and toasted them. Amanda reached her left hand across the table and put it over Rodney's wrist and squeezed. Their eyes met. She picked up her wine and drank it in one go.

She stood up. "No, I'm not going to be sick. We're young and edgy. Drink up, Rodney, come on."

The landlord brought another plate of beef, potatoes and sprouts. Then another red wine and another *Hobgoblin*.

"This one's from Old William. Many happy returns of the day, he says."

They waved another thank you. Old William nodded, picked up his pint and toasted them. Amanda reached her left hand across the table, put it over Rodney's wrist and squeezed. Their eyes met again. She picked up her wine, drank it in one, and set the empty glass back on the table.

"Oh, wow wow wowee," she said. She burped.

"And this next one's from Chris," said the landlord.

At ten o'clock, the men's wives arrived and the pub came alive. The landlord put another log on the fire and poked the embers. Rodney and Amanda got up, fell over, got up, and went to sit at the bar. Everyone was their friend now whether they liked it or not. They held court at the top of their voices.

"There's only one thing I've got to do before midnight," Amanda announced, after ten minutes. "I've got to be the Queen of Paris."

"We can't possibly go to Paris now," Rodney replied.

Everyone laughed.

"Why not?" she said.

"It's gone ten o'clock. Your father's coming in ... in ... soon. Anyway, what's wrong with being the Queen of England?"

"We've already got a Queen of England," Old William said.

Everyone laughed again.

"You could be the Queen of the Fens," Tom said.

The noise of conversation lowered a notch.

"What does the Queen of the Fens look like?" Amanda said.

"I don't know," Tom said, after Old William nudged him. Fewer people were laughing now. "It was just a joke, that's all."

"I want to be the Queen of the Fens!" she shouted.

"Hear that?" the landlord said unsmilingly. "She wants to be the Queen of the Fens." He looked around from face to face.

"Someone do her hair and put a bit more make-up on her," said Old Meg. "It can't do any harm, can it? Let the girl have her day."

"She'll laugh about it in the morning," Chris said.

"Don't be a bloody fool, Chris," Tom said. "You don't know what you're talking about."

"Don't go tempting providence," Old William said.

"It was Meg who said it first," Chris replied.

The landlord stacked six empty glasses. "It ain't right to joke about such things. I'm not saying there's any truth in it, mind you, but it's not a fit subject for laughing about."

"I want to be the Queen of the Fens!" Amanda said.

Meg shook her head. "Don't say such things, girl. You shouldn't have listened to me. I've had one too many, and I'm just a stupid old woman, anyhow."

"What's everyone talking about?" Rodney asked.

"It's nothing at all," Old Meg said. "Just folklore, people's misunderstandings. Pay 'em no mind."

Amanda waited till Meg wasn't looking, then dipped into her handbag. She slid under the table with a small tub of mousse and a lipstick and drew lines on her face and gelled her hair into a spike. She climbed onto a chair.

"Look at me!" she commanded. "I'm the Queen of the Fens!"

Everyone turned to face her. Suddenly, there was complete silence. She struggled out of her dress and bra and stood with her arms rigid in the air.

Outside, the wind howled against the windows. Someone dropped a glass. Old William crossed himself. Someone uttered an, 'Oh, God'.

The door opened and Amanda's father entered looking like an elderly Rodney. His jaw dropped. "Bloody hell."

"Daddy, I'm the Queen of the Fens. Look at me."

The landlord wrung his hands. "We couldn't stop her, Sir. She was too quick. We just couldn't stop her."

Old William groaned. "It's too late. God's truth, keep her ten miles from the coast until next time the moon's this side of Jupiter, otherwise, heaven forbid, they'll claim her."

"I think they've already claimed her," the landlord said. "I don't think anything that's happened here tonight was an accident."

"It was all foretold," Meg said. "Long ago."

Rodney removed his blazer and cravat, folded them together and put them in the fire, where they flared up. "I love your daughter," he told Amanda's father. "And I intend to wrest her from you."

Amanda's father snarled and swept his eyes about. He looked for a moment as if he was held at bay by a flaming sword.

"And I love *you too*, Rodney!" Amanda yelled. "God in heaven! *I love you!*"

LONDON VIRGIN

I saw my picture in *The Big Issue*, yeah, about a week ago, beneath the heading, 'Have you seen this woman?' Fuzzy's all I'll say. Speaks volumes that they couldn't even find *one* decent photo of me. According to what it says underneath, my daughters are 'distraught'.

Makes me laugh, that does.

Let me introduce myself. Hetty Mitchell. Hetty Wainthropp, friends used to call me, after the television private detective (probably before your time). And also as a joke, because Hetty Wainthropp was *interesting* in ways I wasn't: i.e., in just about every possible way. I'm seventy-two now, a widow, short, with cropped grey hair. I generally wear a hat made of peacock feathers, and whatever else I can kit myself out in from the Salvation Army or *Oxfam*, or car-boot sales. In those days, I wore Scholl sandals and polyester top-and-trouser combos in pastel colours from places like Primark. And I'd never been to London.

"You've never been to *London?*" my daughter gasped, one dreary June afternoon, the day of my birthday party. I don't know why she didn't know. It's not like I ever took her there when she was a kid. But then she's probably made a conscious effort to forget those days. Reinvented herself. She's someone posher nowadays, someone like her dad was. And her actual past probably doesn't exist. Or maybe she's just deleted the bits that include me but not him.

Sorry, ranting.

Anyway, for the first time in my life, I was mildly interesting to her. To the point where she told everyone in the room about it. *My* mater (or whatever she calls me to her friends) *has never even been to London!* She couldn't get round quick enough, teetering like an idiot on her too-high heels. It put more of a public gulf between the two of us, I suppose. Made her look cosmopolitan by contrast.

That was my seventieth. The party was my daughters' idea. A golden opportunity for them to tart themselves up and show how caring they are. And of course, they bought me a ticket the next morning. Their bounty knows no limits.

So, two days later, I was standing alone on the station platform, with a green toque on my head, looking down at the railway lines like Anna Karenina. I'd brought a flask of coffee and some ham sandwiches in a travel-bag. A bolt of electricity – that's how it felt – shot through my body as the tannoy announced, "The next train to arrive at Platform Three will be the 13.35 for London Victoria, calling at …"

The space around me began to fill up; people with briefcases sliding purposefully into what looked like reserved positions, pulling their cuffs up to peep at their watches, talking on mobiles, gripping their bags and briefcases. It was a hair-grey morning, rather cold considering it was summer. I clutched my Travelcard.

It's not that I *wasn't* a traveller. I was – a bit. I'd been to France via Southampton, and Germany via Newcastle airport. Just not to London. I definitely *wasn't* a country bumpkin.

Suddenly, my youngest appeared at the far end of the platform, waving flamboyantly. Lavinia is short (she takes after me in that respect), trapped in a skirt-suit and a trendy hairstyle, slightly crooked teeth and three marriages behind her.

"Have a really good time!" she gushed, air-kissing me for what felt like the benefit of everyone else. *This is my elderly mother, I'm a wonderful daughter.* "Have you everything you need for the journey?"

"I've got a pack of ham sandwiches and a flask."

"Ham sandwiches and a flask! That's lovely!"

What does 'lovely' mean in that context? She hadn't brought me anything better. Frankly, I wouldn't have minded one of those Cornish pasties she bought me last Christmas. But it would have been utterly incredible if she'd done that.

Bloody hell, a four-pack of Cornish pasties for Christmas. *For Christmas,* I ask you! The *use by* date was the twenty-seventh. Christmas day, I always have lunch in the Church Hall with the vicar and all the other losers, so I wasn't going to eat one then. That leaves just two days. Two days to eat four pasties - *because they weren't even freezable!*

Back a bit. Sorry, I didn't mean to suggest the vicar was a loser. To have your lunch with a bunch of people like me when you've got a lovely wife and two kids at home, that's the opposite of a loser. A saint. And his missus. Nothing like my two. Won't hear a word against the vicar, no.

But *use by* the twenty-seventh? It nearly bloody killed me, that. Four pasties in two days. And she couldn't bring me *anything* for the journey to London, the bloody fat shite. *Ham sandwiches and a flask. That's lovely.* Right.

I was on the train for about two hours. I wasn't going business class and I didn't manage to get a window seat, so I was next to the aisle. People kept edging past and one or two of them fell onto me slightly. On the other side, the tinted windows made everything outside look maudlin. Mostly bare fields, the occasional glimpse of the wrong bit of a town – why do railway stations always seem to be in the wrong bits of a town? - then trees. Birches, oaks and pines, birches-oaks-and-pines, duddle-de-duh, duddle-de-duh, *parp!* After forty minutes, the sun came out and it started getting warm.

I made the mistake of not bringing a *Woman's Own,* so I just had to sit there and think. And it didn't take me long to realise I was doing this for *them.* I was doing it so they'd: 1. be able to tell themselves they'd 'educated' me, and 2. be able to tell everyone that, since the mortifying occasion of the party, they'd helped their mother lose her London virginity.

Ironically, it was actually a *Virgin* train I was on!

But not for long. When we were still about an hour from London, the train pulled to a halt at a place called Adlestrop. I don't remember much about it now. Only the name. Anyway, we seemed to be there for quite some time, maybe a change of carriages or something. And I got out on the bare platform. Baking hot it was. Proper late June weather for once.

For some reason, I didn't want to get back on that train. Call it an old person's awkwardness; call it a resistance to being patronised by two people I didn't particularly like; call it a rebellion against being managed; call it what you like. Five minutes later, I watched it pull away

And I thought, *What now?* It hit me with the force of a revelation: what I'd done made me a hell of a lot more interesting than any poxy day-trip to London ever could. All I had to do was follow my nose, see where I ended up. And I knew I wasn't going back home, oh no, not ever. I didn't want to be Hetty Wainthropp anymore. I wanted to be me. Maybe I was having some sort of breakdown or something. Probably was, thinking back.

I walked straight through Adlestrop and didn't stop until I came to the first big town. Oxford, I later discovered it was – I must have missed the signpost on the way in. That night, I slept rough on the streets. And the next night. As I've said it was summer, so it wasn't too cold out there. And I certainly didn't starve: people kept stopping to give me food or money. Still some nice people about, don't let anyone tell you otherwise. Eventually, a policeman came along and asked me a few questions – which I pretended not to know the answer to – and pointed me in the direction of a shelter for the homeless.

It wasn't easy. Especially the first few months. It's never easy on the streets, I knew that already. But I was determined to stick it out. Anything - even death - would have been better than crawling back to where I'd come from. If I'd been a 'project' of sorts before, now I could only look like a failure. *So pathetic that even a trip to London defeated her.* Or, *How can we help her when she won't even help herself?* Or, *Such a shame, but don't say anything in front of her.* At seventy, I probably didn't have that long to live anyway. I'd probably despise myself in the end: that's usually how it concludes.

Eventually, I made some friends. All from living at the shelter. We tended to hang out together at night first, then we started going round together in the daytime, meeting up in various familiar places – Christ Church Meadow, Magdalen Bridge, Paradise Square - until we became a proper little 'crew', to use the modern word.

Who are they, these friends of mine? Well, first there's Harry: about twenty-five, thin black beard, dark skin, hollow cheeks, dresses and smells like Worzel Gummidge. Then, Kathleen, an Irish girl: broad white face, smile like a turnip-lantern but pretty, and a champion arm-wrestler. (Harry and Kathleen are a couple.) Then there's Peter, an ex-accountant who lost both his wife and his home in the same year: always sombre, likes everything properly thought-through, still dresses like a suburbanite, turtle-neck jumpers and loafers; fourthly, there's a teenager called Sammy – my adopted granddaughter, that's the joke: skinny, likes a drink and a bet, long fingers and toes like claws, snub nose, long straggly hair. And finally there's Peter's dog, a black and white mongrel called Biscuit – cross between a Border Terrier and an Alsatian by the looks of him, our guardian angel.

They're musicians. The dog excepted! I had to learn to play a tambourine so I'd fit in. Which is harder than you'd think. You see, Peter's the leader, and he's a violinist. Concert standard, I'd say, though I'm not an expert. Harry plays a tin whistle, Kathleen's a guitarist, Sammy plays the bongos and sings. And I thwack the tambourine to bits.

Some days we make enough for a day out, middle-class style – with every little luxury thrown in. Of course, we tend to spend what we get when we get it. Banks don't exist in our world. We've got pockets, that's all. The Grand old Duke of York, he had ten thousand men. When they're full they're full, and when they're empty they're empty.

It was when we all went to the festival at Glastonbury together that they gave me my nickname. For reasons unknown, Harry had made me a hat out of Peacock feathers and, when he presented me with it one evening, I was so overcome – a two-litre bottle of Blackthorn Dry may have had something to do with that - that I promised to wear it forever, or at least until it wore out. And that's when they started calling me 'Mrs Peacock'. I came to forget I'd ever been called Hetty Mitchell, let alone Hetty Wainthropp. Mrs Peacock, that's me.

That was one great excursion. The second came just a few months later. About a year after we first started going around together, they too learned that I'd never been to London. So we walked there together, across country, carrying our instruments. Simple as that. No fuss, no air-kisses, a proper family outing. I'm seventy-two now; I was seventy-one, then, but I did it. Thanks be to God, I did it.

And it felt surprisingly good, losing my London virginity.

THE PREHISTORIC VALLEY

They were climbing a hill. Below them, the valley lay in sunlight interspersed with cloud-shadows. Olivia wore her summer dress and tennis shoes and looked more like a teenager than a fortysomething.

Simon reached into the undergrowth. He cupped a flower head in his fingers. "This is ground elder," he said. "It's a bit like cow parsley or hogweed, but it grows bigger. Normally, you'd expect to find it in damp conditions. Look at the smooth stem in comparison - "

She'd stopped several paces behind him, her hands dangling.

"Are you okay?" he asked.

"Simon, I've something to tell you."

"Yes?"

"First of all, do you love me?"

"You know I do."

"I won't mince words then. I know what ground elder is. I've got a higher degree in Systematic Botany."

He looked as if she'd whipped him. He took a step back and put out his hand for something to steady him. But there was nothing. "Why didn't you say earlier?"

"Because I knew it would hurt you."

He couldn't meet her eyes. He sat down in the grass. "So all this time I've been going on about flowering plants, you've been thinking, 'What a bore'?"

"No, it's not that, of course not. It's just ... oh, I don't know. We've been going out for two years now, and there's the massive age difference. We've got to be honest with each other."

"I've told you. The age difference doesn't matter."

"It will. It might not now, but it will. When ..." She flopped down, dropped her head into her palms and wept.

"What's up?" he said. He forgot about flowering plants, scurried over on his bottom and put his arm round her.

"What hope have we got?" she said.

"We've been through this. It doesn't matter."

"Look, since we've got the Botany thing out in the open, we might as well go the whole hog. I'm not thirty-five. I'm forty-five."

"I know."

"What? You know? How?"

"When you went down to the chemist that day, I went through all your things. I looked at your passport."

"What day? When?"

"About a year ago."

She wiped her eyes and looked at him. "I'm not sure how I feel about that. So you've known all this time?"

"Yes."

"What else did you find out about me?"

"You were born in Kendal, you were abused as a child, you've got a criminal conviction for growing weed, you lost your job with the National Trust, you had shingles when you were thirty-six, you once had a Curly-Coated Retriever called Smiles, which got run over by a white van - "

She laughed bitterly. "And yet you didn't discover that I've got a higher degree in Systematic Botany."

"I didn't get that far. You came back earlier than I expected."

"Oh, if only I'd left my degree certificate somewhere where it could be readily located."

"There's no need to be sarcastic."

"Bloody *hell*, Simon! I leave the house for half an hour and you go through all my *things?* Am I supposed to be *pleased?"*

"It was a one-off. I won't do it again."

"Oh, they all say that."

"What's that supposed to mean?"

"Nothing."

"Who else says it?"

"No one."

"Please."

"Okay," she said. "My dad, amongst others. He used to say that. Then my first boyfriend. He used to beat me up if he found something he didn't like, something that made him suspicious. Did you find out about him too?"

"I didn't need to. You told me about him."

"When?"

"When we first started going out together. He was called Rick. He had a camper van and a beard."

She shuddered. "Oh, that sordid, sordid camper van. I never want to think about him, or it, again. He's coming out of prison soon."

"He won't try to find you, will he?"

"I'm forty-five, Simon. I'm of no interest to any man now. Certainly not to him."

"You're of interest to me."

"Right."

"I want to marry you."

She hooted. "When in God's name did you decide that?"

"About a year ago."

She drew her knees up to her chin and hugged them. She rolled her eyes. "And you don't think the twenty-five-year age gap's going to be a problem? It doesn't worry you that when you're my age, I'll be seventy?"

"Now you're being sarcastic again. No, it *doesn't* worry me."

"Well, it should. Look, Simon, when we embarked on this, this … thing, I didn't expect it to last. I just wanted a fling, that's all, and I couldn't believe my luck when I bagged an eighteen-year-old."

"But to be fair, I'm not exactly an Adonis."

"But you could slim."

"But my hair's never going to come back."

"You're not that bald."

"I am," he said. "Anyway, love is blind."

"And you love me blindly, do you?"

"No, not blindly. You're more beautiful now at forty-five than I am at twenty."

She laughed. "But what if you slim, and they find a cure for baldness? Then you won't want me anymore."

"What if they find a way to reverse the ageing process? Then *you* won't want *me* anymore. Look, this is silly. Do you love me, yes or no?"

"Yes, but - "

"But nothing."

"I've been married twice," she said. "It doesn't work."

"Yes, but maybe you need a more unconventional marriage."

She laughed. "Oh, this one would be unconventional all right."

"That's what I'm saying."

"Can't we just live together?"

"I don't want to 'live together'. I love you. I want to get married."

"What about your parents?"

"They lost the right of veto when they threw me out," he replied. "You know that."

"But don't you think, everywhere we went, people would be like, 'What's he doing with her? She's old enough to be his mum'."

"So what if they were?"

"There's no *if* about it."

"We don't have to *have* friends."

"We do, Simon. What are we going to do on an evening, if we don't have friends?"

"Stay in and watch TV. Anyway, look, I knew a guy once who had a girlfriend with one eye. She used to wear a patch and everything, and he asked her to marry him. He didn't sit there beforehand thinking, 'I wonder if people will approve, maybe I'll have no friends.' He just married her. And I know this other guy. His girlfriend used to be an escort and - "

"It's not the same."

"Not exactly, no, but what I mean is, you've just got to ignore other people. They'll get used to us once they get to know us."

"Wouldn't it be great if we could just win the Lottery?" she said.

"What difference would that make?"

"It would make a difference. If you've got money everyone forgives you."

"I don't know what you mean."

"I mean, people don't mind how different you are if you're rich. Why do you think rich people are all so interesting, and poor people are all so dull and same-y? I'll tell you. Because everyone forgives rich people, that's all. There's nothing else different about them."

They sat in silence. A dragonfly came for a look at them, hovered, then turned round and flew away, bouncing up and down on an invisible rollercoaster.

"Would you rather be twenty with just one eye?" he said, "or forty-five and like you are?"

"That's not the point. It's not about me on my own. It's about me and you. If we got married, I'd ruin your life."

"It's my life."

"Yeah, but you don't want it ruined."

"It wouldn't *be* ruined."

"Look, don't let's talk about it anymore. My mind's made up."

He put his head down to hide it, but after a minute, the tears slid off his face. Then he had to breathe in, and it came out as a sniff.

"Oh, don't cry," she said. "I still love you."

"Not enough to marry me."

"It's because I *do* that I won't marry you!"

"Yeah, right."

Her voice shook. "You're making *me* cry too, now."

They sat with their chins tucked in their necks, weeping and sniffing and wiping their faces. They didn't look at each other. She took a large handkerchief from her bra and blew her nose.

Then they heard someone coming. Another couple. They couldn't see them, but they could hear them talking, somewhere nearby: a man and a woman, elderly and refined.

"What a fantastic view," the woman said.

"Amazing," the man replied. "Look, you can see Welling Castle."

"Where?"

"There. Follow my finger. Look. Just look along my finger. Look."

"Ah yes, I can just see it now."

"It's recent, relatively speaking," he said. "The whole valley was formed in the ice age, and it's been up and down, quite literally, since the time of the dinosaurs, tens of millions of years ago. And of course, after we're dead, it's going to be here for tens of millions of years more. It takes your breath away when you look at it like that. We're so insignificant by comparison. Just two tiny little nothings in the middle of a vast emptiness."

"*Don't*, Charles."

"We're a long time dead, as they say!"

"I said *stop*."

"Vanity of vanities saith the Preacher, all is vanity."

"That's *enough*, Charles. Bloody *hell!*"

"Oh, stop being so damn sentimental, Samantha!"

They walked away. A plane flew over with a roar like chalk on a blackboard. The air suddenly became fragrant with clay and heather. Simon looked up to see what Olivia was doing. He was sorry he'd made her cry now. He was back right again.

"Wouldn't it be funny," he said to her, "if 'Charles' was to have just said that, and 'Samantha' was to turn around and say, 'Actually, Charles, I've got a higher degree in Systematic Geology'?"

Olivia seemed not to hear. Her face was white and she was holding a bunch of dandelions out to him. There were runnels of salt where her tears had been. She turned a haunted glance on the prehistoric valley and smiled.

"Perhaps ... perhaps then maybe after all," she said.

THE WEDDING CAKE

It was going to be the most fabulous wedding County Armagh had ever seen. To plan it, three women and three men sat around a table reviewing the most exotic possibilities with the help of a specialist brochure.

"The oval napkin-holders or the round?" Ellie's mum said.

Ellie pounced. "The oval."

"That's what I hoped you'd say."

"Mum, could I see the catalogue?"

"What's the matter with round?" Ellie's dad said.

Ellie's mum looked sad. "With round, Gerald, there won't be the grip. Napkins probably hang loose in round napkin-holders; depending on their relative diameters, of course, but assuming the oval and the round are about the same size - "

"Mother, could you pass me the *catalogue*, please?"

"Sorry, yes."

Ellie grabbed it when it was halfway across. "We'll go with the oval napkin-holders in silver."

"Yes, I'd go with the silver if it was me," the Wedding Planner replied. "It looks cleaner. Especially in June, with the sun on it."

Ellie was eighteen years old and two months pregnant. She had a thin neck, a drooping mouth and uneven eyebrows. Craig, her fiancé, was the same age, but in some lights looked like an old age pensioner. Opposite him, Ellie's father wore a plum cardigan. Her mother wore an identical cardigan and a pair of horn-rimmed spectacles on a chain. To her right, Father Keogh stared into the deep, black hole of the table: he was here to offer advice on the wedding but no one wanted it. The Wedding Planner sat at the gathering's head. She had lustrous black hair, shining eyes, red lips, and unearthly, almost translucent olive skin. She wore a white suit, and heavy bronze jewellery that looked as if it had been earned on the battlefield. Her name was Athena.

"Definitely the oval napkin rings," Ellie said.

"Can we have a fruit cake instead of a sponge cake?" Craig burst out.
A stunned pause.

"What? For our ... *wedding* cake?" Ellie said.

"Yeah, what the hell's wrong with *that?"* he shot back.

There was another hiatus. Ellie rolled her eyes. "The wedding cake's got to be *tiered,* Craig. Have you ever tried to lift a fruit cake?"

"Probably, yeah."

"Have you ever tried to lift a sponge cake?"

He shrugged.

"If you *had* tried to lift a sponge cake," she continued, "and then you'd tried to lift a fruit cake, you'd notice there's a big difference. A fruit cake weighs a ton. Now, say we're looking at a wedding cake with four tiers - "

"I'd imagine it would have to be at least four tiers," Athena said. "For a wedding on this scale. Maybe even five. Or six."

"Four, minimum," Ellie said.

Craig folded his arms. "So bloody what?"

Ellie sighed. "Well, Craig, imagine the second tier of your fruit cake's one kilogram, the third and fourth together would have to be at least that. So you're looking at two kilograms of cake resting on the bottom layer. Your supports are going to go straight through the base."

"Not if they've got sufficiently wide bases," he replied. "Enough to spread the load."

She gasped. "Yes, but look at the *catalogue,* Craig! Page sixty-five! cake-tier supports!"

"I haven't seen page sixty-five ..."

She hurriedly found it. "Here, look. They don't do them with wide bases."

He scanned the pictures through a frown.

She snuggled up to him and twiddled his penis through his trousers. "Come on, I'll *make* you a fruit cake! *You're* my little fruit cake!"

"Er ... more tea, Gerald?" Ellie's mum asked, by way of dealing with the wide eyes and slack jaws.

Ellie kept looking at page sixty-five. "It's got to be sponge."

Father Keogh guffawed then blushed. The clock struck half-past.

"If we got a really strong icing," Craig said, "that might do it."

Athena frowned. "It'd have to be *very strong indeed!*"

"You'd *make* it strong by making it *thick,*" Craig said. "Say a centimetre deep. That should do it."

"How the hell are we going to cut through *a centimetre of icing?*" Ellie said. "You'd need a bloody *chainsaw!*"

"But we cut it together."

"What's your point?" Athena said.

Craig met her eyes. "I'd imagine that, together, we'd exert enough pressure to cut through a centimetre of icing. We'd have to be pretty puny not to."

"What if there's an explosion?" Ellie said.

"Why would there be?" he replied.

"Don't be ridiculous," Ellie went on, becoming emotional. "We'd have to exert – I don't know – fourteen kilograms per square centimetre. When we get through the icing, the cake's going to fly all over!"

"Or you'll go *through the table,*" Athena said. "Or the table would collapse."

"You'd just have to get us a sturdy table," Craig said. "You could take care of that, couldn't you? You *are* the Wedding Planner."

Ellie's father stood up like he'd had an epiphany. "You could use an electric carving knife!"

Ellie was on the verge on tears. "Don't you get involved, Dad."

"Give him a chance, dear, please," her mum said. "He's your father. Go on, Gerald."

He interlaced his fingers. "An electric carving knife would enable you to saw through any depth of icing, so pressure ceases to be an issue. True, it'd penetrate the icing more slowly than it would the cake itself, but I don't reckon you'd be looking at much more than thirty seconds a slice."

Ellie was crying. Athena put her arm round her and said, "That's very optimistic, Mr O'Connell. But even if you're right, say you have a hundred guests: at thirty seconds a slice, that's fifty minutes to get everyone a piece of cake."

"How long's it normally take?" Gerald said.

"Twenty minutes, tops," Athena replied.

He sat down. "I'm out."

Ellie threw her hands wide. "Anyway, I'm not going to stand at the front of the marquee with an *electric bloody carving knife* buzzing away in my hands! They're for cutting *turkeys!*"

"I think we're missing something important here," Father Keogh said.

The Wedding Planner grimaced. "Oh here we go. You're going to come in on the men's side, I assume."

"Not so," he said.

"I think we should welcome any new diplomatic initiative," Gerald put in. "Go on, Father."

"All I was going to say was: an iced fruit cake? Surely, it's not normal to ice a fruit cake."

"What the hell's a *Christmas* cake, then?" Craig said.

"I'd say there's a difference between Christmas cake and fruit cake," Father Keogh replied.

"I'd second that," Ellie's mum said. "Not just because Father Keogh's a priest, but because a Christmas cake has other things in it besides fruit. Nuts, for example. Besides, we're going to look stupid if we serve up Christmas cake."

"I'm not saying we *should* serve up Christmas cake," Craig said. "My point is that Christmas cake and fruit cake aren't that different."

"Granted," Father Keogh replied, "but then lamb and beef aren't that different. You wouldn't have horseradish sauce with your lamb, would you? Ergo, you wouldn't have icing on your fruit cake."

Athena nodded. "Whereas you've got to have icing on a wedding cake."

"QED," Father Keogh said. *"Quod erat demonstrandum.* 'It stands proven'."

Ellie's mum smiled indulgently. "Father Keogh always likes to get a bit of Latin in. He's a member of Opus Dei, aren't you, Father?"

"No," Father Keogh said.

"Couldn't we have a hybrid cake?" Gerald asked.

Athena scowled. "What the bloody hell's a hybrid cake?"

"I mean, make the bottom level fruit cake, since Craig wants fruit cake, and the second-to-whatever tiers sponge cake. Then the upper tiers would be light enough not to overload the supports, which wouldn't then plunge through the base. Result: everyone's happy."

Athena rolled her eyes. "Except that you don't *have* icing on fruit cakes. And, as we've just agreed, a wedding cake *has* to have icing on. Especially the bottom tier."

"Because it's got to have *writing* on," Ellie's mum said. "'Good Luck Craig and Ellie'. Or, 'Best Wishes For The Future To The Happy Couple'. Something like that."

"Surely, that would be the top tier," Father Keogh said. "Wouldn't it?"

Ellie let out a loud sob. She pushed back her chair and rushed out, slamming the door behind her.

The mantelpiece clock ticked. A fly buzzed.

Athena stood up. She grabbed the wedding catalogue and banged it down in her open briefcase. "I have *never* come across anything like this in all my years of planning weddings! I make it a rule never to involve myself with marriages that are doomed from the outset. Dear *God*, if these two young people can't even agree on something as *simple* and *basic* as a wedding cake, what *hope* do they have?" She sighed. "I'm sorry, I resign."

She locked the catches on her briefcase, swished her hair over her shoulder and strode out of the room. A few minutes later, the clock and the fly were joined by the sound of a Porsche roaring into the distance.

"What are we going to do now?" Ellie's mum whispered.

"Where are we going to find another Wedding Planner at this short notice?" Gerald said.

Father Keogh cleared his throat and smiled. "Well, I wasn't going to say anything, but *I've* planned a few weddings in my time."

Gerald chuckled. "I don't think we've quite reached that point, Father."

"But it was a really nice thought," Ellie's mum said.

Craig got up. "I'd better go and find Ellie."

Ellie was quivering in her bedroom with her face in the duvet. Her bra-buckle stuck out under her blouse like an extra vertebra.

Craig had been in here a few times before, but always just for sex. Now it was as if he was seeing it for the first time. A Westlife poster hung above a rickety dressing table. The skirting boards were lined with Beanie Babies. A giant stuffed panda sat in the corner;

when the lights were out, it looked like Ellie's mum. Two copies of *Wedding Magazine* and a *Sugar* lay on the bed.

"It's me," he said.

She carried on trembling.

"It's me." He decided on a different approach. "I love you like no man's ever loved a woman before." He sat down next to her and stroked the parting in her hair with his fingertip. "We're destined to be together for ever, like Romeo and Juliet. I think you're the most beautiful woman who's ever lived, anywhere, ever, and I feel humbled and privileged that you want to be my wife. Look, we'll have sponge cake. I don't care. I'm sorry I upset you. We'll have sponge cake, okay?"

She turned to look at him, her face a mess of flesh and salt water. She threw her arms around him. "They do make light fruit cakes. I didn't think of that earlier. We could get a light fruit cake if you really, really want fruit cake."

"I think we should just have sponge cake."

She wiped her eyes. "It's just … you won't understand this, being a man … but all my friends will be there and if we have fruit cake, they'll go, 'Why did you have fruit cake for a wedding cake, you stupid bitch?' They'll all hate me."

"Yes, yes, I can see that now. I was just being silly."

"I love you, Craig. I mean, like no woman's ever loved a man before. We're going to be together for ever, like Romeo and Juliet. I think you're the handsomest man who's ever lived, and I feel proud that you want to be my husband."

"Thanks."

"So we can have sponge cake, yes?"

He nodded and sighed.

"What is it?" she said.

"Nothing. It's nothing."

"It's something. What is it?"

He sighed again and cast his eyes down. "The thing is, before I left the house this morning, my mum said, 'I bet you just lie down and let her walk all over you. I bet you can't get a single concession from her. I bet she just gets everything her own way'."

"Really? Your mum said that?"

He nodded. "That's why I fought so hard."

She stood up. "But you *can* have things your own way. I'll show your mum! You *can!* Name something, anything!"

"I can't think of anything."

"No, Craig," she said. "You have to."

Downstairs in the living room Father Keogh began to make his excuses. Mrs O'Connell tidied the table and Gerald sat down with the *Evening Courier*. The door opened, and Craig and Ellie stepped in. He had his arm around her; she was leaning into him.

"That's more like it!" Ellie's mum said, beaming.

"Mum, Dad, Father Keogh," Ellie said, "we've got something important to tell you about the wedding. Or rather, Craig has."

Gerald put his paper down. "Oh?"

Ellie pushed Craig forward a few centimetres. "Tell them, Craig."

"We've … um …"

The adults waited, their faces strenuously non-judgemental.

"We've decided to have round napkin-holders instead of oval," Craig said.

Ellie's mum gasped.

"They're also … They're going to be gold, not silver," he added.

Gerald got to his feet. He and Ellie's mum and Father Keogh swapped looks of amazement and applauded.

Ellie laughed and cried at the same time. "I *tried* to shift him but he just wouldn't budge!" She tickled his penis through his trousers, then stood to one side and joined the ovation.

GIGGLY

The cakes counter was out to defeat them as usual. A literal honey-trap - especially the Greek bit. Julia could pass it without flinching, but it always caught Helena off guard, as if it materialised just to faze her. They were here for coffee. Cakes weren't part of the plan. Julia took Helena's arm and gave it an affectionate tug.

"Come on, there's a free table."

"Four pounds ten," the woman said. She clearly considered it extortionate but, in their case, deserved. She wasn't offering eye-contact, but as Helena paid, she gave the five pound note a company-policy smile. Julia suddenly noticed the custard tart on Helena's tray. How? She hadn't seen her hand move.

They took their coffees and the cake to the window and sat down, sliding their trays onto the table, their coats onto the chair backs, and their bags beneath them, in a single movement. This was CK's. In the words of the advert, *Life for the Living*. Its tiled walls, each with a Futurist 'Coffee Kingdom' logo in a stainless-steel ring, its marble floors, its spot-lighting and aluminium chairs were all modish enough to dissolve whatever little gawkiness still clung to them as a result of having imperceptible creases in their clothes, and sweat glands.

"I wish they wouldn't put nutmeg on custard tarts," Helena said.

"Who?"

"People."

Julia nodded. She was ten years younger than Helena so tended to defer to her. She leaned back and stirred her coffee. "What's yours?"

"What?"

"Your coffee."

"It's…" Helena had to look " … a latte."

"What *is* a latte, anyway?"

"It's one of these. What's yours?"

"A cappuccino."

"Happy cappuccino!" Helena raised her cup.

Their faces crumpled, mainly round the eyes. Dimples appeared in their cheeks. Something inside them began to surge, catching pleasantly in their throats. They leant forward and began to shudder in spasmodic catches of the breath, putting their hands over their mouths to quell their squeaking.

This wasn't entirely spontaneous: it was about *style*. Whereas Julia's school uniform – a navy jumper atop a tartan skirt – might detract from her style at school (where she was just a clone), in town, where everyone was made of denim or knitted cotton, it set her apart. In a good way. And Helena's gabardine, her Grace Kelly headscarf and her wicker heels helped – the fact that she was a stylish friend. And their coffees were stylish. And the venue. And now they were giggling: the essence of style, as confirmed by CK's own poster, alternating electronically with four others high above the mall's epicentre: two giggling supermodels in party frocks, each bearing a fistful of coffee beans and a cafetière. Life for the Living.

"So is it tomorrow?" Julia asked, putting her hand on the table and looking at her new ring. She'd run out of giggles. It was time to flaunt her jewellery. *Jewellorize* – probably where they'd go next if Helena agreed.

Helena scraped the nutmeg off her tart with a teaspoon. "Mm-hm."

"Are you scared?"

"It's only during daylight hours." She bit her tart.

Julia had studied Islam at school so she knew about Ramadan. But how it affected Helena – this real-life adult with a ponytail under her headscarf, freckles, and an ability to magic cakes onto her tray – was a source of curiosity.

Opaque, as usual. Just completely opaque. That had been Julia's mum's verdict eight months ago when she'd discovered Helena had converted. She'd stood with her back to the kitchen units, silhouetted against the window with its unforgiving view of the parked cars that lined St John's Road, tugging at the fingers of her rubber gloves, shaking her head, and murmuring 'Opaque' over and over. Paradoxically, she didn't seem upset, or even to disapprove. After all, her little sister had been unfathomable all her life: this was simply one more manifestation. She brooded for a while then went to the telephone, to ring her. And she made Julia do the same. Helena might be opaque, but there were far worse things. They should both tell her so. Julia hadn't minded. She'd always idolised her aunt. She'd been more than happy to support her.

"Is that halal?" Julia said.

"I'm not so strict that I've got to check every little thing," Helena said with her mouth full.

"I wouldn't like nutmeg on its own but I don't mind it on cakes."

Helena looked at the little mound of nutmeg she'd scraped onto a napkin. "Are you after my nutmeg?"

They both started to giggle again. Another dip into the eternal pool of style. Julia's long hair went into her coffee as she bobbed over the table.

Odd, the things they giggled at never looked funny when she got home. Why was she giggling? Why were *either* of them? But it was so funny! Julia's mum once made her look up 'giggling' in the dictionary. She'd done so to prove it went with 'silly' and 'juvenile'. Since the dictionary never lied, it was probably time for Julia to stop. But she couldn't. And the great thing was, Helena obviously hadn't been to that bit of the dictionary.

"I bet you'll be dying for nutmeg this time tomorrow," she said at last, wheezing.

"Never," Helena replied.

"Are you scared?"

"You've just asked me that."

"And you said, 'I'll only be fasting during daylight hours'."

Helena shrugged. "Something like that. I can't remember."

"Well, that's not even a proper answer."

"Yes, I'm scared."

So she *was*! This was Helena being serious. This was Helena being real! Julia looked at her and tried to reciprocate the solemnity. They both started to dip and catch and splutter breathlessly again like children.

But they were attracting hostility. An elderly couple sat beneath the big 'CK' logo like crows confronted by a rattle. A woman in a skirt-suit had accidentally swallowed the crows' droppings and blamed Julia and Helena. The girl at the cakes counter and the one at the till belonged to a secret organisation whose mission was to send Julia and Helena to Siberia and make them work the salt mines till they lost their sense of humour. They sobered up.

"Shouldn't you have a hen night?" Julia said, sipping her cappuccino with sang-froid.

"A what?"

"Come on, Helena, you must have heard of a hen night."

"Yes, the only problem is - "

"The only problem is, *you're not getting married*. I know that. But you're taking the plunge. I mean, aren't you going to have a big slap-up meal? The biggest?"

"To what end? Anyway, it's a bit late for that now."

"Why?"

"Because it's almost dark," Helena said. "We're allowed to eat after the sun sets."

"Well, let's go to *Jewellorize*."

"What?"

"Let's go to *Jewellorize*," Julia repeated.

"But we've only just got here!"

"It's a bit ... sad ... here."

Julia knew she'd put something important into words. CK's was pathetic. It pretended to be witty and outgoing and stylish, but it did nothing to oppose the spite and envy of people like the woman in the skirt-suit. Once it got its hands on your four pounds ten it just sat quietly back and let the niggardliness poison everything. It was time to move on, maybe for good. They were allowed to giggle in *Jewellorize*. Giggling was encouraged there.

"Drink up," Julia said. "We're leaving."

Everything in *Jewellorize* was sparkly, bright, inviting – and just a little bit the right side of vulgar. Its young shop assistants often had a laugh with each other. Julia had seen them. And they did it shamelessly. Nothing like CK's. She rotated a display unit to look at the bangles. Helena looked at the scarves.

"What do you think of these?" Julia said, holding up a pair of earrings attached to their backing. She put them against her left ear.

"Can't tell," Helena replied.

"What do you mean?"

"All I can see is the label."

"I know. But *think* of them. Then think of my ear."

This should have been the cue for a new round of giggling – the thought of Julia's disembodied ear trailing an earring along the ground as it slithered who knew where - but the shadow of CK's was still hanging over them. They decided to let it pass.

"I can't," Helena said. "I don't know what your ear looks like. Your hair's too long."

"I think my hair's all right, actually," Julia replied, looking into a mirror and plumping it up.

"Julia, your hair's lovely. I didn't mean it like that. I wish I had your hair. It's beautiful. It's your best feature, I think."

"I might buy them."

"What about this scarf?"

"It's nice, but I don't really like scarves. They're for teachers and old ladies. And you're not either. Why cover up your neck? It's lovely."

"That's what *I* just said about your hair."

"Yeah, but I'd rather have your neck," Julia said.

"I'd rather have your hair than my neck."

"But what about your headscarf? I think if you have to wear a headscarf, you're better off with a neck than hair."

They suddenly became aware of something on the other side of the bangles. Two Year Seven girls from Julia's school. She recognised them, vaguely – she knew *of* them: but she didn't know them to talk to, they were far too young. They were obviously eavesdropping because they were laughing. Both had long, brown hair, Alice bands and the school uniform. Julia was enraged. Helena shrugged, her expression halfway between perplexity and amusement.

Julia was about to say something – she didn't know what yet: only, it would have to be something primal and instinctive, something like asking them what was so *funny*, in that caustic tone she could affect – when one of the shop assistants came over, a tall woman, of about Helena's age, with unkempt hair completely at odds with her polished face. She folded her hands in front of her.

"Excuse me, are you two girls going to *buy* anything?" she asked the Alice bands.

They got to their feet, brushed themselves down, stood to attention and blushed. "Um … yes, maybe," they replied together, looking at the floor.

Julia also felt herself blushing. She was connected to them by school and they were obviously going to be thrown out. She wished she'd changed into her home clothes now.

"It's all right, they're with us," Helena said breezily, fixing the assistant with one of her 'looks'.

Helena was about the same age as the shop assistant. They faced each other down for a moment. But just as, 'Are you going to buy anything' came from the training manual, so apparently did, 'The customer is always right'. The assistant gave a frosty smile, lowered her weapons and withdrew.

Helena resumed browsing to find three schoolgirls gazing at her open-mouthed: two with gratitude, one with indignation. She turned to Julia, put the scarf she'd been looking at back on its hook, and took in the two Year Sevens with an expansive sweep of her hand.

"Julia, behold our two new friends," she said.

Julia didn't say anything the rest of the time they were in *Jewellorize*. Helena ignored her and chatted to the two Year Sevens. Once they were outside, they parted company. Helena and Julia went to sit on a bench next to a dwarf chusan, facing CK's. It was early evening. The mall was full now. Three quarters ambling shoppers, the rest, office workers on a short cut to the station. Up on the first floor, a crowd of teenagers was woo-woo-ing at something.

"I take it you're angry with me," Helena said.

Julia looked down at the marmoreal floor. She wondered if it was something to do with Helena's being a Muslim, her being supernaturally friendly to those two little oiks. 'O believers, be ye witnesses to friendly dealing', that sort of thing. If so, she needed to be a bit more discriminating.

"They were nice kids," Helena said.

"I'm having my period," Julia replied.

"No you're not. You had your period a fortnight ago."

"How do you know?"

"You told me, remember? That stupid argument about your mixed grill?"

"It's just – they were *laughing* at us," Julia said.

She blushed. That wasn't the right explanation at all. It was actually worse than none, being so easily refutable. And that emphasis on 'laughing'. She twirled the ends of her hair. She sounded childish, even to herself.

"Four years is quite a difference when you're your age," Helena said. "They challenged you, or seemed to. They showed contempt for that gap. So they deserved to be punished. And I – your best friend – got them off."

This sounded better, though no more defensible. There was a stall selling Russian dolls just to one side of them. Julia tried to focus on it. A Russian doll - did she want one or not? If so, which one? And what would she do with it?

Oh, she wasn't worthy of a Russian doll. She'd only neglect it, she knew that now. Self-knowledge: a terrible thing. Her fingertips were itchy.

"Of course," Helena said, "it's right you should insist on the disparity and they should respect it. I'm not being sarcastic here, Julia, I really mean it." She sat on her hands. "Four years really *is* quite a gap when you're your age. I'd have been livid if some me-equivalent had done what I've just done to you, to me, when I'd been your age. But they didn't mean it. They just got the giggles, that's all. They were about to be thrown out. And they were only little."

Julia sighed. She didn't know what to say for the best.

"Have mercy, Julia!" said Helena. "For goodness' sake, Julia, *have mercy!*"

Julia grinned. Generosity and forgiveness burst up in her like a flower. Helena's *being a Muslim* had broken through. 'O believers, what a storm in teacup'. "You're right," she said, shaking her head. "I *am* being stupid."

"Hang on, I didn't go that far."

"I know, but I am."

Helena scoffed. "Don't go to the other extreme, girl. A moment ago, you were fully in the right."

They watched the pallid faces of the passers-by. Julia still wished she'd put her home clothes on. She yawned and rubbed her temples. "We were almost thrown out of CK's for giggling," she said.

"Exactly. Gigglers of the world unite."

"What made the two tots lose it, do you think?"

"It may have been when I offered to swap my neck for your hair. Or perhaps it was when you said I had a headscarf, so I needed a neck."

"*We* should have giggled!"

"We were still hung over from CK's."

"Well, let's do it now."

"You can't giggle to order, niece. It's got to be spontaneous."

"Well, let's *pretend*, then."

Simulation led to the real thing. Everything they'd put on hold in *Jewellorize* came bubbling to the surface, until they had to clutch each other.

But, just as in CK's, they sobered up as soon as they started to attract disapproving looks. A pair of lovers in faded jeans and T-shirts sneered at them. A group of boys from the grammar school donned supercilious expressions. Two off-duty shop assistants from *The Shop That Gives Its Employees the Right to Judge Others* shook their heads and turned down their thumbs, giving Russell Crowe permission to kill them. They stopped. This time, though, they both felt bellicose, having to brake when they still had fuel in the tank. Propriety was starting to incense them.

Julia's belligerence caught fire when she looked at the window of CK's. A young man of about Helena's age, shaking his head contemptuously at them. His designer stubble, handmade stripy shirt, gelled and highlighted hair, all combined to add to the insult: the fact that he'd managed a distinct conventional *style*. Julia stuck her thumbs in her ears, waggled her fingers and stuck out her tongue. Several passers-by caught what she was doing and emerged from their trances to grin before scuttling back inside again.

Thereafter, events unfolded like a Greek tragedy. First, Helena slapped her on the arm and said 'don't'. Then the man fetched a member of staff, the same woman who'd taken such a fatalistic view of four pounds ten earlier. She took a good, hard look at Julia, pulled a face and withdrew. A few minutes later, one of the mall's security staff turned up in a green uniform. His shoes were like jackboots. He must have been in the army once, because they were polished to a gloss. Eventually, his shoes were all they saw. They didn't dare look up at him.

"Excuse me," he said. "Are you two young ladies going to buy anything?"

As they left the mall, they couldn't help noticing the ubiquity of giggling young women. Every shop had at least two, since it was impossible to giggle on your own. Women of all ethnicities in cocktail dresses, or sarongs, or cheongsams, or sometimes just in their underwear; women in cars, or on scooters, or in the baskets of hot air balloons; women at the office, or at barbecues, or the races, or the seaside tossing beach balls; women trying (despite their giggles) to play tag, or badminton, or catch. All showing their perfect teeth, heads thrown back, elegant fingertips on their ribs as if to modulate the flow.

By contrast, all the real women in the mall – and the men – looked distinctly unhappy. Not just not-happy, but miserable. It was the stuff nightmares were made of. It must always have been there. And yet they'd never noticed it till now. As they cleared the mall's threshold and stepped into the High Street, they took a deep breath. The difference between the recycled, warm and slightly fragrant air inside and the piquant, rather tasteless stuff outside had always struck them as depressing before: they were leaving something well-planned, litter-free and bright for … the world. But suddenly the world didn't look that bad.

"Woo-hoo," said Julia. "Thrown out of the mall. Badge of honour."

They flopped down on a bench, chilly and a little damp. It was still light. Before them, the main road led up towards the school on one side and down to the Pantiles – the older part of town – on the other. They were still surrounded by shops, mostly those that felt confident enough to get by outside the mall but some of which, being smaller, had no choice. In the distance they could see the deciduous woods where the Weald began. It was cloudy and a breeze teased their hair.

"Did you see all those miserable people?" Helena said. "We're better off out here."

"I know."

"Neither entirely serious nor wholly frivolous. Just self-obsessed. The worst of both worlds."

"Exactly."

"They can keep their stupid mall as far as I'm concerned."

"Ay-men."

They sat with their arms folded and their legs crossed. Helena's mobile gave a loud beep. She took it out of her gabardine pocket. Julia looked down at the ground, pretending to be interested in her pumps. She assumed it was Helena's boyfriend. But a moment later, Helena put it away. Just a boring text, then.

"They've just spotted the new moon in Mecca," Helena said. "It's Ramadan."

Julia caught a thrill. "Wow," she said, with emotion. In her mind's eye, she saw an opulent city of domes and minarets, with gatherings of handsome viziers and gorgeous odalisques in translucent veils, pointing to a glistering sky, anticipating something really *serious*. She wasn't a Muslim, but for some reason, she wished she was there, in Mecca. Just for as long as the new moon was rising. It sounded so exciting, yet at the same time, so thoroughly … ordinary. A moon.

"Don't tell Mum I was thrown out of the mall," she said.

"I think she'd be pleased if she knew."

"Er … you have met her, Helena. She's your big sister, remember? Why would she be pleased?"

Helena laughed. She was in a better mood now she'd received that text. "Giggling's our prerogative, Julia, no one can take it away from us. However subversive it may be. And I suppose it is."

"It's a very serious thing, giggling," Julia teased.

Helena's expression grew intent. "Yes, it can be," she said. "I think so. Yes."

Opaque, as usual! Julia thought happily. *Just completely opaque!*

They moved closer together. Somewhere, hidden above the dusk, the new moon was burning. They looked for it for a moment, willing to see through the clouds. They leaned forward and upwards simultaneously. Then they turned to each other, realised they were both wishing the same thing, and smiled at their own hubris.

AN EVENING AT THE BEACH

From *The Scarborough Evening News*, 29 August 2012:

Picnickers Killed as Beach Excursion Leads to Tragedy

TWO YOUNG PEOPLE *died after being trapped by the tide, in an incident described as "profoundly tragic" at an inquest. The bodies of Peter Shippam, 19, of Robin Hood's Bay, and Annabel Peppard, 18, of Scarborough, were discovered at separate locations close to Bempton Cliffs one week after their disappearances on July 7 this year.*

East Yorkshire coroner Michael Jones accepted the coastguard's conclusion that the couple were picnicking in a secluded cove in or near Fylingthorpe when their exit was blocked by the sea. Recording verdicts of accidental death, he said the overwhelming likelihood was that they were swept into the water as they tried to make their way to safety.

Mr Michael Harman, QC, representing both families, described the two teenagers as "caring, intelligent and deeply loved", adding that they had everything to live for. He called for a public awareness campaign to remind young people of the dangers of using the beaches without appropriate safety precautions.

A memorial service will be held at St Laurence's Church in Scarborough on Saturday 26 September.

"We're almost there," Peter said. He braked and went down a gear. The road was down to a car's width now, and had been for the last mile. Judging by the persistent crunch under the tyres, it hadn't been resurfaced for a long time. The foliage was closing in on both sides. A hazel branch brushed the windscreen.

Annabel sighed. "Where are we going? Am I allowed to ask yet?"

"Not yet."

"This is the countryside."

"Er, yes."

"Where did you say we were going?"

He tried to sound upbeat. "Like I said, it's a surprise."

"Because I'd rather not tear my clothes."

She looked mortified in her court shoes, polka dot dress and white shrug. Presumably, she'd taken 'surprise' to mean a restaurant or a club, not a picnic on a stretch of beach accessible if at all (he hadn't checked recently) only by an overgrown footpath. Her heart must have fallen when she saw he was only dressed in a T-shirt, jeans and loafers.

It was six-thirty now. If anything, the road was getting worse. He bit his lip and suppressed a groan.

But just as it seemed they were about to be swallowed by the hedgerows, the road widened and the sky and the sea appeared in two shades of brilliant blue.

Not a moment before time.

A ten-space car park full of dusty pot holes came into view on the left. Peter pulled into it, switched off the engine, and was overcome with desolation. Now he had to reveal the 'surprise'. Now she'd roll her eyes, sigh and call him a dork. She probably wouldn't even tell him to take her home. She wouldn't need to. What sort of prat takes someone dressed like her to a place like this?

Oh, how they'd laugh when he got back to work. She'd tell all her friends and it would enter office lore. She'd probably end up with Stephen from Accounts, since he was always drooling over her in the canteen. Years from now, everyone would still remember him.

Facebook, 2021

> Remember Peter boring Shippam?

> *Shippam? Wasn't he the one who blew his chance with that red hot brunette, Annabel-something?*

> Yeah. She's married to Lucky Bastard Stephen from Accounts now. Don't know what happened to Shippam, though.

> *Who gives a toss? Loser. Fancy taking a girl like that to a place like that.*

> She saw what was going through his mind, though. Out in the middle of nowhere, yeah? Just the two of them? Where's she going to run to, eh?

He slunk back into the present. *Where's she going to run to.* My God. Luckily, there was still time to retrieve matters. He hung his head and blushed. "I'm sorry. I'll take you home."

"We've only just got here."

"You were right. You don't want to rip your clothes."

"So what was the surprise, then? I mean, what was it *going* to be?"

"I was going to take you for a picnic on the beach."

She raised her chin and eyes, then dropped them and fixed her gaze on the glove compartment. "I suppose that would mean we'd have to walk through thickets, etcetera?"

"I wasn't really thinking properly - "

"If you'd told me before we set off - "

"I know."

"I thought you were taking me to a restaurant or something."

"I would have done if I'd had any brains. I just didn't think. Next time – I'm really sorry: I hope there will be a 'next time' – I'll do something a bit more sensible. I won't let you down twice, Annabel, I promise. I know I must sound a bit of a loser and I know you probably don't want to go out with a dud - who would? – but it's - "

"What's in the hamper?"

"What?"

She grinned. "There's a picnic so there must be a hamper, right?"

"There is."

"So what's in it?"

His mind went blank and suddenly it was as if his life depended on it. "Er, honey roast ham sandwiches, a few sticks of celery, hummus, er … some rollmops, salad … Linda McCartney sausages and two Quorn burgers just in case you're a vegetarian … um, a disposable barbecue, er, bread buns, a banana each, ice-pack to keep everything cool, um, two Müller fruit corners, er, two Eccles cakes, a packet of *Sports* biscuits, um, cutlery, obviously, bottle of *Pimm's*, some lemonade … er, wine, in case you don't like *Pimm's*, a carton of orange juice in case you're teetotal, plastic cups, um, paper plates, tablecloth, blankets in case the wind builds up, er - "

She whistled. "No *way!*" She laughed. "It must weigh a *ton!* Can I see it?"

He realised it was a good way of proving he wasn't a rapist, although strictly speaking it only reduced the probability.

They went to the back of the car. He raised the boot and there it was: a wicker basket as big as a suitcase. He undid the straps and lifted the top. Several layers began with the Eccles cakes, the salad, the Pimm's, the hummus and the disposable barbecue.

She laughed. "Bloody hell, how much did it all *cost?*"

"I mean … if you're hungry … I guess you probably are, given that you thought we might be going to a restaurant … we could eat it in the car …"

"We couldn't eat *all* of it. Anywhere."

"No, probably not. I wasn't sure what you liked, and since it had to be a surprise, I couldn't really ask."

"Do you really think you can carry it?"

"I managed to get it in the boot, didn't I?"

"From where?"

He shrugged. "From my kitchen - my, er, parents' kitchen."

"Which was how far?"

"Say ten yards?"

"And how far's the beach?"

"About quarter of a mile." It was closer to half.

"Let's make a deal. I'm willing to risk my clothes if you're willing to carry the hamper. Yeah?"

"Deal," he said, louder than was dignified.

"You lock the car. I'll go and get a stick so we can beat a path through the nettles."

He swung the hamper from the boot to the ground and almost lost his arm. But it was okay: she hadn't seen.

She broke off a switch from an elder tree, stripped its leaves, whipped the air twice in opposite directions and set off, swinging her arms and setting a hopeless pace. He hoped those thickets would appear sooner rather than later.

He was in luck. A few minutes later, they came to a stop. She put the tip of her tongue out to help her concentrate and hacked at a tousle of bindweed, thistles and nettles.

"No one must have been down here for ages," she said happily.

He put the hamper on its side and sat on it. The sweat was pumping out in a continuous stream and he didn't have anything to wipe it away with. His ankles were grazed. His heart was thudding. The temperature was as high now as it must have been at midday and there was nothing in the way of a breeze from the sea.

"Get a stick and come and help me!" she said.

"I'll just be in the way."

"This is brilliant. It was a great idea. Who cares about my stupid clothes? Hell, I'm going to throw my shoes in the sea when we get there."

He wiped his forehead. "It might be dark when we're coming back. You might tread on something sharp."

"You can *carry* me back. If you like."

"Who's going to carry the hamper?"

"You can come back for it in the morning. No one'll get it. Stop worrying."

He laughed happily. "You're on!" He'd probably be half dead by then but it would be worth it. Facebook 2021 was already beginning to take on a very different complexion.

She stopped whipping. She turned to face him and lowered the switch, her expression serious.

"Do you like it … at the office?" she said.

"Not really."

She continued looking at him.

"Er … do *you*?" he asked.

"I hate it," she said. "I utterly *hate* it. I *detest* it. I hate everything about it."

"I didn't realise. I – I often see you smiling."

"It can't be that often."

"I don't know. You've got a nice smile," he said.

"Every day I have to go in, I ask myself, why. Not just, 'why don't I get another job?' because every job's exactly the same nowadays. No, 'why' with a capital 'W'. I'm as trapped as trapped can be."

She bent the switch as if she was going to break it. She turned back to chopping weeds, much more aggressively than before.

"Er, *I* hate it as well!" he called out. He couldn't see her face any more but he had a feeling she was crying. He should keep talking.

"You're right. I sometimes wonder what we're all here for. I'm always having that same discussion with my parents. They've worked all their lives, same thing. He's a GP, she's a lawyer. Their jobs will still be there when they're dead, with somebody else filling them. Yet they've lost any sense that they're anything more than their jobs. Even when they're on holiday, he's a GP, she's a lawyer. I mean, they *are* those things."

He had no idea if he'd helped. She turned to face him. Yes, she'd been crying. Apart from that, he couldn't read her expression. She turned away and went back to slashing the undergrowth.

He could smell the sea, and the hot summer earth, and the seagulls' distant crying seemed like real crying, only more abstract. The insects buzzed and bit and darted. All the way up to the beach, the land was a mixture of greens. A few weeks from now it would be retreating into shades of autumn, then the greys of winter. Never before had the thought of winter so dismayed him. Already, he wanted to cling to this one day – necessarily, somehow, a baking summer's day.

They burst onto the beach as suddenly as they'd arrived at the car park. It was no surprise to find it deserted, though it was hardly the spectacular vista he felt they deserved. Mud, then a belt of sand smeared with dried bladder-wrack, then the sea.

She seemed to share his assessment. "Let's walk along a bit."

Peter fell in behind her. The insides of his fingers were raw where the hamper's handles had dug in, and his arms ached. His head was throbbing. He must be seriously dehydrated. Never mind, his mum had included a packet of Ibuprofen in the hamper. 'You don't want your evening spoiled by a headache,' she'd said as he left the house. As usual, her words were prophetic. He hadn't told her about the *Pimm's* or the wine. She'd never have let him have the car otherwise.

Five minutes later, they rounded the corner of a slight promontory and entered a tiny cove hemmed in by cliffs. The sun was invisible, occupying a point low over the mainland, but it threw the cliffs' shadows far into the sea. Beyond those shadows' borders little whitecaps sparkled. Nearer the horizon the sky was dark blue, a sort of eerie night-in-day in which a few stars were already visible.

The beach inclined steeply towards the sea. Fifty yards of shingle, seaweed, and sand.

"This is what we've been looking for," she said. "Let's go in the water. I'm boiling."

She took off her shoes and threw them far out to sea, grunting like a tennis player, then charged into the water without taking her dress off. "Come on!"

He dropped the picnic hamper and followed her at speed. For a split second he thought he was going to have a seizure. Then he was snatched by a visceral ecstasy that began somewhere in the pit of his stomach and radiated outwards.

Annabel was up to her shoulders now. Then they both were.

She laughed. "You're a bit burned."

"So are you."

"This is outstanding!"

She swam away to the edge of the cliff's shadow then turned to face inland, pushing her hair from her face. "I can see the sun. Come and look."

He swam over and they faced the sun together. He put his arm round her. They were both treading water so it was difficult, and he couldn't help wondering if she thought it contrived. With some reluctance, he withdrew it.

"I'd like to keep swimming out forever," she said.

"You couldn't. You'd bump into Denmark."

"How far?"

"About four hundred miles."

"Are you hungry?"

"Starving."

They swam back, walked ashore and sat down. The shadow here was much darker and they had to keep looking out to sea to remind themselves there were still a few hours of daylight left. There wasn't sufficient heat left in the sun to dry their clothes off. They began to shiver. They stripped to their underwear, wrung their clothes out and put them back on again. Then they wrapped the blankets round themselves and huddled together. Peter put his arm round her again, and she snuggled up to him and drew her knees to her chin.

"Put your other arm round me," she said. "Wait, why don't we light the barbecue? That'll keep us warm. I'll go and get some driftwood. We might be able to make a fire as well."

They ate the ham sandwiches and the rollmops and dipped the celery in the hummus, then went to find tinder. Half an hour later they made a fire and set a row of vegetarian sausages on the barbecue. Roaming the beach looking for fuel restored their circulation. They settled on curling up with their arms round each other.

"That thing you said about your parents," she whispered. "Are you frightened you'll end up like them?"

His joints were stiff. "Yes."

"This has been a perfect day. I mean, almost perfect."

"Just 'almost'?"

"Tell me how much you hate it at the office."

"Well, it's not that I *hate* it, exactly," he said, knowing this probably wasn't what she wanted to hear, "but I can see there are more faults than good points."

"What 'good points'?"

"There's you."

"But I'm not staying."

"Where are you going?"

"I haven't decided yet, but I have to get out. Look." She showed him her arms. They were striated by white scars. He hadn't noticed before. "I'll go crazy if I have to stick around there much longer."

"Does anyone else at work know?"

She scoffed and looked at the horizon. "It's not just the office, Peter. I've looked down on life from a high mountain." She blinked slowly and lifted her chin. "Do you know what I saw? We're all just doing *nothing,* that's what. Every day you get up, just like you did the day before, then you go to work and do just what you did the day before, then you come home and do just what you did the day before. It wouldn't matter if it was worthwhile the first time round, but it isn't. Even if you try to get away from it, and go 'travelling', say, sooner or later the stupidity of it will catch up with you. Because none of it has the slightest meaning."

"But you must - "

"It's getting dark now. Haven't you noticed?"

"Maybe we should be heading back."

"What would you do if you were to look down at my legs now and discover they weren't legs at all? That I'd" – she looked at the sky and laughed – "transformed into - into a mermaid? That where my legs used to be, there was nothing but a fiendish-looking fish tail? It would make sense, wouldn't it, eh, Peter? After all, I threw my shoes away. I can't really have been expecting you to carry me back, can I? Not *really?*" Her eyes blazed and she lurched forward. "And what would you do, Peter, if I grabbed you by the arms and forced you to come into the sea with me? Would you put up a struggle? If so, how much of a struggle, eh, Peter?"

"I wouldn't struggle at all," he replied quietly.

She pulled the blanket away and waved her legs. "Ta-dah! Had you going though, eh?"

"I wish you were a mermaid."

"What?"

"I said, I wish you were a mermaid. I wouldn't struggle at all."

She looked into his pupils and her whole body went soft. He put his cheek against hers and swivelled his head until their lips were touching. He pushed down, squeezing her shoulder blades to him with his palms. She pushed back and slid her tongue along his teeth. Finding his nose blocked by the far side of her face he discreetly withdrew for breath.

"I know we've only known each other a few hours," he said. "And I know you're probably going to say it can't happen that quickly, but – I think I - I love you, Annabel. I know I do … I didn't love you when we came down here in the car. Now I do … I can't explain it. Laugh all you like."

She sat up and broke into a grin. "But you're quite wrong, Peter. I *know* it can happen that quickly. Everything great in love happens in hours or days, never in months or years. Have you ever seen *Titanic?* That's the sort of thing I mean. Over in days, lasted a whole lifetime. And I know because I've fallen in love with you. Oh my God, I'm in love! That's why I told you that mermaid story. Oh my God."

They stood up, facing the sea. They were children again. The whole world shared their astonishment. Creation flowed through them, connecting them more vitally to each other than any mere physical contact. They had the same thought at the same time. *We are alive.*

"Oh, shit," Peter said.

"What?"

The colour had abandoned his face. "My God, *no*. Look."

He pointed to the far reaches of the cove where the cliffs extended farthest seawards. Sometime when they hadn't been looking, the tide had come in. The path by which they'd entered was under several metres of water.

"When did that happen?" she said angrily.

Peter looked up at the cliff. "We can't climb out. It's too steep. And too crumbly."

"We're going to die."

He put his hands on his temples. "Okay, okay, keep calm. The tide's coming in, so it would probably carry us back to shore if we got stuck. There's not much of a wind. We can both swim. So we edge our way along the cliff. Once we're round the corner, we can make a break for the shore."

"What about the picnic basket?"

"Who cares about the picnic basket?"

"I'm frightened."

"Let's drink that wine," he said. "We've still got a while before the water reaches us here."

He rummaged through the basket. They hadn't touched ninety per cent of what was in there. He pulled out the wine.

"Is it a good wine?" she asked.

"I don't know anything about wine."

"Percentage."

He peered at the label. "Thirteen."

"It's a good wine."

"Shit, *shit*."

"What's the matter?"

"I didn't bring a corkscrew."

"Pass it to me." She grabbed it, tore at the cork with her fingernails, then sucked at it and looked at it. Still stuck fast.

"The *Pimm's*," he said.

He took it out, detached a pair of plastic cups from the twelve-pack with trembling fingers and poured two measures. She drank hers at a single draught. "Another," she said.

She was more in need of it than he was. After her third cup, she toasted the ocean. "It's *Pimm's* o'clock."

"Are you ready?" he asked. The tide was nearly at their toes.

"Let's go. No, no, this is silly."

"What do you mean?"

"Well, think. Next to the cliffs, the water's going to be sloshing about more than ever. We're going to get pummelled and we're probably going to get exhausted. Like you said, the sea's calm. There's not much wind. I think we should just swim out from where we are now for about a hundred yards, turn sharp left till we're past the corner, then make for the shore when we're past the cliffs."

He cupped his hands over his face, and smiled underneath them, and looked at her with wide eyes. "You're right! For all I remember, the cliffs might go on for quite a long way. If they do, and we try to get past them by physically edging along them, we're going to get more and more desperate and more and more tired."

"More *Pimm's*," she said.

They drained the bottle.

"You go first," she said.

He ran into the water. It was freezing but as soon as he was beyond touching-distance of the seabed he knew they were going to make it. There wasn't a breath of wind, and the water, if anything, was calmer than when they'd arrived.

"It's lovely!" he shouted. "Come on in!"

A few seconds later, she was alongside him. They grinned at each other and touched hands under the water. She was holding something. She raised it above the surface. The wine.

"We needed an adventure to make the day perfect," she said. "Now we've had one. When we get to safety, we're going to look at the sky and say, 'God in Heaven, we never want to be apart, look after us for the rest of our short lives', then we're going to take all our clothes off and … and have sex. Yes? Then we're going to take the wine, hammer the cork in with a stick or something and drink it dry. When you meet the right person, you just know. You can't be wrong. Don't you agree?"

93

He swallowed. "Yes."

"Have you ever 'done it' before?"

"No."

"Me neither. It's going to be awful."

It took them less than five minutes to reach the shore. They strode onto dry land, shivering. They took off their clothes, lay on the sand, and caressed each other so energetically that their hearts immediately started banging against their ribs and their bodies galloped from cold to warm to hot. She recited her prayer. They swapped nuzzling for foreplay punctuated by awkward laughs, gasps, apologetic grimaces. After an hour, they swapped foreplay for intercourse and began to achieve a mutual understanding. All frivolity dissolved in the rhythm of their skin and bones and he climaxed.

For a moment they whispered incoherencies to each other and listened to the tide. The wind was picking up from the mainland.

She hauled herself to her feet and grabbed the bottle. "Right, now for the wine."

He was utterly exhausted. He'd accumulated the wisdom of a lifetime since turning the car engine off – how long ago? He looked at his hands. They were bleached and crinkly from the brine, like a nonagenarian's. Something had happened, a portal had opened somewhere in time, he'd entered it without knowing and grown old. There could be no going back, no possible undoing. And conversely, no chance of a repeat performance. Because there were no more boundaries to be crossed, just this one now behind him. Everything that was ever going to happen for him had now been achieved. It was the strangest feeling ever, combining the highest elation and the bleakest desolation.

The next thing he was aware of, she was passing him the wine. She'd already drunk half of it.

"Drink the rest," she said coldly.

"Are you okay?"

"I'm absolutely perfect."

"Are you sure?"

She took a handful of sand and ran it between her fingers and watched it blow out to sea. "I'm not going back, Peter. There's nothing to go back for. This has been the most perfect day of my life.

It's everything I've been waiting for since the moment I was born. I can't allow it to fizzle out. It has to end cleanly. I can't do another day of nothing, I just can't."

"But we've got each other now. It's - "

"Not for ever. I will lose you."

"You won't!"

The sea was as grey and dead as mercury. She hitched the corners of her mouth up and looked at the horizon. "Come with me, then. You said you'd come with me if I tried to drag you into the sea. Show me you mean it."

Obviously she was serious, but hopefully, the thought of dragging him along would be too much for her. And yet - it might not be. If not, so be it. He put all his energy into getting to his feet but he was dog-tired. Success only came with the second attempt.

They charged miserably into the water, and swam without looking back for nearly ten minutes, chewing sea-water, fighting the waves, daring each other. She stopped first and began to tread water. He came up alongside her, praying she'd changed her mind.

"I don't want to kill you, Peter," she said. "You go back. I – I didn't think you'd come all this way." She went under for a moment, surfaced, wiped her eyes and took a sharp breath. "You must really love me, after all."

"I do."

"Go back."

"Not without you."

"*Please.*"

"No."

"Why?" Even above the mounting wind he heard her voice crack with emotion. "Why do you want to live? *Why?*"

He suddenly saw there was no point in answering. He laughed without humour. They must have passed the point of no return a long time ago. He couldn't even see the shore. The tide had turned, so the wind would carry them out to sea now whatever they did. He was getting cramp. He thought of his parents, then his friends; his colleagues at the office; his past; his plans; his whole life. He looked up. He didn't want to go back, he wanted to be with Annabel. The sky was aflame with stars.

The muscles in his legs tightened and he stopped treading. He went under the surface and began to lose control.

She swam over in an apparent attempt to bear him up, but she went under alongside him. He saw the rage in her expression as the bubbles shot from her mouth and her eyes bulged. Then his epiglottis opened and he drank and clutched. The pain was excruciating and he lost all sense of where he was.

But then an abrupt calm descended and he somehow saw into the far distance. Everything was just as it should be.

In the icy gloom of approaching death, she held him tight. He saw their lives as they might have been – the long, stoic weathering of all the at-work drudgery, their top-secret, only half-reluctant wedding, their continual stand offs with every conventional expectation from 'the outside world', their several lopsided but loveable children, the unexpected years of genuine companionship, their old-age yes-you-really-could-call-it-happiness inseparability – and wondered where the truth lay: in that world or this one?

It was academic now, anyway. They were mermaids, and going down fast into the darkness.

MISS GREEN'S LAST CASE

According to the local paper, sixty-seven-year-old Miss Black was serving at the till in the Porthcurno horse-charity shop, when a man walked in and asked for a CD that another assistant had reserved for him the day before. Miss Black went into the back to look for it. The man took a hundred pounds from the till and disappeared.

That was the official story.

Miss Green was ninety-seven, and always went outdoors hunched over a walking frame. Over the course of half a decade, she'd won renown in the village for solving crimes the police wouldn't touch. The Case of the Shattered Wing Mirror, The Case of the Missing Allotment Produce, The Case of the Persistent Dog Poo and many others, had all been cracked by her dogged investigatory persistence. The local underworld feared and respected her in equal measure.

The day after the report in the *Porthcurno Advertiser*, she paid the horse-charity shop a visit. She wore her trademark grey overcoat and hat. The bell dinged as she entered.

Miss Brown, the owner, was sorting through some clothes a nice boy from the jumble sale had brought over. She looked up, started unpleasantly – she knew Miss Green of old – and decided to play it cool. She smiled. "Lovely weather we've been having."

Miss Green nodded curtly. She parked her walking frame in the middle of the shop and rested on it.

"So … can I help you?" Miss Brown asked.

"I've found your thief."

"I beg your pardon?"

Miss Green held out a cut-out copy of the newspaper article and sat down on a chair next to a basket of cuddly toys. "Don't act so surprised. Firstly, I happen to know it was Miss Black that was out front that morning, though the article doesn't mention it."

"Er, yes. What of it?"

"Notice the article doesn't describe the thief. Did Miss Black describe him?"

Miss Brown bristled. "I believe he was middle aged with blond hair. I don't know what this has - "

"Height about average?"

"That's what she said, yes."

"As I suspected," Miss Green said. *"Très vague, non?"*

"I'm not sure I follow, and I'm not certain I - "

"There *was* no man," Miss Green snapped. "You both made it up."

Miss Brown's mouth opened. Nothing came out.

"There's a recession going on," Miss Green went on measuredly, "so donations are down, and so are takings. Then, conveniently, you're robbed. Two trusting old ladies, fleeced by a middle-aged con artist. The *Porthcurno Advertiser* loves that sort of thing, so it has a field day. Suddenly, everyone starts giving again out of sympathy."

"For pity's sake - "

"I've been counting the donations, Miss Brown. Four bags a day outside the front door all last week. Seven, since you were allegedly robbed."

"That doesn't mean a thing." But she was blushing now.

"No? All those DVDs at two pounds fifty each? Not to mention the paperbacks and the kiddies' clothing. I imagine things have never looked so good."

"Look, I haven't time for this. Why don't you just go to the police if you think you know what happened? Why bother coming in here?"

"Because I can't prove it. Not yet. But I want you both to know it's only a matter of time."

Miss Brown smiled thinly. "Well, thank you for warning us in advance."

Miss Green stood up and walked her frame slowly out of the shop. It took her three tries to get the door open. Miss Brown watched but didn't try to help. She waited till Miss Green was out of sight, counted to three, then got on the phone to Miss Black.

"We've got to talk," she said. "Face to face."

She heard Miss Black gulp.

Ten minutes later, the doorbell jangled. Miss Black entered.

Miss Brown reversed the 'Open' sign. "Miss Green's just been in," she said. "She knows."

Miss Black sat down on the chair and put her hand over her mouth. "Oh, my God. Oh, my God."

"Don't worry, she can't prove anything. It's a 'theory' she's got, and if you keep your big fat mouth shut, it'll remain just that."

"Has she been to the police?"

"She said she's waiting till she's got some evidence."

Miss Black began to tremble. "I can't cope with this, Shirley. I just can't. I'm not cut out for this sort of thing. It's not me."

"I'm warning you, Susan: don't start getting cold feet. This was never about us, we said that, at the beginning. Think about the horses we've helped. Think of Fancy, Sugar and Lady Tucker. Think of their beautiful, grateful *faces*. My God, each *one* of them is worth a hundred Miss bloody Greens put together! If you hadn't - "

Miss Black put her hand over Miss Brown's mouth. She shook her head and picked up a notepad and a pen.

'*What if she's hidden a microphone?*' she wrote.

Miss Brown looked blank for a split second, then horrified, until, at last, her expression hardened. She reached into the cuddly toy basket and pulled out a mobile phone, switched on and recording. She scowled, threw it to the floor and stamped on it. When it didn't break, she picked up a nineteenth century iron from the antiques shelf and hammered it to smithereens.

Miss Black put her hands on her head and pulled her hair. "That's going to look like confirmation!"

"Of *what*? She's got nothing on us."

"Oh no? What about, 'I can't cope with this, Shirley', and, 'Think about the horses we've been able to help.' What if she was recording the recording?"

But Susan had frozen. Shirley followed her gaze. Miss Green was staring at them grimly through the shop window. She wore an earpiece. When they made eye-contact, Miss Green smiled malevolently, then turned on her walking frame and shot off.

Miss Brown dropped the iron. The bell jangled as she and Susan left the shop in a rush. They scanned the main road.

But Miss Green was nowhere to be seen.

"What are we going to do?" Miss Black said fretfully.

"She can't have got far. You go that way, I'll go this."

Miss Black hesitated. She was beginning to look teary. "I meant: if we catch up with her."

"*When*, not *if*. She's *had* her life, Susan. She's ninety-seven years old, and we'll be doing everyone a favour. And by 'everyone', I mean the entire equine world."

"My God. You're *mad!*" She swallowed. "I - I'm sorry, Shirley, but count me - "

"There she *is!*"

Miss Green stood on the kerbside, fifteen metres away, glaring at them triumphantly. She waited to register their reaction, then made a dash to get across the road.

Miss Brown turned a vehement look on Miss Black. "We've got to stop her!"

Suddenly, there was a screeching of tyres. They turned just in time to see Miss Green and her walking frame disappear beneath a lorry. After it engulfed her, it veered into the front window of the Oxfam shop, producing a spectacular explosion of glass and masonry.

For a split second, the surrounding pedestrians stood poleaxed or screaming, then some of them ran to help. The lorry's alarm blared. The shop's alarm blared. Miss Black and Miss Brown clasped their hands to their mouths. They both went down on their haunches.

"This has been a very bad day," Miss Black croaked. She took a deep breath, then another, and put her fingertips on the pavement, to stop herself from fainting.

Miss Brown put her arm round her. "Just think about the horses, Susan. Think about their faces."

MRS CHALFORD, WITCH

Chrissy ran her fingers through several layers of her client's thin red hair. She stepped back on her heel and looked at the two grim faces in the salon mirror. "Would you like your roots doing, Mrs Chalford?"

"Are they grey?" the old woman said.

"Well ... a *bit*, yes."

"You're new here, aren't you?"

"This is my first week. I'm a trainee."

"Very well, then. Proceed."

Mrs Chalford's roots weren't grey. But 'white' didn't exist in here, not alongside 'hair'. Even 'grey' was against policy. Chrissy would never have said it if Mrs Chalford hadn't first, 'a different colour' being the customary euphemism.

"Just a shampoo and dry, apart from that?" Chrissy said.

"And an intelligent conversation."

Tracy, the proprietress, and Sheryl, the manicurist, were out in the yard, smoking. Tracy had been scheduled to do Mrs Chalford, but a call from school about Annie meant she had to rush off straight after her cigarette. She'd be back to lock up about six-ish, she said. Mrs Chalford was the last customer. Since *Hairfayre* was appointments only, and Sheryl was due to leave just before five, Chrissy would soon be alone with her.

She wheeled the portable basin over and lowered Mrs Chalford's head into it, bringing the hair up from the nape of her neck and making sure she was supported round the collar.

"Is that comfortable?" she asked.

"It'll do ..."

She switched the showerhead on and moderated the pressure. "Not very nice weather we've been having lately," she said, hoping to start Mrs Chalford's 'intelligent conversation'. She checked the temperature with her fingertips and put the VO5 to hand.

"Do you want me to take my hearing aid out or do you think you can do round it?" Mrs Chalford said.

"I think I can probably do round it."

"If it gets water on, it breaks."

"Maybe … take it out, then?"

"Don't make a *statement* as if it's a *question,* girl! Yes or no? *IN OR OUT?"*

Chrissy's eyes grew. "Er, leave it in."

Tracy breezed in from the yard. "Don't forget to take Mrs Chalford's hearing aid out before you get started. And when you've finished rinsing, pop into the back for a moment: Sheryl needs a quick word." She grabbed her keys, took a twenty from the till, slipped on her coat, and plumped her hair in the mirror. "Bloody kids. Girls are as bad as boys nowadays."

Tracy was in her late forties but looked a decade older. Her bobbed blonde hair was an advert for the shop. She wore *Amunoso* and chunky necklaces and ate Fruit & Nut between customers. The chocolate was stress, she explained to everyone who knew, brought on by her teenage daughter. Not only was that Annie's fault, but Annie also made her smoke. And sometimes, thanks to Annie, she drank Lamb's Navy Rum from a hip flask. Nevertheless, she did it all discreetly. She had to, because she was the public face of *Hairfayre.*

"I know I promised *I'd* do you," Tracy whispered, leaning over Mrs Chalford. "But I've really, really got to rush. Absolute emergency. I'm *so* sorry. Is there anything I can get you before you go? Anything I can do to make up for it?" She knitted her fingertips, put her shoes together and bent at the waist like a suppliant.

Mrs Chalford said nothing. She kept a hard stare on her own face in the mirror.

"Take good care of Mrs Chalford!" Tracy snapped at Chrissy. "I'm warning you. *I'll find out if you don't!"*

She banged the door behind her, jangling the bell loudly. Mrs Chalford tugged her hearing aid from the earwax. Chrissy half-expected a slurping 'pop' as it dislodged.

"Here," Mrs Chalford said, handing her it.

Chrissy wanted to shampoo it. She took a tissue from the box on the counter and wrapped it up. She bent down to hide a dry retch.

Mrs Chalford wiped her fingertips on the chair arm. "You know why Tracy's got such a *fat arse*, eh? It's because she can't stop eating. Eat, smoke, eat, smoke. All she thinks about is how to pile more lard on. Looks like a balloon with a slow puncture. Only cares for cakes and *Camel*. No wonder her daughter's such a godawful bloody mess."

The viciousness left Chrissy momentarily lost for words. "Horrible weather ... we've been having lately?" she tried at last.

"Obviously."

She caressed Mrs Chalford's scalp - lifting the hair, and combing it with her fingers to sift the water through - when she met a bump. Without stopping, she looked down. A bald patch with a tattoo. Or perhaps a birthmark? A little number six.

"I can *seeee* you!" Mrs Chalford said.

Chrissy jumped and looked up. She'd forgotten the mirror. She made eye-contact and blushed.

"Curious?" Mrs Chalford said. "And no, I haven't been in a concentration camp, if that's what you're thinking." She paused. "Have you ever seen *The Omen*?"

No, she hadn't. "What's it about?"

Mrs Chalford laughed. "I can't *heeeear* you!"

"What's it about?"

"I still can't *heeeear* you!"

Chrissy's mouth opened and closed four times. She looked in the mirror again and saw her own face: sallow, and topped with what looked like brown cushion-stuffing. She lowered the showerhead into the bowl.

"I'm sorry," Mrs Chalford said, in a conciliatory tone. "I can see I've upset you ... Chrissy. People are always trying to talk to me when I haven't got my hearing aid in. *But* ... I suppose I shouldn't let it get to me. Listen, *you* do the shampooing and dyeing, *I'll* do the talking. I'll tell you the tale of that little mark on my scalp, if you'd prefer. Would you like that? Me to tell you a story? Just nod or shake your head, there's a dear."

Chrissy picked up the shower and resumed rinsing. She'd stemmed the urge to weep, but her hands were shaking. It wasn't just Mrs Chalford. It was everything. This had been the worst week of her life. She couldn't do anything right. Bringing in a trainee had been supposed to help Tracy balance the books. Chrissy was 'tax-deductible' and *Hairfayre* was threatened with 'receivership'. She nodded.

Mrs Chalford smiled. "Good. I believe we're going to get on famously, young lady. I might ask for you every time I come in. It'll make a change to having my hair washed by Gutbucket. Now, story, story. Where to begin? God, it's such a while since it all happened and no one's asked me for such a long time. I've almost forgotten. Let's see ... have you ever come across the notion of the 'mad scientist'? Doctor Frankenstein? Mr Hyde? Jerry Lewis in *The Nutty Professor*? There are more modern versions of that notion than you might think. Another question. Have you ever heard of sociology, the 'science' of society? Because this village used to have a *mad sociologist*, Chrissy. Sounds a bit droll when I put it like that, doesn't it? More Jerry Lewis than Victor Frankenstein? But I can assure you it wasn't funny at all. Not at the time. Now, are you with me? Ready to begin?"

Their eyes locked in the mirror. Chrissy nodded. Mrs Chalford smiled and folded her hands across her stomach.

"Sherman Knox, he was called, this 'sociologist'. His big idea – the one he'd spent his academic career trying to prove – was that human beings are capable of the same depravities today as they've always been, that technology hasn't affected their capacity to take a wrong turn one iota. Apparently, he'd been dismissed from a lectureship at Southampton before he arrived here. We didn't know that when he moved in. Didn't find out till later. His experiments were all a little too ... *intense*, apparently, for the public's liking, and thus for the good name of the university. But being sacked made him more than ever determined to prove the truth of his big idea. He wanted to *show them*, you see, Chrissy, and they'd raised the stakes by giving him his cards.

"Knox was in his late forties, I'd guess. Thick mop of black hair like a Beatle – with just the odd grey strand in - handlebar moustache, long-ish face; quite tall with it, but not very well built. Typical academic, really. Weedy, rather ugly. As for me, I was something of an *ingénue*, I suppose. I lived quietly where I live today, in the old farmhouse on top of Piper's Hill, north of the village. I don't know whether you know the place? You wouldn't see my little hill unless you were looking for it. More of a knoll, really. Old Roman refuse tip, or burial ground. You often see people with metal detectors up there. Luckily, I've five big dogs so they don't usually stray too far from the beaten track.

"In a nutshell, Knox set out to show that, given the right set of circumstances, people were still capable of burning a witch. I mean, actually *burning* one. A *person*. I've no idea whether he intended to step in at the last minute, put a stop to it all, like Derren Brown does when he knows he's gone too far. Have you ever seen Derren Brown, Chrissy? On Channel Four? You should watch him, he's ever so clever. Imagine that though. Actually *burning* someone! That you'd find them so evil and repulsive, you'd be prepared to put a torch to them, then sit and watch as their flesh cooked and peeled from the bone. *A living person!*

"You can probably guess now where this is leading. I was to be that person. Only qualified candidate, really. I was old, lived alone, didn't like company. Sometime shortly after he arrived, he decided he was going to burn me to death. Or rather, the village was. All in the name of his 'big idea'."

She smiled. Then the corners of her mouth dropped off. "He was ingenious, I'll give him that. Incredible as it sounds, he nearly managed it. Soon after he arrived, the village suffered a spate of burglaries and random acts of vandalism. Well, a lot of communal soul-searching went on, the local paper showed interest, the police made the usual enquiries about the secondary school and the pubs. *Nichts und niemand.* Meanwhile, the destruction continued apace. People were upset and angry. Apart from anything else, there were the property prices to think of. No one wants to move into a 'bad' area, now do they?

"About six weeks later, ten or twelve people in the village received letters, hand-delivered and anonymous. Gist: a large London trust had opened one of its 'Homes for Children' just outside the village. Data protection and the law stopped the police, the council or the trust publishing the fact. 'Children' meant disturbed teenagers, all with criminal records, brazen and venal. They couldn't be sent to prison since they were too young, but neither could they be controlled. Owing to the delicacy of the thing, official concealment was *de rigueur*. The trust was picking up a hefty cheque each month from social services. And of course, it was from that 'Home' all the trouble was coming. My house. They were living with me, and I was getting paid a fortune.

"The police, the council and the trust – it *was* a real trust – all denied it. Of course they did: it wasn't true. But the more they denied it, the worse it got. The village was under attack, now it was being lied to by the Establishment. Classic conspiracy ingredients. Obviously, if anything was to be done, the villagers would have to take the law into their own hands.

"From their point of view, there were two distinct problems. The house… and me. Without the house, the fictional children would have nowhere to live, but as long as I was alive and willing to look after them, it was possible we'd relocate somewhere local. No, they had to get rid of both things. I say 'they': not all of them, obviously. Just a few of the more fanatical ones, I guess.

"They started with the building, of course; tried to burn it down. On three occasions, I put the flames out just in time. I never saw who it was, though. Arson is ordinary in this country: ask any fireman. And I was attacked in the street, in broad daylight, by a woman with an umbrella. That's the mark on my head. It was obvious things were heading for a crisis, it was only a matter of time before someone would set the house alight and stop me exiting. Call it the principle of two birds with one stone."

"So what happened in the end?" Chrissy asked.

Mrs Chalford smiled. She chewed her false teeth, got them right, chomped twice, and smiled again.

"Luckily, some members of the Parish Council had clubbed together to hire a private detective. They needed someone impartial to get firm evidence that my house *was* being run by the trust, you see. Turned out to be a nice man, this 'PD'. After I invited him in for a slice of marmalade cake and a cup of Earl Grey, he decided to turn his attention to the anonymous letters and the vandalism. And it didn't take him long to find who was responsible. You see, Knox was like all people convinced of their own genius: apt to underestimate others. He'd written it all down, I'm afraid: both what he'd done and how it was meant to end. Being a scientist, he had to, because that's how science works. You make your prediction, you do your experiment, you match it to your written forecast, and everyone praises your methodology. Your Nobel Prize awaits you, Sire. But not this time.

"The village left me alone after that, although no one ever came to say sorry. Knox was given a five-month suspended sentence. He died in a car crash a few months later, driving home from some dead-end job she – he" – Mrs Chalford laughed and put her index finger on her lower lip – "*he*'d let *him*self drift into. It may have been suicide, or not: the inquest returned an open verdict.

"I learned something, though. Dr Knox might be surprised if he could see me now, I mean from a ... *sociological* point of view."

She fixed Chrissy with a glare. The dye was on now. It just had to fix then the dryer could be lowered. "What did you learn?" Chrissy asked.

Mrs Chalford smiled. "I learned that if enough people start thinking of you as something, you start to think of yourself that way. And make no bones about it, my dear, subliminally people think of me as a witch. They'd never admit it, not even to themselves, but that's how it is. Now," she went on, "I'm not saying I see *myself* as one, but I can't help seeing myself as others do. No one can. Not for long, anyway. And I realised, many moons ago, that it's better to play up to others' ideas about you than it is to fight them. For your own good."

Goose bumps had appeared on Chrissy's arms. It was very cold in the salon now. Perhaps Sheryl had gone home and left the back door open?

She jumped as she suddenly remembered Sheryl 'needed a word'. *God, she'd forgotten!*

It was ten past five. Sheryl would have gone! It could probably wait till tomorrow, couldn't it? It would have to. Which meant yet another bollocking. In the meantime, Tracy would be livid if she came back and found the yard door wide open. Especially now it was dark outside.

"I'm just going to shut the back door. I'll be straight back," she said.

"Say hello to that bitch Sheryl for me," Mrs Chalford shot out through bared teeth. "Tell her I know she's listening. But she's probably worked it out for herself by now."

Chrissy pushed past the beaded screen into the back room. The light was off, and – shock of shocks - Sheryl was perched on a stool in the shadows, her left foot tucked so rigidly behind her right calf that her knees looked bloodless. The door to the yard was firmly shut.

Sheryl was tall and thin with thick brown hair and a BA. Her frilly pink blouse, denim mini-skirt and heels were policy-statements meant to endear her to her critics, of whom there were many. She'd obviously been listening in. She looked up with the thwarted expression of a hobgoblin.

"Hi," she said grimly.

"Oh, hi!" Chrissy replied, raising her voice to magic cheerfulness in. "I thought the door to the yard was open."

"Well, it isn't."

"I thought you had to leave before five."

"Well, I didn't."

"You can go if you want to, Sheryl. It's okay, Tracy said she'll be back around six-ish to lock up."

"Yeah, it's not like she's stupid enough to let *you* lock up. I couldn't help overhearing you both. That bloody old *hag!*"

"I can *heeeear* you!" came Mrs Chalford's voice.

Sheryl went pale. She started to get up but couldn't unknot her legs. "No, I ..." she dissembled, falling forwards and righting herself on the counter. "Mrs Chalford, I didn't - "

"She must have put her hearing aid back in," Chrissy said, wiping her hands on a cloth, and getting ready to help retrieve matters. "No, wait a minute," she continued, speaking to herself, "because she asked me to say 'hello', and she didn't have her hearing aid in then, so ... "

Sheryl rushed through the beaded screening into the shop. Chrissy followed at a walk. They were just in time to see Mrs Chalford's back as she departed with a speed and an energy Chrissy would scarcely have credited her with. As she passed the window, four or five black dogs loomed up like monstrous bubbles and followed her.

"Shit, shit, *shit!*" Sheryl said. "Bloody hell, what have I *done?*"

*

As soon as it was obvious Mrs Chalford wasn't coming back – about five seconds after she'd gone – Chrissy closed the door to stop the cold coming in. Sheryl sat down. She dropped her head. She raked her hands through her hair, re-tied her legs, and cursed.

"She's left me a tip!" Chrissy said, picking up five ten-pound notes from Mrs Chalford's chair. She fanned the money out, grinning.

"Obviously, by mistake," Sheryl said, shaking her head. "It must have dropped out of her purse. Take it at your own risk, I'd say."

"She didn't really give the dye time to fix, did she?"

"Forget about the bloody *dye*, moron. She heard me call her a 'hag', that's all that matters."

"Yes, but *she* called *you* a bitch," Chrissy replied, trying to sound indignant.

"Tracy's not going to see it like that, though, is she? I really need this job, Chrissy. I can't afford to lose it. It's not just the money. I'm starting to look unemployable. Shit, shit, *shit*."

"I quite liked Mrs Chalford," Chrissy said, putting the fifty pounds into her bag. "I'll keep this until I see her again. Maybe it *is* a tip."

"On the other hand, maybe she left it here deliberately and she's ringing the police right now."

"She didn't seem that bad to me."

"Bloody hell, you didn't *believe* all that stuff about the 'evil sociologist', did you? You must be even simpler than I thought! It's all made up, Chrissy. *Made up, comprendez?* You never get the truth in here. Anything anyone tells you is either wishful thinking, half-arsed tittle-tattle, or a downright lie. The sooner you get that into your fat, ugly head, the sooner you'll start growing up and getting on."

Chrissy pursed her lips. She'd weighed Sheryl and Mrs Chalford in the balance and found Sheryl wanting. "I'd better brush the floor if Tracy's coming back at six," she said, to change the subject.

Sheryl clicked her tongue and sighed. "Would you like to know the truth about Mrs Chalford, Chrissy? Would you? Because I can tell you it, if you want to hear it. Your call."

Chrissy shrugged. "Suppose."

Sheryl returned the gesture. "Well, get sweeping then. Go on. I'll tell you while you sweep up."

Chrissy fetched the brush from the yard, being careful to lock the back door as she came in again. As she shepherded the cut hair into little piles, she put on an expression designed to let Sheryl know she could take or leave 'the truth'. For the first time, she noticed Sheryl's glamorous legs looked like chicken-wings – faintly pimpled, bony, insubstantial, oddly drained of life; that she was mainly a skeleton.

"I'll tell you the truth," Sheryl began. She'd discarded her usual clipped, Estuary English accent; this was the voice she put on for select customers: Mrs Collins, the teacher, and Mrs Willis, the solicitor from across the road. "At least what *I* think the truth is. There are lots of stories, there have been for a long time. Most of them are complete bullshit. But not all. First off, there never was a 'Sherman Knox'. That was made up, for my benefit. She knows I've got a degree in sociology, you see. I made the mistake of telling her once. And she knew I was eavesdropping just then. 'Sherman' equals 'Sheryl', yes? Knox: my maiden name. All very droll, ha, ha, ha. Of course you can ask a few of the customers, if you don't believe me. They're all local, every last one of them. A sociologist with a plot to burn Mrs Chalford? Come off it. You might get a few 'looks', nothing else. You won't jog any memories. You can't jog memories where there's nothing to remember.

"No, the truth is ..." She paused, as if deciding whether to go on. She extended her lips and shook her head. "Five years ago, Mrs Chalford was nothing more than an old recluse living on a hilltop with her five dogs. Those dogs were something to behold: black and brawny, big as bullocks. But ... she had two acres of field for a garden and the animals never left it, so no one minded. She was old: indulgence was the order of the day, I guess.

"Things were about to change though. In the run-up to Halloween that year, a group of teenagers was going round the village, tricking or treating. Demanding low-level protection money, in effect. If you didn't pay up you might get out of bed next day to find your house covered in eggs and flour. There were seven of them: three girls and four boys, about fifteen or sixteen. Just kids having a lark, really.

"One night, they turned up at Mrs Chalford's. *Trick or treat?* Mrs Chalford took a bewildered look at them, then rummaged in her purse and pulled out what looked like a pound coin. She beckoned one of the girls over and put it in her hand. Only it wasn't a coin. It was a nail, with a huge round head like an oversized drawing pin. And she didn't just *put* it there. She *drove* it in with her thumb. It went right through the palm and out the other side. There was a lot of screaming and swearing and God knows what else. But Mrs Chalford's dogs came out and the teenagers made off. Ding, ding, end of round one.

"You'd think the parents would have got the police involved, but they probably didn't think the police would do anything. Anyway, next night, three of the lads came back with a can of petrol. Chucked some poisoned meat into the garden and prepared to wait half an hour so they could step over the dogs' dead bodies and raze the house. Not very original. In any case, the dogs weren't having any of it. They took one look at the meat and cleared the fence. Only two boys got away. The third was literally ... well, let's just say he was killed.

"No keeping the police out now. They swooped in numbers. But by this time, the dogs were nowhere to be found. Mrs Chalford claimed they'd escaped. They were never tracked down, ever. They weren't in the house. They weren't in the woods behind it either, apparently. She was arrested, bailed, got off with a caution. The fact that the victim had intended to burn her house down couldn't be overlooked. And yes, she'd put a nail through a girl's hand, but these were known troublemakers. And how was *she* supposed to know the dogs could clear her fence?

"But as the years have passed, it's become common knowledge those dogs have come back. Assuming they ever went away. They live in the house again mostly, or in the woods behind it whenever awkward questions start returning. And she even appears with them in the village occasionally. Quite shameless. Five hulking beasts, always unleashed so she can deny responsibility. Oh, you never see the High Street clear so fast as when Mrs Chalford brings her dogs to visit.

"But that's not the end of the story, by any means. Remember the trick or treaters? Well, after the court case, she started to track them down and terrorize them. With or without her dogs. Wherever they went, she'd be there. Eventually, after she'd reduced them to jellies a few times, they started to have awful nightmares, every last one of them. Psychologists were drafted in, social workers, the police paid Mrs Chalford a return visit, the works. The courts put a restraining order on her, for all the bloody good that did. Because that's when … when they started to, well, *worship* her. All the young people. They're feral, you see. No more than animals. She showed them who was boss, then offered them a place in her pack.

"Nowadays, they're at her house all the time. God knows what they get up to, but I don't think it's anything like people think it is: Satanism, the so-called black arts. I doubt Mrs Chalford even believes in that sort of thing. No, I think she uses them to control the village in subtle ways. Because control the village she definitely does, those things that interest her. Otherwise, I think she's just an old woman not content to accept an old woman's lot. It's a truism that old people tend to lose their teeth. Not Mrs Chalford.

"Anyhow, Tracy's going to go apeshit when she discovers I've upset her. Not just because Mrs Chalford was considering buying the business – there's a *Tesco Express* in the offing: us and the two shops either side of us, and Mrs Chalford doesn't like that sort of thing – but there's … there's Annie," Sheryl said, as if she was saying more than she should.

"Tracy's *daughter* Annie?" Chrissy said.

"She's started going up to Mrs Chalford's house."

Chrissy surprised herself with a sudden thrill.

"I'm leaving now," Sheryl said abruptly. She sighed, taking her jacket from the hanger and her keys from under the till. "If Tracy asks, I didn't say anything. Or Mrs Chalford misheard. She didn't have her hearing aid in, for God's sake. And if you see Mrs Chalford when I'm not here, put in a word for me, yes? Tell her I'm not that bad."

"You're *not* that bad," Chrissy said.

The bell performed its customary jangle as Sheryl left, and all was quiet.

Chrissy sat down and rested her head against the door post. She felt exhausted. After five minutes, the bell rang again. Tracy came in, tugging a stout sour-faced girl in a school uniform. They were obviously in the middle of an argument, but stopped when they saw Chrissy.

"What are *you* doing, still here?" Tracy said. Without waiting for an answer, she went on: "Make yourself useful then. I'm going out the back for a cigarette. Look after Annie for me. Give her a bloody shampoo and set or something, I don't know. Just" – she turned round to lock the door – "keep her amused."

"You can't keep me here!" Annie shouted. *"I'll break the bloody window!"*

Tracy ignored her and breezed out the back. The life seemed to go out of Annie, as if it only her mother's physical proximity had been keeping it there. She turned on Chrissy. "Who the hell are you?" she said, getting into the chair and looking at herself in the mirror.

Chrissy didn't want a fight. "I'm just a trainee, that's all."

"Who-ho, trainee-brainy pudding and pie, kissed the girls and made them cry. Get doing my hair then, slave."

Chrissy swallowed her pride and switched the showerhead on. She moderated the pressure, checked the temperature with her fingertips and put the VO5 to hand.

"Sorry," Annie said quietly. "It's not your fault my mum's such a cow. Sorry I badmouthed you just then."

Chrissy shrugged. She caressed Annie's scalp - lifting the hair and combing it with her fingers to sift the water through - when she met a bump. A little number six.

"I can *seeee* you!" Annie cried out, in a voice that wasn't her own. She laughed. "I can *seeee* you!"

Chrissy jumped and looked up, into the mirror. *Mrs Chalford!* H – *how?*

She couldn't take any more. She tried to leave the shop, but realised the door was locked the moment she started tugging at it. She double backed, and almost flew through the back to where Tracy was, while all the time Annie repeated, "I can *seeee* you!" in what was becoming a shriek.

Then suddenly: silence.

There was no Tracy in the yard; and the gate was locked, so there was nowhere she could have gone.

Which only left one possibility: somehow, she'd never been here to begin with.

The wind sang. There was a dreadful sense of menace now, as if something with lots of legs was waiting round the corner. She peeped through into the shop, where Annie had been. It was empty.

Or almost. In the middle of the floor, a huge black dog lay panting. When it saw Chrissy, it sat up. There was nothing remotely threatening about it, and, in a flash, Chrissy forgot about her terror. She passed through indifference to an inexplicable euphoria, and then, somehow, she knew where she had to go. Because they were all waiting for her: Annie, Sheryl, Tracy, Mrs Chalford - and lots of wonderful people she'd never met, but already craved to.

The dog stood and walked just in front of her, looking back to confirm she was following. Somehow, the door was unlocked now. As she left the shop for the last time, the bell jangled.

NO EXIT

The first thing Bob did when he got there was go round and see his wife. Lyndsay had died twenty years ago. She lived in one of the better areas, near the bus station. He knocked. She answered in a negligee and beamed.

"Bob?"

"Yeah, me," he said. "Died about an hour ago."

"Did - did you suffer much?"

"Why, what do you care?"

"Aren't you pleased to see me again? It's been twenty years."

"What's that smell? You cooking something?"

"I made you a cake."

He scowled. "Made me a cake, but couldn't come and see me."

"Oh God, Bob, don't be like that, please. Everyone's that way when they first get here. 'Why didn't you come and see me?' or 'I was in trouble why didn't you help?' There's a thick wall between here and Earth. *You* try getting out."

"I will. I bloody will."

"You'll see then."

"And I'm going to see Stan."

"Stan? Stan Collins? What on earth for?"

"Because I can. To see his face."

She flinched. "For God's sake, Bob, don't you think *I* wanted to see your face?"

"Is Tom around?"

"Your brother? He's living somewhere better than this. Further uptown."

"Well, I'll be damned. Is he still on his own?"

"We don't see each other that much," she said. "It's been twenty years."

"Does he ever have you round?"

"To his? Once, and he's been round here."

"Think he'd like to see me?"

115

"Probably. Shall I get the car?"

Tom lived in a Palladian-style mansion with a portico and leaded windows. He opened the door with a grin. "Hear you just died," he said. "Congratulations."

"Thanks," Bob said.

"He thinks he can go back," Lyndsay said.

Tom smiled. "Unfinished business?"

"Stan Collins. I just want to see his face."

"Forget it," said Tom. "Listen Bob, if you *could* go back, don't you think Lyndsay would have come to see you?"

Bob shrugged.

"So are you two going to be living together from now on?" Tom asked.

"He thinks I don't love him," Lyndsay said.

Bob frowned. "I don't believe there's no way out. She should have come to see me."

"You've been here five minutes," Lyndsay said, "yet you know exactly how it works. Bloody typical."

"She's right, Bob," Tom said. "You were always a bit like that."

"People on Earth see ghosts all the time," Bob said. "Ergo there must be some way out."

"Bloody trivial reason to go back," Tom said. "See someone's face."

Lyndsay sat down on the sofa. "Ghosts are people who can't get *in*, Bob."

Tom folded his arms. "Imagine, Bob, if you *did* get out, and you couldn't get back in again. Don't forget, Stan will be here himself in a few years' time. He's no spring chicken. Is it really worth an eternity out there, all on your own, just to see his face for a minute?"

"Dunno," Bob said.

"It's a bloody pointless discussion," Lyndsay said. "You can't get out, full stop. No one can."

"So we're stuck here?" Bob said.

"Course we're not 'stuck here', you daft arse. This is Heaven."

"Is there a Hell?"

"No one knows."

"What about a God?"

"No one knows."

"What about pets? Do people have pets?"

"You can have any pet you like."

"Would you like a dog, Bob?" Lyndsay said. "You always said you wanted a Labrador. We could get a Labrador."

"People said Colditz was escape-proof," Bob said.

Lyndsay stood up. "That's it, I've had enough. I've waited twenty years to see you. I even bake you a welcome cake, and that's the thanks I get. If you want to spend the next twenty years trying to escape from Heaven, just so you can go and give Stan Collins a bit of a fright, you go ahead. I won't be here when you're finished."

She wiped her eyes roughly and left. They endured the silence until they heard her car start and drive off.

"You stupid moron," Tom said. "What the hell's a woman like that even doing with a tosser like you?"

"Maybe I was a bit hasty."

"Go after her."

"I just can't believe she didn't come and see me."

"Is there more to this Stan Collins thing than you're letting on?" Tom said. "Are you gay or something?"

"No."

"'I just want to see his face'. Bloody hell, how old are you, Bob? It's the sort of thing you'd expect an eight-year-old to say."

Bob knocked on Lyndsay's door again.

"Sorry," he said, when she answered.

"The cake's ruined."

"Can I come in?"

He wiped his feet and went through into the sitting room. The cake had a sunken middle but she'd iced it and written, 'Welcome to Heaven' on in gel. He felt bad.

"What about séances?" he said.

"Drop it. I've said my piece. Are you staying or going?"

"Staying."

"No more nonsense about getting out?"

"Promise."

They ate the cake and had sex on the rug. She lit a fire and they lay naked in front of it. An hour passed.

"The truth is," he said emotionally, "Stan really helped me."

"What do you mean?"

He welled up. No point in hiding it now; might as well get it out. "If it hadn't been for him I'd have been completely alone, Lyndsay. Honest to God, no one else ever came to visit, not even the kids. Day in, day out, rain or shine. I just want to tell him it's okay up here, that's all; that there's nothing to be scared of."

She wiped his tears and produced some of her own in response. "You can't, Bob. No one can."

They had sex again and she fell asleep in his arms. He looked into the fire. There were no answers. No one knew what it all meant, even up here.

He remembered his last night at the hospital. That blizzard. Stan walking to his battered old Ford van, shivering. On the way home to an empty flat, not even a cat for company.

The embers died in the grate. Lyndsay turned over in her sleep.

NOT FROM THE EMBASSY

Bear in mind this was twenty years ago. I'm an old man now, but what occurred that morning still feels like yesterday. I mean, it's clearer than my graduation, every single miserable event in my failed marriage, the deaths of my parents; clearer than half an hour ago. Yet it lasted ten minutes.

Let me tell you how it happened. My elderly sister, Charlotte, and I were holidaying on a small island, described in the brochure as having 'beautiful beaches, azure seas, guaranteed sunshine, and' – a touch of whimsy – 'a tourist-friendly volcano.'

When we arrived, only the sunshine lived up to its billing. The beaches were mostly restricted entry, the 'azure sea' was full of stinging jellyfish, and the volcano was extinct, inconsequential and surrounded by a barbed wire fence. Contrary to our hopes and expectations, we spent more or less our whole vacation in the resort, being waited on hand and foot by men and women wearing hospitality uniforms and dour expressions.

By the last day, however, we'd decided enough was enough. It was time to venture out and get a taste of the local culture. Which, as Charlotte interpreted it, meant a trip to the Saturday bazaar.

Personally, I didn't think that really counted, and I'm not keen on shopping. Yet I couldn't let her go alone. By way of a compromise, we decided that, when we reached the town centre and had the bazaar in sight, I'd strike out on my own; do a little solitary exploration. We could meet up again later.

The taxi picked us up just after breakfast and took us to within five hundred yards of our destination. After I'd paid, we stood face to face on the pavement, regarding each other with indulgent expressions.

"Where do you want to rendezvous?" she said. "I mean, how long do you want?"

I shrugged. "I've no particular destination in mind. I'm completely flexible as regards time."

"An hour? I'd like two really …"

"Fine by me."

"Don't start worrying if I'm late. And before you protest: yes, you will: you know what you're like."

"Allegedly. Meet you back here, then?"

I watched until she'd gone. She was eighty-two - twenty years older than me - and I didn't like leaving her. She knew that. We had frequent fights over it (never that acrimonious, but always irksome).

Anyway, once I was sure she was safely in the bazaar, and probably amongst people who'd at least try to help if she was mugged or had a fall, I put my hands in my pockets and wondered what to do with my new-found 'freedom'.

Then I felt something fix aggressively on my elbows. I juddered forward slightly under the impact.

Two men in uniform, both several inches taller than me. The crowd around me widened, like something ominous was occurring.

"You speak English?" the one on my left said.

I was too stupefied to answer. Twelve days cooped up in the resort had accustomed me so completely to people in uniforms that, idiotically, I thought two staffers must have followed me out here to offer some sort of guidance, or possibly tell me I'd missed an excursion.

They shifted their grip to my armpits and actually lifted me off the ground. We took a sharp right turn into an alleyway with high concrete buildings on either side. In the adjacent wall, a door opened, as if automatically. All this, before I even had a chance to get my bearings, much less to complain.

Then it sank in. You read about these sorts of things in the papers. You never consider them as happening to you. We were in complete darkness. They hurled me through an internal door. I landed on my hands and knees, and it slammed behind me.

For the first time, I heard myself hyperventilating. Okay, so yes, I was scared.

My eyes began to adjust. Actually, it wasn't particularly dark anymore. I stood up and I wiped my grazed palms on my Bermuda shirt.

I was inside a room - a cell? - about ten metres square, with a low ceiling and a grille admitting a sallow light.

But why? It had to be a mistake, obviously. But who to tell? How could I -

Then I registered another man, naked, with his back to me.

Instinctively, I went into fight-or-flight mode. The adrenalin would decide, not me.

But - he was weeping. People don't do that when they're going to attack you, do they? So… maybe we were in the same boat?

He turned to face me, and my stomach almost flipped. He was completely covered in welts and lacerations. *"Can't we just agree I'm sorry?"* he yelled.

I reeled, then dimly recognised: he was – was that a *Home Counties* accent? He was *British?*

Underneath his lesions, he looked about thirty. Clean-shaven, lean, round shoulders, big, flat feet. He shook his head vigorously, like a dog shaking its ears.

"Surely that's the *purpose* of punishment?" he went on. "To make the person feel sorry? Not to *exterminate* them like some little *fly who's landed on your dinner?* Because that would be right for a *fly.* But I'm a HUMAN BEING, FOR GOD'S SAKE!"

How to respond?

"Are you from the embassy?" he asked quietly.

"No," I managed to say.

He grinned. "You *are* from the embassy. I know you are."

"I'm not. I'm - "

"Oh, I know what you're thinking. You're thinking no one will care. I'm just one little person among hundreds. A *few* people might kick up a fuss, but I'll soon be forgotten. I'm a nobody." He laughed. "It's the *project* that matters. And even the project doesn't matter anymore, only the *organisation!*"

"I'm not from the embassy."

"I - *matter! - to me!*"

"Look, I don't know why I'm here."

"My mother's still alive," he said softly. "I matter to her."

"Who *are* you? What have you done?"

He was pacing the cell now, turning around every two seconds. "We're all going to die in the end, yes, yes, I accept that. If I get a reprieve, it's only thirty-, forty-odd years, probably, then I'll die of natural causes, old age."

"I'm not from the embassy."

He cackled. "I've tried to tell myself it's like a disease. Some sort of terminal disease I've got, you know?" He broke down. *"But what sort of a disease only gives you AN HOUR TO LIVE?"*

"If I can only find out what embassy you mean ... What nationality are you? British?"

He flopped onto the floor, sat up, and pulled his knees against his face. "If you're not from the embassy, then who are you?"

"They asked me if I spoke English. So perhaps - "

"Who did?"

"I - I don't know."

He clambered to his feet. "You *are* from the embassy!"

"No, I'm not. I'm *not* from the embassy. Look, I don't know who brought me here, or what you're supposed to have done, or anything!"

"People die all the time in this country," he muttered. "It's normal. All sorts of reasons, things you wouldn't imagine. Diarrhoea, even: people die from that. Death means nothing here. But – but, you see, I can't bring myself to think that way. Death *isn't* nothing to me. I want to live!"

It seemed pointless to repeat myself. He wasn't going to tell me anything about himself. He was utterly fixated on the future.

He smirked. "They'll come for *you* next. Naturally they will. You think you're safe. You're *not* safe, *absolutely* not. You think you are, but you're *not!*"

"I'd really like to help you," I said, going back to the beginning. "But - "

"No, what am I saying? Of *course* they won't come for you! I can tell, just by looking, the sort of person *you* are! People like you – what has your life been worth? They won't come for *you!*" He retched, and covered his face with his hands.

Suddenly, he lunged at me, and doors burst open on two sides. Before he reached me, two men wrestled him to the floor. His eyes bulged. *"Oh my God! No! Oh God! Oh, God! I'm sorry! PLEASE, GOD! OH, NO!"*

They pulled him up and dragged him through an open door in the opposite wall. His yelling seemed to intensify, even as it became more and more distant. Then it abruptly expired.

Meanwhile, they'd grabbed me beneath the armpits, just like before. They turned me bodily, lifted me through an exit, then through another, and finally, flung me out of the building onto the street. The ejection was so forceful, I stumbled and landed on all fours again.

None of the passers-by seemed to notice... although, looking back, how could they not have? There must have been an element of wilful blindness in there, a kind of see-no-evil.

The sun was suddenly blinding. I struggled to my feet in a daze, stood gasping for a few moments, then began to stagger.

I don't know where I went, except that I seemed to go in circles. I twice came back to my point of origin. There was no sign of any life behind that door, no windows in the walls, nothing to indicate a purpose of any kind. It wasn't even possible to tell what the building was.

Finally, I found Charlotte at the bazaar. "Did you have a good time?" she asked. "What happened to your shirt, by the way?"

My mouth opened but no sound came out.

She looked harder at me, and gave a nervous chuckle. "What's the matter, Jack?" She frowned. "You're scaring me! My God, what happened?"

We went back to the hotel. I lay down, at her insistence. Half an hour later Sheila, the rep, turned up: she'd somehow heard something was wrong, and how could she help? I explained, as well as I could – I was still in shock - what had happened. We teamed up with the hotel manager and another travel agency rep, and went to where I'd been accosted. We banged on that door as hard as we could, but there was no answer. We went to the police, but, of course, they didn't want to know. We rang round the embassies – British, American, Canadian, Australian, all the English-speaking ones – but no one knew of a missing person. And no one ever contacted me to suggest things had changed in that regard.

Charlotte died (of cancer) a few months afterwards, and I think the ensuing loneliness may have unhinged me slightly. Try as I might, I couldn't forget what had happened on that island. Every summer, for years afterwards, I went back, and doggedly relocated that same street. Needless to say, the door was never open, nor did I ever meet anyone who'd ever seen it open.

And then, about a decade ago, they demolished the entire building to erect yet another mega-hotel.

You'd think that might have drawn a line under it, but no. I bought a villa on the other side of town. And I came to stay here permanently.

After I learned to speak the language, I discovered something mind-blowing. That volcano's far from being 'tourist-friendly'. It's vastly more extensive than I could ever have imagined, even in my worst nightmares: in fact, according to what I've learned, it's all the island really is. And it could erupt at any time. Very occasionally, I hear people talk about it in hushed tones. But never on request, and definitely never to tourists.

Why don't you emigrate, I hear you say? Why not go anywhere else, and as soon as possible?

Well, I still haven't told you the half of it. You see, it's general. *The entire Earth's crust* is floating precariously on a never-ending ocean of simmering lava. We all think we're secure, but in fact, everything's hanging by a knife-edge, everywhere. The calmest places are often the most dangerous.

Clearly, you don't get dragged unceremoniously into a prison compound if you really are part of a diplomatic mission, but even so, I often ask myself what I'd have been able to do, that day, if I actually *had* been 'from the embassy'.

But the truth is, I already know. Nothing at all.

SMUGGLER'S RETURN

One rainy January afternoon, after an agreeable hour browsing the *Beckford Getaways* brochure, Florence Evesham picked up the phone and booked a room in a favourably-reviewed sandstone guest-house in a forest clearing six miles south of Aberystwyth Bay. Six months' later, on the Saturday of the second fortnight in July, she arrived at Smuggler's Return in a tweed skirt and new brogues, so full of summer contentment that she gave the taxi driver an exorbitant tip. As she watched him drive away, and mentally prepared herself for the first day of the rest of her retirement, a heavy goods vehicle veered off the road, narrowly missing her but ploughing into the guest-house, where it demolished half of its frontage, including its front door and two windows.

Once she overcame her shock, her first thought was for the driver, but he stepped out of his cabin, swearing and apparently unscathed; then, for whoever was inside, but a woman emerged from the back yelling who the hell had blown up her bloody guest-house, which would surely have been her last concern if there were casualties. This had to be the landlady, Ria Jenkins. She wore a multicoloured peasant-smock quite unlike the sort of thing Florence expected from her phone voice, and she had a shock of unruly red hair.

The driver examined his tyres, looking sorry to be alive. After a long row with Ria Jenkins, he put his hands in his pockets and walked off towards the nearest village, pointedly ignoring Florence's offer of the use of her mobile.

She was about to dial 999 when Ria Jenkins strode over holding her palm up. "I know what you're about to do," she said. "Don't. I was the only one in there and I'm fine."

They locked eyes. Mutual incomprehension.

"What about the lorry driver?" Florence said. "He's obviously in shock. Should we even allow him to walk? A strong cup of tea - "

"Jim's okay. He's got bald tyres. That's why he didn't ring himself."

"You know him?"

Ria Jenkins shrugged. "Everyone knows everyone round here. Look, I don't want him getting in trouble: he'll lose his licence. I'll just check the damage, then I'll help you in with your things, okay?"

"I think you're in shock, Ms Jenkins. 'In' where?"

"You're Miss Evesham, I presume. I'm Ria. The back half's fine."

Florence scoffed. "I can't possibly stay here now, I'm sorry. You can keep my deposit, if it helps. And I'm sure you'll get the insurance."

"You could stay in the folly. It's actually better than the room you booked."

Florence drew her eyebrows together. "Excuse me?"

"The folly. It's a tower. In the back garden. There are stairs to get up and down, but it's got an *en suite* bathroom."

"I don't know... I'd have to - "

"And the view's lovely. You can see for miles."

She shook her head. "I'd better be going. Really."

"I'm not insured," Ria told her irritably.

"What?"

"I never bothered with any of that rubbish. I'm seventy years old and a child of the nineteen sixties. If you don't stay here, I don't eat. Your choice."

"Well, I - "

"And you won't find anyone else to take you. Not at this short notice. July's peak season. Please. *Please.*"

Florence shrugged and sighed. "Well, I suppose the least I can do is have a look. Obviously, I'm not promising anything."

"Just keep an open mind, that's all."

As she followed Ria to the back of the house, Florence cast a backwards glance at the lorry. Its tyres hadn't looked bald. Ria noticed her looking.

"They have higher standards for HGVs," she said.

The folly was a drum tower with a cupola and a spiral staircase. It had been built in 1920 by a Massachusetts millionaire who was on the verge of demolishing the guest-house as surplus to requirements, when he was ruined in the Wall Street Crash. Both buildings, on one plot of land, had been sold to Ria's grandfather, a fashionable painter, and passed down the family line to Ria, 'The Last of the Mojenkins', as she liked to call herself. The room at its pinnacle had a bed, a bookshelf, two chairs, sea views to the west and mountains to the east. The bathroom, on the next level down, was screened by a sliding glass door.

"If you like it," Ria said, "I'll come and make up the fire for you later."

"Does it get very cold?"

"Not at this time of year, but a bit of extra heat never goes amiss. And feast your eyes on the view."

Florence looked at the mountains again and felt her reservations dissolve. "I'll take it," she said.

Ria breathed a sigh of relief. "Thank you."

"But what about you? Where are you going to sleep?"

"In the annex tonight. It's structurally independent of the rest of the house. I'll be fine."

"Are you sure I won't be in the way?"

"I guarantee it. If you want anything, let me know."

That evening, Florence went for a walk through the ancient forest that fringed the coastal path, and afterwards watched the sun set from the west window. Ria came in to make the fire at nine, although it was still warm outside. Florence got under her continental quilt and blew out the gas lamp at eleven.

She dreamed she'd inherited money and bought the folly, but not the house. She and Ria went for a walk together on the sands, talking freely about people they both somehow knew. Yet it quickly became obvious Ria wasn't just Ria but also Lucy Benson, and, as usual, Lucy Benson brought up the question of why Florence hadn't done more. Suddenly, there was no Ria any more, only Lucy Benson, plodding along the sands in her colossal bare feet and black dress, like she knew she was dead. "Why did you just cut me off?" she said.

Florence awoke with a start. It took her a moment to remember where she was. It was dark. The trigger must have been when Ria mentioned the nineteen-sixties, yes, that would have done it.

Outside, metal clanged, motors roared, and Jimi Hendrix sang, 'All Along the Watchtower'.

It felt for a moment like she was still in the dream. The '60s, then that song?

But it wasn't the dream. It was real. And it was annoying.

She looked towards the house, where the noise was. There were lights beyond it, but she couldn't see anything more. Presumably, it was builders, repairing the guest-house. Very late for that sort of thing, but then Ria didn't seem like the conventional type of landlady.

She should probably ring over, see what was going on, perhaps ask her to keep the noise down. Some of it probably couldn't be helped; but Jimi Hendrix was definitely unnecessary.

She tried both coat pockets, her travel bag, then her suitcase. Her mobile was gone. She groaned.

She put her coat and shoes on and went downstairs and round to the front of the house. The crashed lorry was being pulled free by a tractor with six chains. Ria stood with a group of ten men, solemnly watching it bring yet more of the masonry down. She wore a fur coat and she was tapping her foot to some new guitar anthem. One of the men nudged her and indicated Florence.

Ria nodded and came over. "Sorry, we must be making a bit of a noise. - *Gerry, switch the music off!* - Tonight only, I promise. I'll give you a day's refund."

"I wasn't sure what was happening," Florence replied, straining to see.

"Once we've freed the lorry, we're going to rebuild the house."

"Tonight?"

"No time like the present. There are lots of us. All working *gratis.*"

"You must have some very good friends."

Ria smiled. "All these men owe me one way or another."

"Incidentally, have you seen my mobile phone? I can't find it."

"I'll keep a look out. Did you have it when you went out for you walk earlier this evening?"

"I don't think so."

"We'll find it in the morning. You probably dropped it between here and the folly."

As she walked away, the music came back on, just a notch lower. Florence had the odd feeling Ria knew where her phone was. She'd taken it to stop her ringing 999 and exposing Jim's bald tyres.

But what if someone wanted to contact her? Tom usually rang to check she'd arrived. He'd probably called Air-Sea Rescue by now. That was how he was.

She passed the annex at the back of the building and – shock of shocks! - heard her ringtone. It was quite distinctive: an obscure Pickettywitch song called, 'I'll Say Bye Bye'.

It was coming from inside somewhere. She looked to check the coast was clear, then tried the back door. It opened smoothly. She swallowed, looked around herself again and went in.

She removed her shoes to keep her incursion quiet and found herself walking along a white-walled carpeted passageway. Her phone rang and rang. There was a door with a bright light under it at the end. She was scared now, but she tried to swap fear for indignation. This was *her* mobile, *her* holiday... *her* chance to put an end to Tom's risible paranoia.

She opened the door and was blinded. She recovered sufficiently to see her phone on a shelf. The ringing stopped abruptly – as if the phone was just as startled as she was - and her eyes adjusted. Rows and rows of pot plants beneath gantries hung with arc lights.

Oh my God. She'd seen enough *Crimewatch* to realise she was looking at a cannabis farm.

She picked up her phone and turned round to find herself face to face with Ria and five rough-looking men, wearing scowls.

"I can't help thinking you're a little bit of a jinx, my lady," Ria said coldly.

They frogmarched her back to the folly and locked her in, presumably so they could decide what to do with her next. For all she knew, they might kill her, although she didn't think that was very likely. It all depended how big their operation was. She might have stumbled on a miniscule part of it, but enough to allow the police to deduce the whole. Failing murder, they might decide to let her off with menaces. They might be researching her nearest and dearest right now, in order to give any up-and-coming threats the dark stamp of authenticity. Well, they'd find that task an uphill struggle.

It didn't matter what they did to her, not really. Apart from Lucy Benson, she'd lived a good life and there wasn't much to look forward to now. Let them kill her if they wanted. She wasn't in a position to stop them, and what you can't prevent, you have to accept.

At four o'clock, she watched sun rise over the mountains. Now that she came to think of it, there was a deep resemblance between Ria and Lucy. They were both lawbreakers, and they probably needed saving from themselves. Lucy certainly had. As for Ria, what sort of person doesn't insure their house? Why grow drugs when you live in an idyllic getaway guest-house?

At five o'clock, there was a knock. Ria slipped into the room and leaned her back on the closed door. She didn't speak.

"What are you going to do with me?" Florence said.

Ria smiled. "Let you go, of course."

"Obviously, I'll go to the police. I've no objection to people growing cannabis for medicinal purposes, but - "

"I texted 'Tom', by the way. I told him my – your – batteries were low, so you couldn't call or receive calls. I told him it was lovely here."

Florence shrugged. "I don't suppose you did it for my sake, but I'm grateful."

"We're in the process of relocating the nursery as we speak. When we let you go, there'll be nothing left to show anyone."

"Presumably the 'guest-house' is just a front."

"Allowing us to launder the money, yes."

"Do you manufacture other drugs?"

"A few. Not the bad ones."

Florence smiled dourly. "I had a friend in the 1960s. She started on cannabis but she soon moved to other things. She died of an overdose in 1971, just twenty-four years old. Looking back, I should have done more to help her – I've never forgiven myself for that - but without the slippery slope, she'd still be here. It's the story a lot of corpses might tell. Don't expect my support."

To Florence's surprise, Ria looked chastened. She ground her teeth. "Believe it or not, I give most of the money to charity," she said eventually.

"Has it occurred to you that the reason 'Jim' crashed into your house might have something to do with it all?"

Ria laughed harshly. "It occurred to both of us. What's to be done? It's too late now."

"What do you mean, 'too late'? You've a perfectly good guest-house."

Ria stood up, hunched, shot through with something resembling despair. She went to the window and touched the pane. "After we locked you in here, I saw myself through your eyes. I didn't like it. But then, I've not liked myself for a long time now, truth be told. I don't meet that many normal people, and when I do, none of them get to know what I really do for a living. Well done for finding out."

"You don't sound very happy with your lot."

"When did I say I was? It's a living, that's all. Anyway, what do *you* know? It's too bloody late to do anything about it now. My bed, I'll lie in it."

Florence put her head on one side. "You keep saying that: 'too late'. What do you mean?"

"You mentioned 'medicinal'. Earlier. You said you'd no objection to people growing cannabis for medicinal purposes."

Florence scoffed. "You're not going to pretend - "

"Back in '67, I believed it was, yes: good for people, I mean, and in *that* sense 'medicinal'. Curing an ill world. Trouble is, it wasn't just me. Jim, Gaz, Dai, Sharon, Alan, Angharad, Rick – we grew up together. They're getting their livelihoods from it now. They're good people too. But even if they weren't, we're all linked to people we don't even know. In a sense we try never to think about, we're slaves, bound head and foot. All of us. The best we can hope for is to mitigate it with charity. I don't want to talk about it, anyway. You're free to go."

"Go where? What's the point?"

Ria drew a sharp breath. "Say again?"

"I came here for a holiday. Now you've moved the nursery, even if I go to the police there's nothing for them to find. I might as well stay."

"You're no longer welcome. I'd only be uncomfortable."

Florence exhaled a bitter sigh. "I'd better start packing then."

"Right. And, er … there's nothing to pay. I'll post your deposit back to you."

They could no longer meet each other's eyes. Ria left without locking the door. Florence looked out of the window for the last time and swallowed her misery. She stretched out on the bed and, now Ria's visit had assuaged her anxiety about being murdered, she fell asleep. 'All Along the Watchtower', 'I Feel Free', 'Mr Tambourine Man', 'Purple Haze' – everything they'd been playing as they rebuilt the house, music she hadn't heard for decades – came flooding back. She'd forgotten how much a part of her it was. She dreamed she was in Ria's gang. Jim, Gaz, Dai, Sharon, Alan, Angharad, Rick. And it was nice. God help her, it was like being twenty-four again.

When Florence wheeled her suitcase out of the folly and along the path to the bus stop, she found Ria sitting on her front doorstep with her head in her hands and her eyes glassy, as if she'd been poked by a spectre.

"Are you all right?" Florence asked.

Ria grimaced. "You'd better get going before the police arrive."

"What do you mean? *I* haven't said anything."

"Someone in Port Isaac tipped them off yesterday. They've raided three houses already. It's only a matter of time before they reach mine. A few hours if I'm lucky."

"I thought you'd moved everything out."

"All the plants, yes. Not all the tables. Not all the lights. And they'll bring sniffer dogs. They're probably on their way now. You'd better vamoose."

Florence called a taxi and rode to Llansantffraed. She returned twenty minutes later with two mops, a litre bottle of bleach, two bags of rubber gloves, scouring powder, a 24-pack of firelighters, a box of matches and two axes. Ria was still sitting on the step. She thrust an axe into her hand.

"I'll make a start on the tables," she said. "Any 'spliffs' or anything, bring them to the middle of the garden or flush them down the toilet. And boil a kettle."

Ria looked dazed, but she stood up and went inside. Florence took off her cardigan and went into what used to be the nursery and started swinging her axe.

The police arrived an hour later to find a huge bonfire in the garden and a house that smelt of bleach and scouring powder and drying cement and plaster. As Ria predicted, they'd brought sniffer dogs. They searched the premises with obvious frustration and took Ria away for questioning. She returned by taxi two hours later looking shaken. Florence stood in the kitchen, wearing an 'I love Caernarfon' apron and stirring a hot pot.

"I found a few things in the fridge," she said. "I thought you might be hungry."

Ria sat down at the table without saying anything.

Florence served the casserole she'd made into two bowls. "Don't be despondent," she said neutrally. "You've still got the guest-house."

"I know bugger all about running a guest-house."

"I'm sure it's not difficult."

"You really liked being in the folly, didn't you?"

Florence sighed. "Yes, I did."

"Would you like to live there permanently?"

Florence put her fork down. "On what basis?"

"Hear me out," Ria said. "You've got get-up-and-go. You're a doer. And you saved me. I owe you. We could help each other."

"I'm still not sure what you're proposing,"

"I thought about it while I was down at the police station. I'd put the deeds in both our names, fifty-fifty. I'm no good at being a hostess, never have been, never will be. My relatives all disowned me yonks ago. I don't want to die alone."

"I'm in roughly the same boat, yes."

"What about 'Tom'?"

"Tom's my brother. He's eighty-seven and he's got his wife to look after."

"So ..."

Florence looked around the room. "If you're really serious, I think we could make a go of this place."

"You'd have to be nice to everyone. I'm the reclusive type."

Florence shrugged. "I could probably manage that. And no, actually you're not. If you're thinking of surrendering to self-pity, get someone else."

That evening, they sat in the garden on deckchairs. There were no clouds, no moon, and the Milky Way smouldered and spangled. They sipped cider, listened to *Sgt. Pepper's Lonely Hearts Club Band,* and talked about what they'd do when Jim, Gaz, Dai, Sharon, Alan, Angharad and Rick got out of prison. Ria didn't know exactly what she'd say to them, but she was sure it would be okay. Florence gazed at Ursa Major, all those millions of light years away, and 'Lucy in the Sky With Diamonds' came on, and, for the first time in years, yes, she was actually all right with it.

TELL IT ON THE MOUNTAIN

Bryan and Lakshmi Bates put on their puffa jackets and hiking boots. They did each other's zips and laces up as they'd done since Lakshmi's mother died a year ago, telling themselves they only had each other now. It was one of the things that kept them together when things started going wrong.

But things were back right now. That night, at two in the morning, they began an ascent of Scafell Pike to watch the sun rise. This was to be their new beginning. They wanted to symbolise it. The sky was starry and the wind was gentle. When they reached the top, they were alone. They sat down on the granite and held hands.

"No more lies then," Lakshmi said.

"No more lies. I meant what I said."

"And I'll try not to be jealous anymore."

"Are you cold?"

"No, not now. Just out of breath."

He took a flask from his haversack. "Here, have some soup."

"Not yet, thank you."

"Mushroom? Chef's special?"

She blew a flute of air and grinned. "I'll have some when I've caught my breath."

"Do you think we can make it?"

"You mean, back down? Or our marriage?"

"The latter," he replied.

"Connie said it was mainly my jealousy. You haven't done anything wrong."

"She didn't go that far."

Lakshmi snorted. "She didn't have to."

"She's a marriage guidance counsellor. She doesn't apportion blame."

"I'm the one who's got to do the work, though."

"If I wasn't such a liar - "

"They're only white lies. And you only lie because you're afraid I'll read stupid things into the truth."

He shrugged. "Maybe."

"Well, from now on, I won't."

He drew closer to her and put his arm round her waist. "I would never hurt you, Lakshmi, you know that. Deep down, you do."

"What time's the sun due to rise?"

"Five o'clock. Ten minutes' time."

"Thank goodness we made it," she said. "I thought we were going to get lost at one point."

"I've done it before. I know the way."

"What? You never said. When?"

"When I was younger."

The smile fell from her face. She turned to look at him. "Er, how much younger?"

"When I was at sixth form."

"So – what? – twenty years ago? About?"

He shrugged again. "About that, I suppose."

"And you haven't done it since then? No, no, you'd have said. You wouldn't have said, 'I've done it before', you'd have said, 'I've done it before *recently*'."

He withdrew his arm. "Er, where's this leading?"

"I'm only thinking. Twenty years ago, and you still remember the way."

"So what?"

"It's just that ..."

"That what?"

"There was that business trip you went on, to the Lake District, last year ... with Miss Pargetter from Accounts."

He clicked his tongue and scowled. "Oh, here we go."

Her hand trembled. She put it to her forehead. "I'm just saying."

"And you think I brought Miss Pargetter from Accounts up Scafell Pike?"

"It's just ... no one would remember the way up Scafell Pike twenty years later."

"I'm not going to argue with you, Lakshmi."

"Are you blushing?"

"No, I'm not bloody blushing! It's dark! How the hell can you tell whether I'm blushing or not?"

The tip of the sun rose blood-red on the horizon, making everything scarlet. But he wasn't blushing.

"Why won't you argue?" she said. "Haven't you any defence?"

"It's not about me defending myself. We established that with Connie. It's about trust. You either trust me or you don't."

"I don't know, Bryan. Miss Pargetter's so attractive. You're so attractive. I'm so … frumpy."

"We've been through all this at counselling, remember. You've got a negative body image, and if anyone's frumpy, it's me."

"Just tell me straight. Did you come up here with Miss Pargetter, or not?"

"No. I didn't."

She took a deep breath. "I don't believe you, Bryan."

"Fine. That's fine. This was supposed to be a new start. But that's fine. At least we know where we stand now. There's no getting past our problems. Divorce, here we come."

"I brought you up here for a reason, Bryan. If you don't love me anymore, I don't want to go down."

"What do you mean you 'don't want to go down'?"

"I mean, it's a mountain. I'm going to throw myself off."

"Oh, don't be ridiculous."

"I've thought about it. You're all I live for."

"Bloody hell, stop being so melodramatic."

"I'm not."

"So, I'm just supposed to leave you here, am I?"

"You've no alternative. I'm an adult. I'm allowed to make my own decisions."

He paused. He looked at the ground. His eyebrows contracted. His mouth fell open and he sat up straight and beamed. "My God!"

"What?"

"Lakshmi, can't you see? That's exactly the problem!"

"What is?"

"All those sessions in therapy, having our lives picked over by that bloody maudlin Connie, and she - we never spotted the elephant in the room!"

She wiped her tears with her mittens. "You've lost me."

"What you just said."

"What?"

"'You're all I live for.' That's what you said. 'You're all I live for.' You did say that, didn't you?"

"Yes," she said.

"But that's precisely the problem. Don't you see? You only obsess about me because you haven't got anything else."

"I don't want anything else."

"It's me! I'm the problem! I'm the one who'd never have children, even though I know you love them; I'm the one that took Biffo to the rescue centre when we couldn't look after him – or so we told ourselves … or so I told you; I'm the one that moans about you spending all that time at the Mandir - "

"It isn't you. Connie said - "

"Sod Connie, she's a moron. Look, Lakshmi, let's get Miss bloody Pargetter out of the way, then I'll tell you what we're going to do."

"What do you mean?"

"Miss Pargetter's engaged to be married. She came up to the Lake District under protest and she spent all her free time with Marie. Marie: Mrs Bowles."

"You *would* say that, though."

"And I wasn't the only man on that trip. There were five of us. And – and I shared a room with Bill Hamilton. If I'd been up to anything Bill would suspect, and he'd tell his wife. So ask Francesca."

"I - "

"Look, Lakshmi, we're going to walk down this mountain and when we get to the bottom, we're going to stay together. But I'm setting conditions, okay?"

"What sort of conditions?"

"We've got to stop prioritising me and start prioritising you. We're going to - yes, that's it: foster some children."

"*What?*"

"With a view to adopting one."

"But – but – hang on, aren't we too old?"

"Or we could even try for one of our own. You're only thirty-eight. There's still time. You do still want one, don't you?"

"I haven't thought about it for years. You're serious?"

Suddenly, the sun disappeared. A thick mist fell, enveloping them, and it darkened. They could see each other and the rock they were sitting on and nothing else.

"Oh, my God," Lakshmi said. "They said this could happen. The hotel manager warned us."

"Beauty, it's fine. It's only a bit of mist."

"*A bit of mist?* Bryan, we're at the top of Scafell Pike! People have got lost and died in less than this!"

He stood up. "Trust me, we're going to be okay."

She was about to object again, but it was pointless. Arguing wouldn't make the sun come back. She stood up and faced him, and for some reason her panic subsided.

"I should have brought my mobile phone," she said. "I've been a fool."

"No, you're not. I don't even own one. That's being a fool."

"You're old-fashioned, that's all."

"Trust me. That's all I ask."

She hesitated then kissed him and nodded. They joined hands and set off into the opacity.

THE BACCHAE

When Frederick got in late that night, there were two empty wine bottles on the kitchen table. His mother was dressed in her red party frock, silver-clasp belt and heels, and she'd had her hair done that afternoon, but she was alone. No sign of her friends, thank God. She was sitting at the table cupping her ears in her palms.

"Are you all right?" he asked.

"I've had too much to drink," she said. She picked up a bottle from the floor and set it alongside the other two. "And one more makes three," she said.

"Three? Three bottles?"

"One more bottle standing on the wall, and if one more bottle should accidentally fall - " She swiped the bottle. Frederick caught it as it left the table.

"You've had three bottles?" he said, his voice panicky. "What on Earth's got into you?"

"What's the matter with having three lovely bottles of wine?"

"You're normally stewed after one *glass!* But three *bottles!*"

"And what have you been doing at work today, Frederick?"

"Never mind that. My God. You're going to be ill. How many fingers am I holding up?"

"What? On your hand?"

There was a pause. "Yes," he replied.

"Two? Three? Five?" She giggled. "How many tries do I get?"

"How long ago did you drink the last one?"

"About ten minutes ago. No, hang on. It may have been ... may have been ten days ago. Anyway, what have you been doing at work today?"

"Drink some water." He went to the cupboard and got out a pint glass.

"No, I *won't* drink any water. Not until you've told me what you've been doing at work today."

"Stop it. We never discuss that, anyway. You know that."

"Yeah, well I had a bet with Jeannie and Beth and Ali that I could *make* you discuss it."

"You've had your friends round?"

"Yeah, 'sright."

He brightened. "So you didn't drink all this … on your own?"

"Yeah, I did. Yeah. Drink it all myself. Yeah."

"I don't understand. Here drink this."

"I won't drink that, no."

"Didn't your friends drink any wine?"

"No."

There was a pause. "Are you sure?"

"They brought it, yeah. Then they left it and went home. Then I drank it. And do you know what? It was superb. Except that middle one. That's shit."

"Mother!"

"What?"

"Here, drink this."

"What have you been doing at work today?" she said.

"I'm going to call an ambulance."

"Do you want a cuddle?"

"Look, you're going to be ill! I mean, seriously *ill!*"

"Well, if you want a cuddle, tell me what you've been doing at work today."

"Bloody hell! What would be the point? You'd have forgotten it in half an hour's time anyway!"

"You'd tell me if you cared about me. We had a bet, me and Jeannie and … and …"

"For God's sake!"

"Anyway, if I'll have 'forgotten it in half an hour', what's it matter? It'll be like that tape recorder on *Mission Impossible*." She giggled again. "Do I mean *Mission Impossible*? Or *The Man from U.N.C.L.E.*? 'This tape recorder will self-destruct in fifteen seconds'. That one. Is it fifteen seconds?"

"Look, okay, if I tell you what I did at work, please will you do whatever I tell you?"

"Yes. Because you're my son and I love you."

"Will you drink this and let me call an ambulance?"

"Yeah, sure thing."

"Don't joke, Mother. I mean it, really."

"Cross my heart and hope to die. With a Playtex bra."

"This is going to be the one and only time I'll do this. It's not a precedent, understood?"

"You've got to *promise* you'll tell me."

"What?"

"You've got to *promise* you'll tell me about your day. Hurry up. I'm starting to feel ill. Say it. Say you promise you'll tell me."

"Okay! Okay! I promise!"

"Right. Get on with it, then."

He took a deep breath. "I took on a new client. Okay. Unusual story. I suppose it bears telling. But you must never, never repeat a word of this to anyone else, understood?" He saw she was past the point of understanding anything. "His mobile went off," he said, "during a production of *The Bacchae* at the Royal Court. You know how touchy actors can be about that sort of thing. To be fair to the theatre, it wasn't as if he wasn't warned. They'd told everyone to switch their phones off at the start, and it was printed in the programme. Anyway, he claims his wife was in hospital and it was someone ringing about that. The actors stopped the play, Dionysus told him to switch the bloody thing off, the lighting engineer shone a spotlight on him and everyone started booing him. He's suing the theatre company for emotional distress."

His mother put her hand over her mouth and jerked her chin down to forestall a retch.

"Everyone's been ribbing me all day about how unlucky it is to sue Dionysus. Ho, ho, hilarious. Anyway, it's not a cut and dried case. I expect there'll be some out of court settlement and everyone'll retire with their egos intact. I'd really just like to forget it all, if you don't mind. And whatever smidgeon of this you might remember in the morning, I also want you to remember that you promised not to tell - "

There was a cacophony of women's voices shouting, *"Surprise!"* Jeannie burst in from the living room, Beth from the larder and Ali from the back door. All were in party frocks, and Jeannie was blowing a party horn. Suddenly, 'Never Can Say Goodbye' came on at top volume. All the women danced, including his mother. Ali let off a party popper. Beth turned the TV on.

There was a crash, completely unnoticed under the sound of Gloria Gaynor and the ten o'clock news.

Fifteen minutes later, his mother knelt down next to him and raised his head into her lap. She began to shake. "Switch the music off!" she screamed. "He's not breathing! My God! *Frederick's not breathing!*"

THE HIGHLAND CLEARANCES

The Present.

As Charlie Campbell MBE stood before his wardrobe mirror deciding what to wear that night – holding each tie, jacket, shirt, against himself before tossing it onto the bed with a grunt - he dropped one of his silver cuff-links. He stooped to retrieve it, and when he got up, he accidentally caught sight of himself in the glass. For a split second he saw himself as others must see him. His annoyance evaporated. He looked younger, much younger, than he tended to think.

He added to this act of self-congratulation another: he'd bent right over, then straightened, without even a creak. Pretty damn good for sixty-five.

Normally, none of this would have mattered. But it did tonight.

He slipped on a pair of expensive black loafers. Were they too old? He'd last worn them for the Palace, over two years ago. Never mind, they'd have to do. And the white shirt? Yes, of course: there was nothing to beat the plain white shirt.

He supposed he must look pretty dapper. Of course, you never saw yourself as you really were. The mirror nearly always lied. But as he looked himself over – his thick, steel-and-snow hair, his straight shoulders, his broad chest tapering towards his cummerbund just the way the ladies liked, his Roman nose, square jowls, eyebrows trimmed to just the right degree of formidability – he couldn't help thinking his reflection was almost a perfect match with the accidental sighting he'd just experienced. Yes, pretty damn good.

Maybe the peach cummerbund, not the cream. The peach was more striking. He undid the cream one, and flipped painstakingly through those on the hanger.

The peach wasn't there; and it hadn't fallen on the floor. Maybe it was in the next section of the wardrobe. After all, he had a lot of clothes. A lot of clothes in a big wardrobe in a big house.

He'd only moved here six months ago – London to the Highlands, not for the faint-hearted. It was amazing he could even find the right clothes for an occasion like this: a lot of his stuff was still in tea-chests. Never mind: if the peach cummerbund had gone the way of his *Times* atlas, his beloved peace lily, and his ornamental desk-lamp (a present from his replacement at *The Independent*) – if it was missing presumed lost, in other words – it was pointless getting worked up. Every house-move has its casualties; the greater the distance, the higher the toll.

He opened the next wardrobe door along and experienced a momentary shudder of discomfort, like something his conscience might have inspired in him when it caught him doing something shifty. For a moment, until he closed the door again, he was face-to-face with his *alter ego*. A green wax-jacket, a cloth cap, six check shirts neatly folded, several pairs of jeans. On the floor, six or seven pairs of walking boots coated with mud from those wretched walks with Rabbie, most of them through the driving bloody rain.

His alter ego was elsewhere in the house too: in the oaken walking-stick he'd bought from an exclusive catalogue; in the collection of Scottish dance and folk-music CDs and DVDs in his kitchen-cupboards; and in Rabbie himself.

Rabbie was the West Highland Terrier he'd bought from a breeder in Fulham, last thing he did before moving. The little maggot was probably skulking in his basket now, down in the lounge. God willing, he was on his way to a rescue-centre in about a week or so. If they wouldn't take him, he'd just have to be put down. Which would probably cost an arm and a leg, but never mind.

The irony was, they'd taken to each other so well at first. But he'd been closer to his *alter ego* then.

That was before Kitty Hamilton.

Thirty Hours Earlier.

"So, I can rely on seeing you tomorrow night, Charlie?" Kitty said. There was something in the way she emphasised *rely* that made him think things were about to move to what was sometimes called 'the next level'. He'd managed to slip in the information that he was a widower several days beforehand - discreetly he thought: not in such a way as to scare her. An invitation to a party at her house had followed.

"I'm very much looking forward to it," he replied.

"There'll be lots of people there. It'll be an opportunity for you to spread the word."

"Spread the word?"

She laughed, as if she didn't believe he was being serious. "About your *theory!* About your *book!*"

They were sitting outside a little pub overlooking the Strathspey with purple mountains in the distance. The sky was overcast and the air was cold but invigorating. Wisps of grey hair kept escaping from beneath Kitty's boater; she kept retrieving them and pushing them back beneath her hat. She had a glass of orange juice. His was a single malt whisky – the sort of thing his *alter ego* liked to drink.

"I'll knock 'em dead," he said, raising his glass.

"I wouldn't be so sure." When she became solicitous, her Home Counties accent took on soft edges. "Some of them are dyed-in-the-wool SNP. They won't take kindly to being told that all nationalism is fascism."

"I'll keep quiet if you think it'll ruin things."

She laughed. "Oh, *no*. That's the last thing I want. Every hostess likes a lively soirée. And they all know where you stand. They know you're not the sort of person who shies away from a fight - "

"I won't provoke one unnecessarily."

"Some of them are a bit afraid of you!"

"Really? Which ones?"

"I won't name names. Very well," she said, as if he'd insisted, "just one. Tom Lawrence, maybe …"

"*Tom Lawrence?* Isn't he the local SNP *candidate?* I mean, I know they lost to Labour at the last by-election, but only by a handful of votes - assuming that what I've heard is true. What possible reason can *he* have to be afraid of *me?*"

"Oh, come on Charlie, don't be modest. Lots. For a start, you've been the editor of one of the biggest dailies on the planet. That's enough to strike the fear of God into anyone, let alone someone like Tom Lawrence. And your MBE: he may not believe in that sort of thing, but that's not to say he's not intimidated by it. Finally, you're actually from *round* here. You were *born* here, you *grew up* here. You're not some outsider, with no claim to speak … Dare I say it: someone like him?"

"So, it's true he's not actually Scottish?"

"That depends how widely you interpret 'Scottish'. Is Greg Rusedski English? He wasn't born here, no. I rather like Tom," she added. "He's sweet on me, you know."

"Is he?"

"It's pathetic, really. I don't encourage it. The only reason I'm inviting him tomorrow is he's something of a local dignitary. Anyway, I know *you'll* protect me. Your reputation precedes you, let's just say. Apart from all the things I've just told you, there's this book of yours. It's well known that people like Tom Lawrence are going to find it very uncomfortable reading when it finally comes out. Even though you've kept your cards very close to your chest so far; even though no one knows specifically what it's about. Although… what am I saying? That's precisely the *genius* of it!"

"The truth is, I'm not entirely sure myself. Ostensibly, it's about the Highland Clearances - "

She waved her hand. "It's no use explaining that sort of thing to me. It'll go completely over my head. All I know is your book's supposed to make the intellectual case against rogue movements like the SNP. Rumour has it that even Alex Salmond's a bit worried about it."

"That's nonsense of course," he scoffed, trying to hide his pleasure. "Since when have politicians – any of them - worried about intellectual refutations? They appeal to emotions and prejudices, not arguments. Anyway, I'm not even sure what I'm going to say myself yet."

"You are still *writing* a book, aren't you?"

"I'm still *trying* to. I've drafted bits. I'm trying to keep an open mind. I don't want to have to make the evidence fit the theory."

"In my view, it's utterly admirable."

"Thank you."

"You know, I really believe in the Union," she said looking dreamily at the distant mountains. "Not only the Great British Union, but the European one too – in fact, all unions: all humans together, everywhere. I'm a child of the sixties, maybe, yes, but it's just an objective fact that the more we split into little factions based on culture, the more we regress. Culture's a gift you give to others. It's not some totem pole for you and your friends to congregate round."

"I expect the Tom Lawrences of this world would say Scotland's cultural 'gift' has been declined – the English have either ignored it or tried to stamp on it - so the world's in danger of losing it."

"That's wrong though, isn't it?" She laughed. "Tell me it's wrong! If I thought it was right I *would* join the SNP!"

"Well, a lot of any culture's in the language, and Gaelic's probably dying out. They'd probably say it's dying out because of Scotland's relative poverty, and that Scotland's relative poverty is the result of things like its North Sea oil being sequestered – then squandered - by Westminster."

"But surely that's silly?"

"It may be wrong. I'm not sure it's silly."

"But isn't it *better* that we all speak one language? I mean, I know English is a fairly clumsy tool, but if we all spoke one language – be it English or Gaelic or Latin or ancient Egyptian – I'm sure the world would be a much better place. I know people are always going on about minority languages 'disappearing', and how terrible it is that we lose all these idiosyncratic 'concepts' and we're all forced to 'carve the world up linguistically' in exactly the same way for ever and ever hereafter. But think of the *gains!*"

"Wouldn't it be even better if everyone was bilingual?"

"Do *you* speak any Gaelic?"

"A bheil an t-acras ort?"

"Meaning?"

"Are you hungry?"

She clapped her hands delightedly. "Not right now, Charlie. I had a big breakfast. But I will be tomorrow night. You're definitely coming?"

"Wild horses couldn't keep me away."

Three hours later, as he stretched out on the back seat of the taxi home, he reflected with a smile that falling in love with Kitty had been the exact opposite of why he'd returned to the Highlands. Having been in journalism all his working life, he'd always assumed the newspaper editor side of him – 'Roaring Charlie Campbell' with his handmade suits and ties, his big swivel chair, his firm handshake and ready opinions on everything from the 4.15 at Doncaster to the strength of the euro - wasn't his true identity. The *real* him was a very different animal, only properly at home in the literal wilderness, or in a croft in front of a poky log fire. The *real* Charlie Campbell could brood for hours in the corner of an old pub, guarding a half-finished pint, staring fixedly at the carpet, saying nothing. So he'd thought. It was why he returned 'home'.

But the best laid schemes o' mice an' men gang aft agley. Kitty was English. And so was he, really. He was now, anyway. He'd left the Highlands when he was sixteen. He'd stayed in London till he was sixty-five. Forty-nine years, after which it should have been no surprise there was no 'real him' to come home to; that it had all been a fantasy. Nevertheless, it had taken Kitty to show him.

When they were married, they'd go and live in one of the Home Counties. There was nothing left for him here.

He got out of the taxi, took a deep lungful of air and straightened. It was early evening now and the sun was setting. He paid the driver, adding a precise ten per cent tip as was his custom, and skipped up the drive to his house.

As soon as he opened the front door his mood was killed. The smell hit him at once. Rabbie had had another 'accident' – and now he could see it in the middle of the hall carpet! And suddenly, there was Rabbie, wagging his tail.

"*Bad dog!*" he bellowed. "Bad dog! *Bad dog!*" Then something inside him snapped and he decided to stop treating Rabbie as anything worth relating to. "*You filthy little worm!*" he screamed. "*Get out of my bloody sight!*"

Rabbie scampered to his basket, lay down with his face flat on the bottom and expelled a sigh through his nose. Charlie Campbell went into the kitchen to fetch the carpet cleaner.

Two hours later, he lay in bed unable to sleep. He'd pretended not to know Tom Lawrence for Kitty's benefit. Over the years, pretending not to know someone was the way he'd taught himself to underline that person's insignificance – both for himself and for others.

But he *did* know him. Maybe not to speak to, but by reputation and by sight. Tom Lawrence was taciturn, larger-than-life, bearded loner - in many ways, the sort of person he'd once seen himself becoming, before Kitty brought him to his senses. They were even about the same age.

Tom Lawrence had been a gamekeeper at one time, but drink – so the rumours said - had forced him to retire, or possibly prompted his sacking. In any case, he wasn't a gamekeeper anymore, though he routinely dressed like one. Flat cap, waterproof trousers, thick worsted jacket with his neck tightly bound in a grey scarf. People said he never changed his clothes. After his wife had left him ten years ago, he'd taken up with the SNP.

The irony was, he was English. He'd been born somewhere in County Durham. His mother had been Scottish, yes, but his father was a Bedfordshire man. And he'd gone to public school in England. He'd lived there till he was nearly sixteen.

There would almost certainly be some sort of confrontation tomorrow night. Kitty couldn't see it of course, because she was sweet and trusting: she saw the best in everyone. But Tom Lawrence had something to prove. Being nominally English, he had to fight doubly hard to prove his 'Scottish' credentials. And there would be drink there, naturally there would.

Charlie Campbell got out of bed and went over to his desk. Maybe he should rehearse the main outlines of what he was going to say in his book, just in case he was called on to speak about it.

His writing desk was a simple table, with a monitor and keyboard. There were a variety of print-offs of draft chapters and assorted web-pages, and two academic textbooks – Eric Richards's *The Highland Clearances* and Marianne McLean's *The People of Glengarry: Highlanders in Transition 1745-1820*. On these, stood a dirty plate and a half-finished cup of coffee, long since cold, with a milky disc floating on top.

His own book dealt with the mass evictions of the nineteenth century in which tens of thousands of Highlanders were expelled from their homes so the land could be turned over to sheep-farming. Its primary thesis – if it could be called that: it was more like an empty shell that needed filling with evidence – was that these clearances were the precondition of modern Scottish nationalism. If they hadn't happened, he wanted to assert, the Highland villages would ultimately have developed into thriving urban centres like those in the South – Newcastle, Bradford, Leeds, Manchester - importing labour from England and thereby dissolving the mandate for home rule. Scottish nationalism was thus the product of an historical event, or series of events, which it was conscience-bound to condemn. Its position was intrinsically self-contradictory, hence untenable.

There were lots of problems with this. The most obvious one was that all political parties whatever were dependent on conditions they claimed to want to remove. There could be no communists if it wasn't for capitalism; there could be no anti-racism if there was no racism. Any resolution of this difficulty depended on his finding a difference *specific to this case* – a discovery he was by no means confident of making.

The book's second thesis was that all nationalism was fascism. The newspaper editor in him liked the sound-bite in that. And he felt it was easier to prove. All it required was a distinction between 'a desire for independence', which was frequently defensible, and 'nationalism', which never was.

If there was a problem here, it had to do with the hidden subject. A desire for independence could never be free-floating; it had to be *someone's* desire. In this context, though, whose? The most natural political candidate was the nation. This meant that if there was a distinction to be sustained, it would have to be between 'national independence' and 'nationalism'. The difficulty lay in showing that they weren't just two sides of the same coin.

He closed his eyes and tried to imagine what it would be like to drop off to sleep right now. He hoped no one would ask him about his book tomorrow. As things stood, he wouldn't have the faintest idea how to reply. It was beginning to look like a disaster. Even as he tried to refute it, Scottish nationalism – or at least its coherent possibility - was threatening to seduce him.

He was so glad he'd met Kitty when he had. Looking back, she hadn't arrived a moment too soon.

The Present.

He tried to ignore the proliferation of Rabbie-related paraphernalia in the second section of his wardrobe, and eventually found the peach cummerbund in the pocket of one of his jackets, of all places. It needed ironing, but otherwise it was good as new. He rang for a taxi and poured himself a brandy to drink while he was waiting. Oblivious to the looming prospect of the rescue-centre, Rabbie came to the door to see him off.

It was eight o'clock, and dark, when his taxi pulled up outside Kitty's house, a six-bedroom mansion set in several acres of hardy grassland relieved only by pine trees, rocky outcrops, a few disused shooting huts, and an imposing pond. The roof was clay-tiled and sagging slightly. A four-panelled green door stood beneath a grandiose white portico.

He was welcomed into the house by a stranger, an Englishman, slightly younger than he was, with dyed black hair, a hollow chest and a public school accent.

"I'm Clive Jones," this man said, offering a handshake and breaking into a grin composed of two rows of perfectly white, perfectly aligned teeth. "I'm one of Kitty's oldest friends," he went on. "I'm in the second-hand book trade. You must be Charlie Campbell, the newspaper editor. Of course, I knew who you were before she told me about you. *The Independent*, eh? That must have been a job and a half. And an MBE. She's very excited you've moved here. We both are. Can I get you a drink?"

"Pleased to meet you, Clive. I wouldn't mind a double brandy."

"Double *brandy?*" Clive hooted, showing his teeth again (which, it suddenly struck Charlie, were almost certainly false).

"Is there something wrong with … double brandy?" Charlie asked.

"Nothing wrong with the French of course: just ask Bonnie Prince Charles Edward Stuart! No, we only serve single malt in here. It's the only drink we *do!* And Irn-Bru!"

"Well, I, er, wouldn't mind a double single malt, then."

"'Double single malt'!" Clive repeated, suppressing a giggle. "I love it! Of course, the whisky-only policy's driven by our concern for local businesses. I hope you like haggis, by the way: there's a lot of it about tonight!" He laughed again, then became more serious. "I hear you're writing about the Highland Clearances? I expect there aren't many books on that. It's not as fashionable as, say, the Irish Potato Famine, is it? But I can get you any book you like. For your research, I mean. Just ask. No matter how long out-of-print. Just ask. *Kitty! It's Charlie! Charlie's here!* Hang on, Charlie: I'll just get Kitty."

He led Charlie into the living room then walked away, still chuckling to himself and repeating 'double single malt' in an undertone.

The 'living room' was as big as a small warehouse. The carpet was patterned and worn in random places, like a pub-carpet. The high ceiling was hung with two enormous chandeliers that came halfway to the floor. All the wall-lights had been switched on to give the impression of overwhelming radiance. Tables and chairs had been moved to the side, the former draped with tablecloths and laid with snacks, jugs of orange and full whisky decanters. All told there were about forty people in the room, mostly couples; the men in dinner-jackets, the women in evening dresses. It was a grander, more formal occasion than Charlie had been expecting, but he was glad he hadn't dressed down for it. Nevertheless, he merely blended in rather than standing out, which was rather a disappointment.

His first instinct was to look not for Kitty, but for Tom Lawrence. He caught sight of him standing alone on the other side of the room, dressed in an old grey suit creased at the back, and a blue tie, the thin end of which was too long. He had obviously combed his beard and hair and pruned his eyebrows hard, because, relative to his usual look, he was almost unrecognisably spruce. He was holding what looked like a quadruple single malt in both hands and gazing into it as if he'd looked everywhere in the room for something he'd lost and now he was looking in this one last place, and he knew he wouldn't find it there either. Kitty's words, *He's sweet on me, you know* came back to Charlie, then, *It's pathetic, really*. It certainly was pathetic.

He had to find Kitty.

But before he could act on this resolution, there came the sound of repeated tapping on a glass, clearly the prelude to an announcement. The conversational rumble died down and everyone looked to the front of the room. Clive Jones stood on a podium, and fired shafts of light from his teeth. He lowered the glass and the teaspoon.

"Ladies and gentlemen," he said, "a select few of you know why you're here tonight. The rest of you: prepare to be delighted and amazed. I won't beat about the bush. *Kitty Hamilton and I are to be married!*"

There were cries of glee, then a collective 'Aaaah!' of affection, then a long round of applause in which Charlie participated only with his hands. Tom had dropped his quadruple single malt on the carpet and he began to clap stupidly, as if afraid his hands might miss each other and make him lose balance. His face was a picture of pain and indignation. He looked exactly like Charlie felt.

Suddenly Kitty herself was on the podium, next to her fiancé. She was dressed all in tartan with a tartan turban. She looked hideous.

"Obviously," she said, "I won't be renouncing my surname. It's the one thing that still ties me to Scotland – besides my love and affection for the country," she went on. "My ancestors were *proud* to be Hamiltons, and so am I! I'd like you all to have an *excellent* time tonight: eat, drink and be merry, and don't forget to pick up a wedding invitation on the way out. *Lang may yer lum reek! I wish you all every happiness!*"

"I'd just like to thank Kitty for making me the first-happiest second-hand book dealer in the world!" Clive quipped.

There was another delighted 'Aaaah!' and another round of applause. Then suddenly a piano broke into the opening chords of 'Bonnie Banks o' Loch Lomond'.

"Oh ye'll take the high road!" Clive sang, putting his arms round Kitty's shoulders.

"And I'll take the low road!" sang Kitty, leaning in to him.

Suddenly, Charlie felt a rough tug at his elbow. He turned around to find himself face-to-face with Tom Lawrence, who was gripping a one-litre cut-glass whisky decanter, full to the top.

"The bloody bastards," Tom said, loud enough to make everyone in the vicinity to turn round.

Charlie didn't know what to say. Like everyone else he was clapping in time to 'The Bonnie Banks o' Loch Lomond'.

"Come on," Tom said.

A moment later, they were outside on the heath, Tom still clutching the full decanter, and walking determinedly side by side. The wind had built up, it rained, and a mist was falling. Tom obviously knew where he was going; Charlie didn't. But it could have been a death-march for all he cared. It probably was.

Three-quarters of an hour later, they arrived at an abandoned thatched stone hut with a single window and a wooden door whose white paint had almost completely peeled. They went inside and into complete darkness. It smelt of paraffin, candle-wax and moist earth, like the entrance to an old kirk. Tom fumbled about for a few moments then lit four candles in slow succession. There was a bed in the room, an old wardrobe, a table and two wooden chairs. With each new candle, they grew a little more distinct.

Tom took two cups from the wardrobe and banged them on the table. Then he put the decanter down.

"Ha' ye e'er seen a ghost?" he demanded, out of the blue.

"I don't think so," Charlie replied.

"Go an' tek a look oot the windee. There's plenty aboot tonight. All your Highland Clearance laddies. That's whit ye'r book's aboot, isn't it? Go an' tek a look."

It was a strange Scottish accent, too forced somehow. Charlie suddenly recalled the gamekeeper in *Lady Chatterley's Lover*, shamming a regional accent or not as the mood took him.

He stood up and looked out of the window. Yes, he could see them, the ghosts – just. They were traipsing through the mist, forever on their way out of this place. Just as he was.

'Who *am* I?' he murmured softly to himself. He felt like he was dreaming. 'Who *am* I really?'

Thanks to the candles behind him, and the increasing darkness on the other side of the single dirty window, he caught an accidental glimpse of himself for the second time that day. This time he looked much, much older than sixty-five. He looked about two hundred.

Tom poured two full glasses of whisky. Charlie sat down opposite him. They grimly toasted each other's health and drank.

It was Irn-Bru.

Twelve Years Later

They must be eighty-five or ninety now. Something of an institution round these parts. Callum McReady - you must know Callum McReady: leader of the SNP? – anyway, he came up from Edinburgh last year, specially to have his photo taken with them. They agreed to it, but they were hardly bowled over. Nothing much impresses men like them: they've seen too much.

They don't say a lot, either of them. They're not brothers, but in their matching jackets, baggy trousers, heavy boots and pulled-down caps, and with their gnarled hands and sombre weather-beaten faces, they might as well be. Every night, they sit dourly in the corner of *The Black Watch,* each nursing a pint, saying nothing.

Rumour has it the older one ran a newspaper once, somewhere down south. But frankly, that seems unlikely. Who knows where those sorts of tales come from, and who can explain how far-fetched some of them are? More likely, he worked on the land. Because that's what he looks like: a fencer, or a thatcher. I don't mean that to sound prejudiced. He's supposed to be writing a book in defence of Scottish nationalism, if you can believe such a thing. Or he was. He's got severe arthritis now, so I'll be surprised if he can even hold a pen any more.

As for the younger one, you may not believe this, but technically he's English. His parents were Scottish of course, and they brought him back over the border the same day he was born. Agatha McDonald, his mother was called. She used to live hereabouts. Wild one. He used to be wild, too. A real Braveheart.

He's got a singular accent when he speaks. A couple of years back, some expert, a professor from some university in America, came and listened to him. Apparently, it's how Highlanders used to inflect their speech in the days of yore.

There's another story about them. It's said they were both rivals for the heart of a Gaelic woman called Kathy Henderson. She loved both equally, and couldn't bring herself to disappoint either of them. She sacrificed herself by marrying a visiting Englishman on the spur of the moment. He took her over the border with him. She died shortly afterwards of a broken heart. The rival suitors never got over it.

That must have been seventy years ago, though, if it was a day. Obviously, they never fell in love again.

When you look at them, you can really see the spirit of the Highlands. I mean the real *human* dimension. They're the last of a dying breed, I suppose: a last link to the bygone days of the clans. The real Scotland, if there is such a thing.

Aye, if there is such a thing, they're its embodiment.

Them, and that cute little West Highland Terrier one of them owns. Rabbie, I think it's called.

AN UNHAPPY FAMILY TURNS THE CORNER

Rows of Edwardian terraced houses stretched miles either side of them and met other Edwardian terraces at T-junctions, and these stretched miles to meet yet more Edwardian terraces at T-junctions, and so on for all eternity. The windows had the haunted look of hospital patients in sepia photos. The only concession to Christmas day and the century – presumably, therefore, a mistake - was a square of fairy lights, two doors away.

Alicia, blonde and plump, stood on the second step up under a grey sky. She gripped a bottle of Pinot Noir. Tom, twenty-eight years her senior, six feet tall and greying, stood below and behind his wife, dangling two bags of presents. They'd rowed about this moment for a year and they'd stared blankly through Sunday pm silences. Zoe, in a ballet dress and a tiara, tugged at her father's sleeve.

Alicia blinked slowly. "Maybe they've gone out."

"Try again," Tom said.

She raised the knocker, paused, then brought it down three times hard. It was the sort of thing you'd hear if you were in. If you chose not to answer it, there could only be one reason.

Tom sensed the neighbours switching off the lights and retiring a few steps to watch. "They must be out," he said.

"Where?"

"I don't know. A meal."

"It's four o'clock."

"Shall we come back later?"

Alicia frowned. "It's Christmas Day. No one's serving at this time."

"Maybe they're visiting friends."

She closed her eyes and put her hands on her face. "What a disaster. We'll have to wait, though."

"So, what'll we do in the meantime? Sit in the car?"

"Maybe. And then we could see if - "

The door opened. The occupants – an elderly man and woman - stood touching shoulders like a Gilbert and George installation. Hugh hadn't changed since a year ago, when he'd fractured Tom's skull with a poker: everything about him was crepuscular and moribund. Betty looked older, and there was hatred in her eyes. Only her feet were the same. She always wore shoes in the house, so Alicia claimed, except for bed.

Tom passed his wife the carrier bags then looked at the ground to show that none of this was his idea.

"Happy Christmas, Mummy and Daddy," Alicia said.

"Bring Zoe in," Betty said.

No one moved. The wind bit.

"We're not coming in without Tom," Alicia said, her tone part plea, part ultimatum.

Hugh and Betty made to look at one another but stopped halfway. Presumably a conference would look like weakness. Betty shrugged and stepped aside. Hugh swore under his breath and walked back indoors.

"Come on in, Tom!" Alicia said jauntily.

The dining room was roughly as Alicia remembered it, except for the impalpable sense that it was decaying. Two easy chairs faced a cast-iron mantelpiece where postcards from friends jostled with inexpensive knick-knacks from camping holidays. A wide screen TV with an old-fashioned video player took up one corner. On the far side, the dining table was pulled away from the wall.

Betty went into the kitchen. "We haven't eaten yet," she said, as if the intrusion was to blame. "Sit at the table."

Alicia took Zoe on her knee and folded their bodies onto the chair next to the wall. Tom sat opposite her. Betty returned with two empty biscuit plates and banged them down and went back. Hugh sat at the head of the table without making eye-contact and clutched his cutlery.

Betty brought in two dishes piled with dinner for herself and Hugh. "There's some turkey in the kitchen," she told Alicia. "Get it if you're hungry."

She jerked her chair in without looking up, stuck her knife and fork into a roast potato and ate it with her mouth half open.

"We've eaten already," Alicia said.

"I'm sure Zoe wouldn't mind a Yorkshire pudding," Tom said.

Alicia blushed. "Zoe's taken this real liking to them. She'd eat them all day if she could."

Betty scowled. She fished a Yorkshire pudding out of her gravy then scraped the liquid off as if she was ceremonially disembowelling it. "Pass her plate, then."

"You didn't have to give her yours!" Alicia protested.

"We haven't got any spares. Just pass her bloody *plate*, will you?"

"I think we should go," Tom said.

But Alicia had already passed Zoe's plate.

After dinner, Betty went to do the washing up. Alicia followed with Zoe, leaving Tom and Hugh alone. She was astonished by how far things had slipped into apparent neglect since her last visit. Piles of roughly stacked plates with dried-on ketchup, egg-shells stacked and left, shards of peeled or torn vegetables, countless different coloured stains, the tracks of dried-up trickles on walls and the units, a film of grime on the floor, a dead woodlouse on the washing machine. Betty pulled on her rubber gloves.

"I'll dry, shall I?" Alicia said, swallowing her incredulity.

"Please yourself."

"Don't be like that. It's Christmas Day. Don't you think we should open the presents?"

"I've no intention of 'opening the presents'. You can take them back with you."

Her words were slurred. Alicia registered a half-drunk bottle of Courvoisier hiding between the bread-bin and the kettle. Then she saw her mother noticing her noticing it.

"It's – it's for the Christmas pudding," Betty muttered. It was the first time she'd been on the back foot and suddenly she looked vulnerable. She marched to the bottle, unscrewed the cap and took a long pull. Then she wept.

In the living room, Tom and Hugh were silent. Their armchairs were at an obtuse angle whose intersection was the coal fire. On the TV, a carriage clock stood next to a photograph of Alicia in her University of Essex gown, clutching a scroll and smiling. Through the wall, the neighbours could be heard singing, 'Have Yourself a Merry Little Christmas'.

Hugh leaned towards his son-in-law, put his chin in his hand, and poured all the detestation he could muster into his gaze. He didn't care if Tom thought he was mad. He *was* mad.

"Mind if I help myself to a few nuts and raisins?" Tom asked.

"Keep your filthy hands to yourself," Hugh said.

Tom put up his palms, leaned back and sighed. "Know what this reminds me of? When you and I were at school together. Remember those long winter evenings when we were allowed into the canteen, but we weren't allowed to touch the food?"

"I wouldn't know. You were in the year above me."

Hugh immediately regretted speaking. It implied Tom was worth it. And it had compromised his odium. He stood up and went to the window behind Tom's chair.

Then he had an idea how he could repair his mistake.

He could kill Tom. He could smash his skull with the poker, finish what he'd failed to last year.

"It's always the women who suffer when the men fight," Alicia said.

Her mother had abandoned the washing up and her tears had dried. She poured herself a large brandy and one for her daughter. But she wasn't speaking. It was as if she'd gone through a tunnel of vulnerability and emerged reinvigorated.

Alicia kept speaking. Even in her most optimistic daydreams, this was the best she'd expected: a miniscule breach in the walls. She just had to keep working at it.

"Look, I know this isn't what you and Dad expected. Me marrying someone who's a year older than him. And I know Tom was always Dad's big enemy at school and he's supposed to have bullied him and so on. And I know Dad thinks he made a move on me to wreck your lives and that he's going to reduce me to utter dependency then leave me." She looked at the ceiling and spread her hands on the table. "But none of that's true. The way divorce law is nowadays, I could take him to the cleaner's. You can't make it all about you. I still love you. You've got to try and move on."

Betty downed her brandy and banged her glass on the table. "He left his first wife high and dry. Twenty years they'd been married. And then you come along." She laughed and shook her head. "Don't think he'll stay with you, oh no. He didn't stay with her. Ten years on, your face'll have dropped and you'll be pudgy like I was. Then who's going to want you? Not him. He just wants to frolic in the grass with a young bunny and he's realistic enough to realise that, at his age, marriage is the price."

In the living room, Tom knew Hugh was somewhere behind him. His scalp tingled, presumably at the memory of last time. He tried to calm himself. Lightning – never twice. Speaking was partly a way of easing his nerves, but he'd already made him respond and that was what he and Alicia had agreed: get them to open up, only ever so slightly, then appeal to their better natures. It might take a day, it might take a year ...

"Hugh," he said, "I know you think I've some kind of long-standing grudge against you and that I'm using Alicia to satisfy it. Nothing could be further from the truth. I'm very sorry for that day, before we were married when you discovered us upstairs, making love in such an... *unusual* way in your bed, but I swear to God that wasn't intended. I love Alicia. I wouldn't be here now if I - "

Tom's skull caved in with a muffled crunch. As Hugh was to put it later in court - and as he was to tell a succession of counsellors and psychologists - he was 'surprised by the amount of give'. Tom only knew that something had landed on him. The last thing he was conscious of was his teeth clapping together. He let out an involuntary gurgle of surprise.

Hugh raised the poker again and brought it down with even greater force. But Tom had slumped to one side, so it landed with a loud crack on the back of the armchair.

"What's that?" Alicia said.

Betty shrugged. "What?"

"It sounded like a firework." She got up, hauled Zoe wearily onto her hip and went into the living room.

Her father stood to attention resting the poker on his shoulder. Tom dangled over the side of the armchair.

"Call the police," Hugh said. "I've just killed your husband."

Betty gripped the bottle of wine. She formed the advance guard, facing the front door. Hugh stood behind her, holding three carrier bags with presents in. They knocked and waited. Inside, through the glass on either side of the door, they could see a decorated spruce.

"Maybe they've gone out," Betty said after two minutes. Her voice trembled.

"Knock again."

She paused then knocked three times. There was an uncanny quiet. Even the birds weren't singing. Overhead, cumulonimbus clouds went by like snails.

"They must be out," Hugh said.

But suddenly the door opened and Alicia stood holding Zoe's hand. In the background, they could see Tom in a wheelchair, one hand on each tyre.

Hugh handed his wife the carrier bags.

"Happy Christmas, Ali," Betty said.

Alicia clenched her teeth and glared, and everything about her – visible and invisible - blocked their entry. Zoe hid behind her.

"We'll – we'll leave the gifts here," Betty said. She put them on the ground. Hugh nodded. The door closed.

Betty turned to her husband and welled up.

Then they heard a little click. The door re-opened. This time, Tom was foremost. He had a blanket over his legs and he looked as if he was in pain. He forced a smile. Although Alicia and Zoe had taken a step back, their faces hadn't altered.

Tom held out his hands. "Come in, come in. Betty, Hugh. For God's sake, come in."

The couple sprang apart as if electricity had compelled them. They exchanged anxious glances then stumbled separately into the interior.

A STUDY IN REGRET

I shouldn't have gone into the study. Of course, that's obvious.

Still, what's done is done. No point crying over spilt milk.

As for what's going on now ... well, it beats me. Plush red seats, marble flooring, amiable receptionists. And those people in green jackets marching back and forwards, obviously important bods. An altogether classy establishment. And Mr Smith – Ron - from next door, well, he was so, *sentimental* on the journey over. I've never known him like that before and we've lived next door to each other for – what? Must be twelve years. Probably doesn't get out much, not to places like this.

No, I don't understand it. Harriet should have turned up for *this*– whatever it is; I'm guessing some kind of special occasion. It's been a full three days now since I last saw her. She always liked us to be together, before. Which is the operative word, perhaps. Before. Before the study, we were virtually inseparable. It's sad how just when you think you know someone ...

But I must say, everyone's being very nice. I ate before I left home. Really well, actually: one of the best meals I've had for ages. I have to hand it to Mr Smith – Ron. Whatever Harriet sometimes says about him in her dark moments, he can prepare a meal. And as soon as I got here, they offered me a drink. Always loved a good stiff drink, me.

Mind you, I'm not comfortable with the way they're so free with my Christian name. Soon as I checked in it was Colin this, Colin that. *Are you okay there, Colin? Would you like another drink, Colin?* I don't like to sound fastidious, but it's Colin *McReady*. I'm not such a stickler that I insist on "*Mr* McReady", but surely, just "Colin" is a bit familiar on a first meeting. Wait till we've been properly introduced is all I ask. It isn't much.

Thanks, I've just had a drink. Just put it down there, there's a good fellow. I'll get it in a minute. Thank you.

I guess Harriet's stuck in traffic. The Blackhurst Junction's a nightmare round about this time. Bloody commuters, why can't they just move closer to work or get bikes? Too often we've both had to sit there at a complete standstill, grumbling or listening to the radio. Radio Four, as a rule, although I sometimes drift off during the *Today* programme. Politics has never been my forte. A great philosopher, name of Immanuel Kant, once said 'ought' implies 'can'. Well, I can't. Can't get involved in politics or world affairs, I mean. Makes me sleepy.

Not her. Things I love tend to make her go 'yuck' and vice-versa. Maybe that's why we hit it off so immediately, so passionately, so deeply. Opposites attract. *The Archers* is one of the few places we converge. But even there, I love it for the music; she loves it for the fifteen or so minutes in between. Chalk and cheese.

She's probably frustrated as anything she's not here, enjoying a relaxing drink before whatever's going to happen. Probably cursing. She should have set off a bit earlier, that's what I'll say. Then she'll blow up and I'll tell her I was only joking and we'll have a bloody good laugh.

My guess is it's some kind of surprise party. That would make sense, wouldn't it? Mr Smith's probably nervous. Thinks I'll guess what he's been up to, the sly fox.

Of course, Harriet will have organised it. Harriet and I love each other, you see. Oh, I know what you're probably thinking. One of those mugs who still believes in love? It's all sex and celebrity and money nowadays. Who can believe in *love* anymore? Well, I can, and Harriet can. Ours is of the old-fashioned sort, I suppose. She told me recently she didn't think anyone had ever loved her like I love her; and that the feeling was mutual: she loved me with a completeness that transcended the vagaries of life and chance. Made me blush, you bet. But she wasn't joking.

There's a corollary to all that, naturally. Which is why I know Harriet's stuck in traffic. Fidelity. Let's say she's stopped loving me (which she won't have), our love doesn't stop with our emotions. It's got a moral dimension. Because even if I stopped loving her, I'd still be *there* for her. So I know she'll be here for me.

Although, even saying that ever so confidently, I can't pretend there isn't another possibility. She's annoyed because I went into the study. That was a mistake, I admit. A big mistake, yes, I can see that now.

Three days. It seems a lot longer. I mean, a *lot* longer. But then, that's love. Time goes slowly when you're apart. You're counting the minutes sometimes.

The study. No, I'm sure she'll have forgiven me by now.

There's a woman in the next-door room.

"Are we ready for Colin?"

"I think so." Another woman. Comes out, all smiles. The receptionist.

Golly, this is it! But for goodness' sake, I don't want to start without Harriet. Where can she be? I'm thinking back, trying to search for clues in what she did the last time we were together.

Nothing much. I'd been in the garden for twenty minutes, pottering around between the patio and the flowers. I came back in for a biscuit and something to wash it down with, and there she was, on the kitchen floor, having a sleep. The vegetable knife was in her hand and she'd dropped an onion. I nodded it towards the bin. I know she doesn't like mess. She doesn't usually sleep face down like that but I guess everyone gets really tired some time.

"What is he?"

Harriet's thirteen. Unlucky, when you come to think of it. That's … eighty-four in human years. Humans age a lot more quickly than we do.

"He's a Labrador."

"Hello, Colin."

I shake hands with the person in the green jacket, the organiser of the surprise party presumably. There seems no reason not to.

"He's been crying non-stop since it happened."

I don't remember her waking up. Mr Smith banged at the front door for a long time and came in, and I was allowed into the study. I'm not usually supposed to go in there, so I jumped at the chance. Obviously, I hoped Mr Smith wouldn't wake Harriet up for a few minutes. Not until I'd had a good nose around. I knew I'd have to be quick, but I made the most of it.

"Poor thing. Shame he's so old. They never settle anywhere else when they get to his age."

The woman in the green overall points her squirter – whatever it is - in the air and gives it a squeeze. I remember this place now. I thought so. Harriet brought me here when I was a boy. So that's what all this is about. Another round of injections. I knew she was behind it.

And to make matters even better, I hardly felt that one.

So it wasn't a surprise party. Mr Smith's putting on his coat. I suppose we'll be off home in a minute. Nice of Mr Smith – Ron – to bring me out here. Probably thinks it'll get him in with Harriet. I wonder if he's got a *thing* for her. Most men have. Not that she'd look twice at him, however well he cooks. She's mine.

Whoops. Sorry, everyone. Yawned. Won't happen again. It must be the injection I suppose. How rude, my apologies, I can't seem to help myself. I'm not normally like this. Maybe if I have twenty minutes, Harriet will be here. Yes, then I'll have a peek. She's bound to be here, half an hour at the outside. The roads can't be that busy.

I wish she was here *now*, though. As I remember it, the study wasn't half as much fun as I'd expected it to be.

I wish I'd waited in the kitchen with Mr Smith, now.

IN MUNRO HOUSE

You trust to the undertaker, that's the thing. No one thinks not to, ever. Moreover, I was actually *with* my wife when she died … or when I *think* she died, as it now turns out. Between the removal of the body and the burial of the coffin, I suppose anything could have happened. *Was* she really in there? I never thought to question it. Nor would anyone, not at that point. Anyway, I didn't have the letter then. The letter – handwritten on cartridge paper, unheaded, undated, unsigned – that said: *Germaine, your wife, is still alive and living in Munro House, E14. Tell no one.*

You can imagine my state of mind. Standing in the hallway, midway between the electricity bill and a junk letter about car insurance. My first instinct was to go to the police. But tell them what? What if they thought I'd written it myself, that I'm some kind of attention seeker? It didn't demand anything. It wasn't an extortion note, but then, that's often how extortion begins. *Tell no one.* It's a test. If you obey orders and keep quiet, you're already caught in the net. Otherwise, God help you.

I'd never heard of 'Munro House', but with E14 as my search-term it was a straight road from Google to Wikipedia. It's a high-rise monstrosity on the Isle of Dogs, visible from virtually everywhere in London. Mind you, for something so unmistakable it's odd no one seems to know what goes on inside. It's one of those things that gives Wikipedia a bad name: so many strident opinions, so much editing, counter-editing, plain editorial vandalism. It's a finance institution, a world administrative centre, the true home of MI6/MI5/ the CIA, a hotel whose guests never leave, a husk abandoned after the building costs spiralled out of control … I could go on: Rosicrucians, Freemasons, Opus Dei, you name it. Obviously, it's impregnable otherwise there couldn't be such discord. Someone would have reported back.

Now, I'm not the sort of person anyone sane would try to extort money from. For a kick off, I'm not rich. You don't get junk mail about cheaper car insurance if you're rich. And I'm not impressive either. I'm sub-editor at *Paulin's* a commercial printer on an industrial estate in Swindon. It's not the world's greatest job but it pays for a fortnight in Cornwall every year and it keeps the Ford Focus on the road. Physically: well, I'm fifty-seven, just short of six foot tall, gaunt, not terribly sociable. I stopped dyeing my hair when Germaine passed away. There didn't seem much point any more. I took time off work and when I went back my hair was white. Of course, everyone put it down to shock. They may have been right, for all I know. I'd never been far enough behind with the dyeing before to find out. What I'm trying to say is, I'm not the sort of person you'd 'tap' if you were in the business of tapping people. I'm nondescript.

Anyway, I held onto the letter. I had it down as a sick joke for a while. But then, a joke needs a joker, and no one seemed to be laughing. In fact, no one gave any indication of knowing anything about it.

In the end – after several days – I decided to act. Since Germaine's death, I needed something to occupy my mind. And since this *involved* Germaine, however obliquely, it was probably as satisfying as anything was likely to get anymore.

It was raining hard when I got off the train at Victoria. Ten minutes later I alighted from a black cab, paid, and told the driver to take my luggage to my hotel: The City Lodge, a good distance away. Clasping my overcoat round my neck, I ran as fast as the slippery pavements would allow to the nearest place of shelter: Munro House itself, its porch. Fifty yards, no more, but I was half-soaked when I arrived.

Munro House stood midway along a characterless street whose pavement was lit by sodium lamps. It was five-thirty. Office-workers under umbrellas, or with newspapers over their heads, rushed home. Two lanes of traffic stood waiting before red lights at both ends of the road. The crackle of the rain, the growling of the cars, the lorries, the horns, combined to make a dispiriting cacophony. No one had taken shelter alongside me.

Munro House looked shut up and forgotten. Four sets of glass double-doors were blacked out. Stepping outside the porch and looking up, I couldn't discern so much as a glimmer from its hundreds of windows. Obviously, I'd called on a quiet day.

It seems ridiculous in retrospect, but I wondered if there might be an entrance *at the back somewhere*. Perhaps a door ajar, an open window. Perhaps I could knock, explain my predicament. I'd come a long way and I didn't want to arrive at my hotel empty-handed.

So, I went through the motions of looking for my 'back way', even though I saw the absurdity of it now.

It didn't take long. The sides of the building were fenced off with railings that met the next building along on both sides. And the same went for all buildings in that street. For all practical purposes, impregnable.

Since I was clutching at straws now, I thought I might as well turn onto the waterfront, see if I could come at it that way. But that was fenced off too, this time by a small regiment of security guards.

I had no choice anymore but to go back to my hotel. And I wasn't sorry either. But what an idiot I'd been. Time and money down the drain, and I was soaked.

A few minutes later, I decided to cut my losses: get the early train home tomorrow and put the whole fiasco behind me. Thank God for small mercies: I hadn't told anyone what I was doing. The whole thing was over before it had begun. I had no idea anymore what I'd even been expecting. Suppose Munro House *had* been open, what would I have done? Marched into reception and presented the letter? *Excuse me, I received this. It says my dead wife is still alive and living here. Is she?* It wasn't funny. It made me shudder.

But it was odd. Seriously: what *had* I been I expecting? It was as if I'd come to London ... not *against* my will: no, no, that's not it ... but by a process in which my will played no part. God help me, maybe I was in the early stages of dementia.

Which was a distressing thought, to say the least. When something like that strikes, you've no choice but to try and forget it. After all, there's no cure.

Forgetting it proved harder than I anticipated. Waiting behind the reception at The City Lodge, the manageress looked remarkably like Germaine. Both were about the same height, tall and thin, with straight, dark hair, and cheekbones so high their eyes seemed to be resting in them like stones. After what I'd been through, I couldn't help the peculiar feeling that this was more than coincidental. How, I don't know. But it refused to go away. As for an explanation, well I'd been thinking of Germaine a lot since receiving the note. Perhaps this was a side-effect. I probably needed a complete rest.

Anyway, as soon as she spoke, the illusion was temporarily dispelled. Germaine had a south-coast accent; Mrs Clitheroe was a Geordie.

"We took receipt of your luggage, dear," she said. "It's all in your room."

Just as Munro House was much bigger than its maisonette-sounding name might suggest, so The City Lodge was much smaller. The reception area was hardly bigger than a box-room and nothing had been done to make it feel less claustrophobic. There was a plain desk with a safe built into the wall behind it, and a notice saying 'No Valuables Kept in Here'. The wallpaper and the carpet were new, but their sombre colours merely enhanced the sense of being confined. It was a relief to get my key.

There were just four rooms in The City Lodge. Mine was at the back, looking onto a line of allotments with the Victoria-Portsmouth line in the distance.

At eight o'clock, I went down to the bar-stroke-restaurant for the evening meal. I sat alone at a small table against a radiator, and chose the Liver and Bacon Casserole. Pig's liver: bitter, but not unpleasant. I washed it down with half a pint of Old Speckled Hen and was about to retire to bed or to the lounge – I hadn't decided yet – when the manageress approached, wearing a smile and carrying a notebook and pencil. Clearly, she wasn't anticipating a complaint. I wasn't about to make one.

"Did you enjoy your meal?" she said.

I nodded. "It was very nice."

"Just to let you know about tomorrow morning. We normally serve a continental breakfast, brought to your room around eight o'clock. You can have it earlier if you like. Or later, up until nine."

"Eight o'clock will be fine."

"Breakfast is two croissants, jam and butter – or would you like marmalade?"

"Jam, please."

"Bowl of cereal: cornflakes? Rice Krispies? Special K?"

"Cornflakes," I said. "Yes, I'll have cornflakes, please."

"Cornflakes, right-ho ... Tea or coffee?"

"Tea."

"Tea, right. Yes, *I* like tea ... Anything else?"

"Is the milk UHT?" I asked. "I don't really like that."

"We don't do UHT milk with food." She smiled and I saw Germaine again. "Not if we can avoid it. Yes, we leave it in the Teasmade, in those little cartons, along with the coffee capsules, the teabags and the pot, just in case anyone wants a cup of something hot during the night, but we wouldn't serve it with food. It's emergency fare. Of course, there are some who like their UHT; some actually *prefer* it; some people can drink it by the pint! But we never presume."

"I suppose you can't really get sealed cartons of fresh milk," I said.

"You probably can, but there's the worry of it going off, and some customers would take that as a reflection on The City Lodge. They'd remember us for milk that had turned. They might not like UHT but everyone accepts there's nothing wrong with it. That's the way it's meant to be. You might find it unpleasant, but you're not going to get diarrhoea - if you'll pardon my French."

"And I suppose you can always ring down and order a jug of fresh milk if that's what you want."

Incredibly, we went on like this for some time. I don't know how we got so much from the topic, but soon she'd drawn up a chair and we were laughing like a couple of close relations. Suddenly, she said:

"Would you like to look at what's on for tomorrow night?" She was already passing me the menu. "I could bring your meal to your room if you'd prefer to eat there."

"I won't be staying another night," I said. "I'm going back tomorrow morning."

Her eyebrows touched the underside of her fringe; she looked disbelieving and disappointed. "That's a pity," she said. "You're booked in for three days."

"I'll pay for the three days. It's just ..." I realised I couldn't explain without sounding ridiculous.

"The chicken casserole's very good," she said. "Just in case you do change your mind. Shall I put you down for the chicken casserole? I mean, just on the off chance?"

"In the unlikely event I do change my mind," I said, to please her, "then, yes, I'll have the chicken casserole."

She scribbled in her notebook, snapped it shut, stood up, and disappeared into the kitchen; so abruptly that I wondered if I'd offended her.

A point of clarification. All the above might give the impression I'd warmed to her, even that I was attracted to her. True, whilst she was in front of me I enjoyed her company; but now she'd gone, I felt deflated. There was something ... *strange* about her. Her sudden departure didn't strike me as unforeseeable any more: rather, it was of a piece with the rest of her. She'd no more been interested in the ins and outs of UHT milk than I had; or any normal person would have been. It was merely a pretext to keep me talking.

She'd been *looking into me* somehow. That remark about bringing my meal to my room there was nothing suggestive in it; nothing to indicate a tryst. It was as businesslike as I was entitled to expect. But it wasn't innocuous. Rather, it felt like part of some other agenda.

Did it? ... Or was I adding paranoia to my list of problems now? Anyway, who in heaven's name was *I* to judge Mrs Clitheroe?

The stairs to my room were steep, and the walls were lined with aquatints. I quickly forgot about Mrs Clitheroe: as a professional printer, I've always been unable to resist tints of all types. You can keep your oils and watercolours, as far as I'm concerned.

Anyway, the stairway was the one place in the house that wasn't cramped, so I reckoned I wouldn't be obstructing anyone if I stopped to browse.

There were five pictures in total, all biblical depictions of angels. The three angels appearing to Abraham before the destruction of Sodom were followed by the angel of death in the Exodus story. In both, the attention to detail was outstanding. None of them was signed in any way: perhaps the minutiae were meant to identify the artist to his colleagues. I guessed they were all eighteenth century: individual artists were less significant in those days. Anyway,

Balaam and his donkey was next, followed by Gabriel's appearance to Mary in the Annunciation. Both equally exquisite. In all my years of examining aquatints, I'd never seen workmanship of such remarkable quality. They had to be worth something. I wondered what they were doing hanging on the walls in a place like The City Lodge.

The last picture showed the seven angels of the Book of Revelation blowing their seven trumpets. They were depicted floating above the Earth, shoulder to shoulder, in conventional flowing dress. What set this one apart from the others wasn't the angels, however, but the expressions of the people below on Earth. Every shade of misery and desolation was represented there in compelling genuineness.

But the most disturbing feature of the whole picture was what it didn't show. Somehow – how can I put it? - it *conveyed the conviction* of an unimaginable catastrophe just out of sight, beyond the horizon. The longer I looked, the more I intuited something of that cataclysm until – without yet comprehending it – the feeling became unbearable. I tore myself away.

It wasn't the sort of picture you'd want hanging in your home. I wondered what sort of person Mrs Clitheroe was, to have it hanging prominently on the wall in her hotel (as opposed to, say, locked in a trunk somewhere). I took firm hold of the stair-rail and didn't stop till I got to my room.

It wasn't a bad room, as hotel rooms go. Two pine dressers with a wardrobe and chest of drawers, a dressing table with a mirror, a sliding window and a single bed. The bathroom was *en suite*. No television for some reason. Not that I wanted one. I'm not a great fan of the box.

I took a last look outside, across the allotments. Two trains passed each other in the distance, going in opposite directions, I drew the curtains. Thankfully, the railway was inaudible from here. I wondered if that meant the room had been soundproofed, or whether the railway line was just too distant. It was getting too dark to judge distances now and I couldn't remember from earlier in the day.

It wasn't until I'd showered and changed into my pyjamas that I realised I'd forgotten to pack my book. Another sign of encroaching feeble-mindedness. *The Island* by Victoria Hislop. I was looking forward to making good headway with it tonight. I'd earmarked page two hundred for the train home. But no: presumably, it was still on the kitchen table.

And I'd thrown away the newspaper I'd bought this morning.

There were probably heaps of books downstairs in the lounge ...

But it was only ten o'clock, and I hadn't brought a dressing gown, so I'd have to change back out of my pyjamas. I couldn't go downstairs like this. I said my prayers, got into bed and switched out the light.

I thought I'd drop off immediately. But no. I suppose it was because The City Lodge was so small that every sound was magnified. I could hear the other guests conversing. I could hear a radio. I could hear chairs being scraped back, pots and pans being washed and put away. All at low volume but enough to put an unbreachable barrier between me and sleep. After twenty minutes, I switched the light on. I needed that book.

But I was too tired to get dressed and go down to the lounge. Going by all the noises I'd just heard, there were lots of people about, and I wasn't in a fit condition to meet them. Not after today. Besides, I hadn't even been in the lounge yet. For all I knew, there might not even *be* any books down there. The annoyance of two wasted journeys in one day would only fuel my insomnia.

So, I didn't have any choice, I suppose. I opened the top drawer of my bedside table and felt around. I wasn't really in the mood for it, not after those aquatints, but beggars can't be choosers. Yes, there it was. *Presented by the Gideons.*

I started at the beginning. God created the Earth, threw Adam and Eve out of Eden, Cain killed Abel, God got Noah to build an Ark then flooded the Earth. I fell asleep at Genesis 11, the Tower of Babel. 'And they said, Go let us build us a city and a tower, whose top may reach unto heaven: and let us make us a name, lest we be scattered abroad upon the face of the whole earth'. With this sort of thing whirling round in my head it wasn't surprising I dropped off.

As often happens, my dream picked up where my reading left off. Germaine and I were on the Tower of Babel. I say 'on': ascending a spiral staircase wound round its outside. The whole construction was a solid cylinder reaching into the sky and with its foundations in the Earth's core. It was a beautiful day and Germaine and I were breathless with excitement. We were on our way to the top. Something important was about to happen up there.

Sometimes when you dream about what you were thinking of before nodding off, it keeps revisiting you, until the whole experience becomes unpleasant. That didn't happen this time. I had the dream once then I fell into oblivion and wasn't conscious of anything till my alarm went off the next day.

I'd set it for seven forty-five. I didn't want to look too bleary and dishevelled when breakfast arrived. But when I looked across at the dresser, I saw breakfast was already there. Someone had obviously been in while I was asleep.

I won't say I wasn't annoyed. I got out of bed and felt the teapot. Hot. I shrugged. It was probably well intentioned. Pointless making a fuss the day I was leaving. I'd probably never come back.

When I returned from the bathroom, I became aware of an insistent hiss … coming from outside the window? I realised it had been there all along; since I'd awoken. Perhaps a storm had blown up during the night. I flung the curtains open.

At first, I didn't know what I was seeing.

Where was everything? Gone were the allotments; gone the railway-line. In their place, a blue sky with cumulus clouds. I went right up to the window. I looked up and down. Below me I could see … a city. The City of London: I could just make out some of the landmarks. I thrust my head as far against the pane as it would go, stood on my tiptoes, looked directly down. Yes, it was: it was the street I'd visited so briefly yesterday evening.

I was inside Munro House, somewhere near the top.

So, I must still be dreaming. I stepped back and walked to the bathroom – just to walk to the bathroom – sat on the bed – just to sit on the bed – and returned to the window. I was inside Munro House!

Yes, I must be dreaming then. How to confirm it? How to wake up?

But of course, you know when you're *not* dreaming. True, we all occasionally have a vivid dream and afterwards we say it felt just like reality. But how many of us have ever given sustained consideration to the question whether we might be dreaming *on this particular occasion,* concluded we weren't, then awoken, thereby confirming the opposite? I've never heard of such a thing. I *wasn't* dreaming; this was reality. My God, I was inside Munro House.

I looked again at my breakfast on the dresser. Croissants, jam and butter, an empty bowl with a variety-packet of cornflakes beside it, a pot of tea, a bowl of sugar, a jug of milk. Mrs Clitheroe must be somewhere around. I went for another look outside the window. *My God, I was inside Munro House.*

I dressed at speed and went out into the corridor. Only now, it wasn't the corridor. Not the corridor of The City Lodge. The floors were bare concrete, and thick with polythene sheets. The walls were unpainted plaster. I had to struggle across scaffolding in various stages of assembly. The air smelt of cement and brick-dust. If there was building work, though, there had to be builders: someone else close to hand, in other words.

All the doors along the corridor were open, so I could see into the rooms. They were all unfinished; partway through the process of construction.

At the end, I stepped through a fire-door onto what looked to be a long marmoreal floor with a wall about five metres away, rising at one side and falling at the other, like an enclosed staircase, but without any stairs: a man-made ramp, disappearing round corners to the right and left.

I went into the ramp's centre and looked up and down. The slope disappeared into obscurity both ways.

Okay, so I was at a high altitude – the view from the window had revealed that - but if I just kept walking down, I could get out. It was going to take a long time, but it was definitely doable. I went back to my room, packed my suitcase and set off. I won't say I wasn't panicking slightly.

All that happened sixty years ago. By rights, of course, I should be long dead now. But looking at myself in the mirror on the dresser, I can honestly say I don't look any older than I did then.

I never did reach the bottom. As far as I'm aware, there *is* no bottom, despite the view from the window. I must have been walking for about twelve hours when that fact sank in. Each floor had a set of corridors leading off it you see, and from there I could walk into any of the half-finished rooms and look out of the window. And the ground wasn't getting any closer.

But turning around! What was twelve hours downhill was closer to eighteen going up. And the anxiety, thinking I wouldn't even be able to find my room again, and all the corridors looking exactly the same, so that I wasn't even sure I'd know I was back when I'd got there … And the hunger, and the thirst …

When I finally made it, I was actually in tears. More, I was on the verge of a breakdown – not just mental, but physical: I'd been walking for over thirty hours. I went straight into the bathroom and drank from the tap. When I staggered into bed, the last thing I noticed before falling asleep was what looked like a hot meal on the dresser. And a distinct smell of chicken casserole.

Over the years, I've come to the conclusion that somehow, we managed it. Somehow, we – I say 'we': some of us: some secret minority - built the Tower of Babel. And the crowning glory of the achievement is that, even today, hardly anyone knows it.

But how I ended up inside it, or why, I still have no idea.

It's academic really, I suppose, because there's no way out. The windows don't open and they can't be broken. Maybe they're not even windows in the conventional sense. Looking out from them, time and geography sometimes seem to fuse. Sometimes, I can see the end of the world on the far horizon: a purple vapour shot through with yellow flashes. And sometimes, the distant past.

Breakfast and an evening meal, always the same thing. I've never seen who - or what - brings it. For all practical purposes, I'm completely alone.

Except for Germaine. The past and the future merge in here and they're of a piece with some third thing: a kind of 'no-time', for want of a better term, where everything stays still or repeats itself. The note was right. Germaine *is* alive, and she *is* somewhere in Munro House. I know that now.

Of course, whether I'll ever find her is an entirely different matter.

Occasionally, absent-mindedly, almost by accident, I open my Gideon's Bible hoping to find something to read. But then – God help me - I remember.

For some reason, all its pages are blank now.

THE UTTER TAT MILK JUG

It was killing her just thinking about it. It wasn't just the thing itself, that was bad enough. It was the craving.

"Time to make our way to the beach soon," Kenneth said.

Down in the clear water of the harbour, the fish swam in between each other. No troubles for them. Meanwhile the sun was becoming unbearable. She poured herself another glass of water and took her flip-flops off under the table.

"Maybe it *is* silly," she said. "It's only a jug."

Kenneth sighed. "That again?"

She smiled. How could he be expected to understand?

"It's a milk jug," he said, "that's all. They're in every gift shop."

"I like it. Anyway, it's only ten euros."

"Get it then. I'm just saying, that's all."

"Saying what?"

"It's tat."

"*Très* sophisticated evaluation, Kenneth."

He shrugged. "It's a tatty imitation of a black-figure *oinochoe* showing Apollo riding a dolphin guiding Cretan sailors to Delphi."

"And that's no more than a straight description with 'tatty' in front."

"I doubt any Greek people have them in their homes. It's not meant for anyone living in the real world. It only exists for us tourists, to shaft us."

"Yes, you've made your point."

"Look, I can see you're dying for it. So, let's promise ourselves that we *will* buy it, okay? But on the penultimate day, so that, when it's finally out of your system, nothing else creeps in there."

"Are you trying to say I'm showing signs of mental disturbance?"

He smiled. "Everyone goes mad on holiday, Sally. It's well known. Including me, if it's any consolation. I've been looking at an alabaster figurine of Athena all week, thinking how nice it would look in the study."

"You never said. Where?"

"Where we bought the sun cream."

"Price?"

"Fifteen euros."

"So why don't we *both* buy our things, then we can relax and enjoy the rest of the holiday?"

"It doesn't work like that."

"Why not?"

"Because we don't really want them in the first place. We'd just transfer our affections to something else. You'd have your milk jug but then you'd be inveigled by an icon of Saint Cyril of Alexandria."

"I don't think I would."

"Because you're underestimating the craving for holiday tat."

"I'm not keen on icons."

"But you could *become* keen on icons. You can be anyone you want to be on holiday, that's why people have them. Not for the sun or the beaches: they're just a backdrop."

"It's only a jug. I'm not going to put it in an illuminated frame and hoist it onto the roof."

"Will you use it to put milk in?"

"Maybe."

"We haven't even got a milk jug at home. We pour it straight from the carton, remember?"

"It would look nice when people come round."

"It's probably made of terracotta. Lots of things out here are. So it'll absorb your milk. Then what are you going to do? Take it back?"

"Keep it as an ornament."

"And put it where?"

"On the window ledge, in the kitchen."

"It's all Wedgwood on the window ledge. It'll stick out like a sore thumb."

"Stop being such a bully, Kenneth. It's ten bloody euros."

"Listen, when we're at home, we love to go shopping, yes? It never occurs to us that we might be addicted to shopping, because we buy stuff we're sure we want. But addiction's addiction. It reveals itself where it's most irrational."

"What do you mean?"

"Like in Greece now, where we can't even grasp the meaning of the local alphabet. But where we'll carry on merrily buying things. It's only when we get home that we'll look at what we've bought and realise there's something a teensy bit wrong with us."

"Maybe there is."

"Yes, Sally, there is. We're a materialistic society and we're all addicted to shopping. It's not a profound or original observation."

"Perhaps we should all become Buddhists then."

"Except that in our society, a Buddhist is just someone who collects Buddhist stuff."

"You're the one who's being silly now."

"Okay, let's buy the milk jug and the alabaster figure, but let's not kid ourselves we really want them. Let's indulge our failings with open eyes, like adults."

She thought for a moment. "Yes, I suppose so. Maybe you're right."

"I am."

"So, I can have my milk jug, and you can have your figurine?"

"You get your milk jug. I'm going to wrestle with the figurine for a while yet for the good of my soul."

"How patronising."

"There's nothing to stop you wrestling with your milk jug."

"And we'll have a thoroughly miserable holiday. You wrestling with a figurine and me wrestling with a milk jug."

"Oh, come on."

"And when we go back to England, your mother will say, 'Did you both have a good time?' and I'll have to say, 'We would have, but Kenneth spent the whole time wrestling with a figurine while I wrestled with a milk jug'. What do you think she'll make of that?"

"She'll say, 'Let's have a look at your figurine and your milk jug', then she'll say, 'Shame you couldn't have got three falls or a knockout. They're tat.'"

"Let's just say, for the sake of argument, that you're right. Let's just say that, once I've got the milk jug, it'll only be the pretext for a new craving - "

"Which it will."

"It doesn't matter. All of this takes place in time, yes? First of all, the elation of having secured the milk jug has to run its course and subside. Then my desire for something new has to kick in again. Then I'll have to find it."

"What's your point?"

"That it's going to take a while, because not just anything will do: I'm not *wholly* undiscriminating. I find it, then I buy it, and the elation of possessing it has to run its course and subside."

"Yes, and so on and so on *ad infinitum*."

"No, because very soon we'll be on the plane home. Probably twenty or thirty euros worse off than if we'd spent the holiday wrestling, yes, but a hell of a lot more relaxed. Because, Kenneth, wrestling's wearing. It's *hard work.*"

He looked at her with mild astonishment. "You're absolutely right. We didn't come on holiday to do spiritual exercises."

"You're not being sarcastic now, are you?"

"Absolutely not. Bloody hell, this holiday cost us thousands of pounds. If we're going to spend the next week sweating over a few measly euros, we might as well have gone to Penzance."

"Precisely."

"I've been an idiot. Sod the beach. We're going to eat our Cephalonian meat pie then we're going to Poros for the figurine, then to the pottery factory for the jug. And tonight, we'll celebrate. Thank God for sanity. Bravo, Sally."

They bought the figurine as planned and rang Claire at the Thompson office for a taxi. As they raced along the dirt track to Sami and the milk jug, the sea air blew in their faces. Cicadas grumbled. Old people sat on their porches with worry beads.

They pulled up in front of half an acre of dry mud surrounded by tall wire-fencing with rows of pots and statuettes. A shed with a cash register stood by a closed gate. It looked ominously quiet. They paid the driver without Kenneth's usual attempt to barter and watched him disappear, trailing dust.

"Bloody hell," Kenneth said.

"What?"

"It's all locked up. Look."

She groaned. "Greek siesta time."

"Now what?"

"We go into the village for a lemonade, I suppose."

"I wonder how long till it reopens."

"We could ask around. Have we got the phrase book?"

But he was already on the phone. "Hi, Claire, Kenneth again. We're at the pottery shop in Sami – the one in the compoundy thing with the wire netting round it … Don't know what it's called, no. It's got a shed-thing where you pay. Pots and statues in lines. We wondered if you knew when it opens …"

"She must know where it *is*," Sally said. "She must have told the taxi driver."

"She's gone away to find out what time it opens." He looked at the sky and tapped his foot. "About five? Thanks then, Claire. Bye-ee."

"Five sounds about right."

"Should we go into the village, then?"

Sally looked through the wire netting. "I can't see it, Kenneth. It's gone."

"Don't be - "

"Somebody's bought it. They must have. It was there, by those plant pots."

"Maybe they've moved it."

"Oh, what a waste of a journey."

"They'll have others. They probably don't put *all* their stock out."

She shook her head. "Where do they keep the rest? Look, there's just this yard and there's the shed. There's no warehouse. What you see is what you get."

"Let's not be pessimistic."

"There's no point in me building my hopes up if it's gone."

"It might have fallen down the back of the display unit somewhere."

"I've been a fool. I should have just bought it. All that bloody soul-searching over ten euros."

"I feel quite bad about having bought this Athena now."

"Well, don't. At least one of us has got something to show for this little outbreak of sanity."

They walked into the village and found the tourist quarter where the menus were. Kenneth ordered two lemonades, and they sat down and slumped in their chairs.

"We've got three hours till five," Sally said. "What are we going to do for three hours? I didn't bring my bikini, and you didn't bring your swimming trunks."

"Nor did I bring my book."

"So here we are, trapped in a small Greek village - "

Kenneth paid the waiter. "Thank you."

"With only an alabaster figurine of Athena for company."

"And two lemonades now. Cheers."

"If only I'd kept my big mouth shut," she said, "we'd be lying on the beach now. What's got into me?"

"I've an idea. After we've drunk up, let's go and have a look in some of the local shops. They don't all do siesta-time. Some of them actually want to make money."

"What good will that do? I'm not ready to buy anything else yet. I wanted that milk jug."

"Yes, but it's a milk jug. It's small enough to fit on the shelf in a shop. If the pottery shop sells them, maybe they're *made* round here. Maybe they're in other shops round here."

"We didn't see any in Poros ..."

"Exactly. Because they're not *made* in Poros. They're made *here*, in Sami."

"Do you think so?"

"I'm sure of it."

"But what if they're made *by* the wire netting pottery shop *for* the wire netting pottery shop?"

"That seems unlikely. Like you said, apart from the soil and the wire netting, there's only a shed, and all that's for is paying for what you pick up. There isn't a workshop there. We'd have seen it."

She sat up. "So they're probably made elsewhere. Like you just said. Somewhere nearby."

"And it's unlikely the wire netting pottery shop's got a monopoly on them."

She was a lot more cheerful now. They tossed back their lemonades and set off.

It took them an hour to find what they were looking for. There were two in the shop, slightly dissimilar.

"Which one do you prefer?" Kenneth said.

"Oh, my God."

"It's not that exciting."

"It *is*. They're not the same."

"Er, so?"

"Don't you see?" she said. "They must be handcrafted."

"Yes ... yes, I suppose so."

"Just ten euros for something as exquisite as this. A genuine one-off. Come on, Kenneth: you know yourself how much 'handmade' costs in England. You've got to pay through the nose for it."

"Let's not get carried away, Sally. It's still tat."

"*What?* How can you *say* that?"

"Because it's only ten euros."

"But that's ... that's circular."

"That's what 'tat' is. What everyone thinks they want for about five minutes, then they can't wait to get rid of. What stays on the shelf in Oxfam shops. Like this milk jug, no disrespect to the 'craftsman'."

She looked at him as if she'd been slapped. But not – he realised later – as if he'd done the slapping.

"Let's just buy one and get out of here," he said. "Let's get back to the hotel and chill out, shall we? Which do you want?"

"I want both of them. I want every single one I can find."

Even though she had two milk jugs, Sally withdrew into herself in the taxi back and became unhappy. She was okay until she was getting dressed and putting her makeup on, but then she cried. When they were ready to go down to dinner, she sat on the bed, still tearful. Kenneth sat beside her in his suit.

"I'm sorry," he said. "I suppose you're going to say you want a divorce. I'll resist, of course. In court I'll argue that I didn't mean to hurt your feelings. I love you. I'm sorry."

"I'm not crying because I'm angry with you."

"What then?" he asked.

"What you said: that really *is* the definition – if there is such a thing - of 'tat'. It hit me between the eyes. What's wrong with the world?"

"Keep them as long as you like. Put them on the windowsill. So long as you're happy, that's all that matters. I'm just saying: they've got no resale value, that's all. None at all."

She smiled. "I know."

"It's a strange world. But that's the world."

"I know."

"Friends again?"

"We were never enemies."

"Let's go down to dinner, shall we?"

She didn't move. "I've been thinking about what you said this morning. You said – do you remember? 'Everyone goes mad on holiday. It's well known.'"

"I remember, yes."

"But maybe it's only when we're on holiday that we're sane. We don't care then whether something deserves a right to sit on the window ledge based on its resale value. We see something beautiful, we buy it. We make fools of ourselves in sombreros and what have you, then when we get home we revert to the old, old insanities. And we call them 'real' because they're so long-standing."

"Maybe. Maybe."

"During the taxi ride back to the hotel this afternoon, I kept looking at the two milk jugs, one then the other. It was like there was a different ... world in there, calling me in. As if they *contain* something, like a tunnel or a doorway to a place where everything's sane."

He laughed. "Wow, now that's what I call value for money!"

"I can't put it into words. I know it sounds mad. And that the feeling will subside, I know that too. But I can look at them now and... still see it. And it makes me feel so *sad*, because I know the door's closed, and it'll always be closed for as long as we're both alive. And it's so close, and yet so ... far." She wept again. Her tears dripped onto her dress. "Oh, I know what you're going to say. You're going to say it's all an elaborate performance by Greek shopkeepers and hoteliers to lull us to sleep, and we're complicit in it."

He put his arm round her. "I wasn't going to say anything at all."

"And yes, I know all that. But I feel as if I've stumbled onto a group of actors performing a play they despise to an audience that's indifferent, and suddenly I *see*: the play's about something real, something crucial, and no one else *at all* can see it … Yet I don't know what its reality consists in. Whether it's something that *has* happened, or *will* happen, or *is* happening, whether it's far or near or… nowhere."

He kissed her hair. She drew up her feet up and wiped her eyes roughly with the back of her hand. "We have to get down to dinner," she said.

"If, and only if, you're ready. Anyway, we don't *have* to eat in the hotel. We can eat out, later. Don't force yourself. Especially not for my sake."

She kissed him. "Come on. I am ready."

She awoke at 3am, and couldn't get back to sleep. She slipped from beneath the bed's single sheet without disturbing Kenneth. She picked up the milk jugs and went to the open window to marvel at them anew in the moonlight.

A breeze whispered through the olive grove in the yard. Beyond the woods and the shoreline, the faraway island of Ithaca stood silhouetted in a milky sea.

She stood without moving for a while, dreading getting home in a few days and then knowing – 'knowing' wrongly, but she realised now it was inevitable – that she'd bought something 'worthless'. A nocturnal bird sang, the cicadas picked up, the smell of pines intensified. In the far distance, where the ocean met the sky, and where the first glimmerings of dawn were already appearing, she saw Apollo guiding the Cretan sailors to Delphi.

A HOMECOMING

He was aching to see inside, but they'd closed the curtains. Anyway, the downpour was so thick it'd probably have made no difference. He briefly considered going home, but pulled himself up. Home? This *was* home; at least, as much of it as he'd ever known! He grabbed the window sill to steady himself against the gale and caught sight of his hands, bleached and crinkled by the rain like an old man's.

Maybe they'd feel sorry for him. If he looked as defeated by the weather as he was by life, they might relent. *I was a stranger and ye took me in.* God, if only. He removed his hat and cast it away, to make himself look more pathetic.

He'd come here on foot through miles of deep heather, and he must look awful. They'd pity him for that, at least. They'd have to, wouldn't they?

No, nothing was certain any more. He ran his hand over his head – his hair was thinning now, but that was stress: it'd grow back under the right circumstances – then gathered his courage. He went to the front door and knocked.

He waited a minute. But it sank in more quickly than that: no answer.

Surely not – surely, they weren't *out?* He looked at his watch. Eleven. How - how long could he survive out here if the house was empty? Could he even make it to morning?

He began to panic. Because, actually, it wasn't impossible: they might have gone out somewhere, and put up overnight rather than risk the journey back. He knocked again, harder. "Please," he heard himself say.

Suddenly, the door opened. For a moment, he was blinded by the brilliance, and also by a primitive, only half self-conscious kind of relief.

Bryony, his sister, stood holding Laddie on a taut chain. People didn't stop by at this time of night unless something was wrong. Or *they* were wrong. His eyes adjusted and he saw his mother in the armchair. Thank God.

"Can I help you?" Bryony said.

"It's - it's me."

She appeared to lose her composure for a second, then recovered. "Neil."

"Can – can I come in?"

She turned to look at their mother – not for a conference, he realised, but to see whether she'd heard. She hadn't. She sat in the living room, side-on to the front doorway, watching the television on full volume. She'd looked like she'd aged in the three years since he'd last seen her. Everything about her was bonier. Even her hands seemed more desiccated and angular.

Bryony, too. "What do you want?" she said. "What are you here for?"

"I've come back because I was … wrong." He'd planned something like this – a scene, to weaken her – but deliberately left the details vague, trusting to his instincts. Now, though, he was surprised to be speaking from the heart. If only she could see his tears as well! "I admit, I was wrong."

She looked back into the room at the old woman. "Keep your voice down."

"Can I come in? Please?"

Laddie snarled and reared. Without Bryony to restrain him, he'd probably have attacked. Astonishing: a dog's friendship wasn't supposed to turn sour like that. He experienced a renewed sense of the absoluteness of his rejection.

"Please," he repeated.

"Come down into the scullery," she said. "And don't let Mother see you."

She didn't ask him to take his coat off. She walked ahead of him and downstairs. The scullery was windowless with a washing machine and a sink. She closed the door behind them.

"Laddie, lie down!" she snapped. She leaned back against the wall and folded her arms. "Well?"

"I've come back to say sorry. To tell you how sorry I am."

"Ah."

"I really am, Bryony. God, I'm so sorry, it hurts."

"Sorry about what? There's nothing to feel sorry for, is there?"

"I know I let everyone down. I thought I could do it on my own."

She laughed. "And you couldn't."

"It's not that. That's not it. I never want to … write again. I don't want to be a writer. I just want what we had."

"Well, sorry to disappoint you, Neil, but that doesn't exist anymore. You wrecked it, remember? That night you revealed we'd had a stranger in our midst."

"It was a mistake. The biggest I've ever made. I'm here to try and put it right. I know it's going to be difficult, but I'm prepared to devote my whole life to it from here on. Nothing else matters. Nothing."

"You've got a job round here, then?"

"Yes."

"Pays well?"

"No."

She smiled. "Somewhere to live?"

"I managed to get a caravan."

"A caravan."

"I - I left London yesterday. I won't ever be going back. Look, I don't expect you to forgive me now. I just want you to know I'm determined to make up for what I did. I don't care how long it takes, and I know I'll have my work cut out trying to persuade you I'm sincere, and - "

"Is it because you're a failure?"

"What?"

"You're a failure. Don't pretend otherwise, Neil. Exmoor's not some little end-of-the-world place where news never reaches. We've read all the reviews of all your plays. We've followed your progress in minute detail since you left us. You were only a success so long as we helped you, rattled off suggestions, improvements, revisions, cuts. But you didn't believe it was us, did you? You thought it was you."

"And I was wrong."

She smirked. "We both know what this is about. You want us to start 'helping' you again. Slaving for you, so you can salvage what little's left of your reputation. Because you've finally realised what side your bread's buttered on. It's not remorse, though. You're not capable of that. Or any other human emotion."

He could see he was talking to a brick wall. "Look, all right, fine; I'm going to appeal to mother. She'll understand."

"You mean that woman upstairs?"

"Yes?" he said, temporarily flummoxed by the oddity of her question.

"That's not mother."

"Er, what do you mean?"

She unfolded her arms and put her hands in her pockets. "Mother died two years ago. Shortly after you left. We didn't bother telling you, because we didn't think you'd care."

"Wh – who *is* it, then? Where are the children?"

"*My* children? They're dead too. I don't *know* who the old woman is. But she's not mother."

This was too much. Could she be joking? Not from the look in her eyes. Was she *mad*? Whatever the truth, it was beginning to look unspeakably horrible.

She looked much, much older now – like a nonagenarian.

How? The air in here was doing something unpleasant to him. He was going to be sick.

"It's time for you to leave," she said.

He wanted to vomit. But he'd expressed a firm intention. He *had* to see their mother, with or without his sister's permission. He rushed to the door and flung it open.

But he stepped out of the room straight onto the moor. Where the stairs had been, there was - nothing. He heard the door bang behind him - a bang so loud, it might have been a bomb – and awoke with a start.

He looked around the hotel room, then at his bedside clock.

He put his fingertips to his forehead. How ...? What ...?

Nine o'clock. Breakfast would be over now. Never mind, he wasn't hungry, anyway. The curtain gently billowed and deflated. The traffic roared in the street below.

It was okay, everything was fine! Thank God, *thank God!* He gave a single laugh.

Someone knocked. He got leisurely up and opened the door.

The 'bellboy', in his waistcoat and bow tie: a living embodiment of the Roaring Twenties. That sort of hotel. "Post, Sir," he said.

Neil exchanged the five newspapers, and a letter with a handwritten address, for a hefty tip. He scrutinised the letter first. *Neil Sullivan (Playwright), The Belfry Hotel, Mayfair.* His sister's handwriting. He shuddered and tossed it onto the bed.

He sat down nervously at the dresser and opened each newspaper in turn. It took him a while to find what he was looking for, but when he did, it was as if the sought-for articles had lined up to form a firing squad.

The Daily Mail: '… a long time since I found a trip to the theatre this tedious. The author, once so promising …'

The Daily Telegraph: '… Such fine actors wasted on such a poor script. One feels sincerely sorry for …'

The Times: '… The author has mined every available cliché to produce a story as hackneyed as …'

The Guardian: 'One hates to see actors and audiences suffer and die nightly …'

He emitted another single laugh, but from a different psychological source. Not a single good word!

His chest hurt. Maybe there had been some mistake. There must have been. Oh, God.

Then the mists cleared and he saw. This was the end of the road. No one ever recovered from this sort of thing. He was finished!

Unless, of course …

He had another play: *Of Sunny Countenance.* He'd have to beg. Maybe it wouldn't be possible to open in the West End this time, maybe somewhere smaller. The provincial papers were supposed to be kinder, weren't they?

Anguish and despair quickly became indignation. He strode the length of the room to the window. The *morons* couldn't see what he'd intended! Bloody *London crowd, raging snobs* the lot of them!

He turned and strode back to the door. Future generations would get him! No one had understood *Ibsen* when he started, oh no!

He swivelled, still full of adrenalin, and went back to the window. And they'd said *Chekhov* was dull! This lot would live to rue their mistakes! He'd *keep the reviews*, he'd *remember their names!*

He put his hands on his hair and strode back to the door. His time would come and as he waxed, they'd *wane*! He'd see to that, oh yes!

Suddenly, he was physically depleted. He felt weary enough to faint. He remembered Bryony's letter. He skulked over to the bed, knelt abjectly down, and tore it open.

Neil,

I trust you're well and that everything in London is as you expected. I am sure you'll be a great success. I would like to say I hope so, but of course your manner of leaving makes that impossible. I am writing simply to tell you that mother is ill. I am not sure she will even agree to see you if you come back now, but I would be failing in my duty if I was not to keep you informed.
Your call.
Regards, Bryony.

He read it through twice, before – in one final burst of adrenalin - tearing it to shreds. *They'd* be laughing at him too now, once they read today's papers! *Bastards!*

As he binned it, it broke his dream. He took four deep breaths. He couldn't remember exactly what had happened, something to do with Bryony, and his mother, and Laddie.

Getting up to collect the post must have shaken the whole thing out of him. But an unsettling fragment had somehow just returned: two harridan faces and a sense of wretchedness.

There was another knock at the door. He ignored it. He lay face-down on the bed and wept. Whoever it was knocked again, then presumably left. Five minutes passed. He gently closed the window to block out the noise of the traffic. Silence.

He peered at the pieces of Bryony's letter in the waste basket.

It was the newspapers he'd wanted to tear up, not *that*. Why in God's name had he torn *that* up?

Before he knew what he was doing, he'd picked up his mobile.

Not that it would achieve anything. She'd see it was him, and switch it off.

Still, he could say he'd tried. One day, he could tell God.

"Hello, Neil." To his amazement, she didn't sound hostile. "Neil?" After a pause: "Neil? This is you, isn't it? Say something, Neil, if it's you. Speak to me."

"I – I - " he said.

"Neil? Are you crying?"

No, it wouldn't do to stay on the line. Not while he was weeping. He pressed 'end call' and lay face down on the bed.

Then it started to ring. *Bryony.*

He decided to leave it.

But he suddenly realised what should have been obvious long ago: he'd forfeited the right to choose the time, the place, the manner.

Five rings.

He wiped his eyes, swallowed his pride and picked up.

THE MESSAGE

I first went to Tubbercurry about thirty years ago, had to do a delivery there. I was working as a lorry driver in Liverpool at the time.

Anyway, Tubbercurry was across the sea in Ireland, and it sounded like it might be a bit of a holiday, so I decided to take my girlfriend along. I was quite good-looking in those days, lots of blond hair, soldier's back: not like I am now, old and defeated-looking. We split up shortly afterwards, me and her, but the memories remain. Good ones.

Before we set off, I had to report to the boss's office with my vehicle inspection sheet. Of course, as far as I was aware, he didn't know I was taking someone with me. He wouldn't have let me go if he had. Small man; thick neck and bald, only ever wore open-necked Oxford shirts and polyester trousers with creases in; tended to shout a lot and fire people. We were all a bit scared of him, though we pretended not to be.

Anyway, I'd done all the safety checks. Still, he looked at my sheet the way he looked at everyone's: like he couldn't believe anyone could do anything so complicated so quickly.

Then he grinned. "You're going to Tubbercurry?"

Not like him to look cheerful. For a moment I thought he knew what I had planned.

"Be sure and look up Tommy Healey," he said. "When you find him, say, *I'd like to see you mash tyres with a pair of six-inch sprouts!*" He laughed, like it was hilarious. "Tell him it's a message from Barry Timms!"

"Say what?" I said.

"'I'd like to see you mash tyres with a pair of six-inch sprouts'," he replied soberly. "I'll write it down for you."

He wrote it in block capitals on the back of a brown A4 envelope. Then he signed it, and printed his name underneath, also in capitals.

"He won't get angry, will he?" I asked. "I mean, it's not a dig of some sort?"

"God, *no!* He'll laugh till his sides split! He'll buy you all the drinks you *like!* Trust me!"

In the end, it wasn't an issue either way. I forgot all about Tommy Healey the moment I got in the cab, and I didn't remember till I got back to Liverpool.

Of course, the next day, I told Barry I couldn't find him.

Barry didn't say anything, but he must have known I was lying because he took against me from that day on. A couple of months later, he fired me on a technicality. Then, shortly after that, he had a heart attack, and died.

Not my fault, obviously. And with his stress-levels, he probably had it coming. But I felt stupidly guilty. I wondered whether, if I'd delivered his message, it might have, say … given him an extra week?

I don't even know why I cared. He'd fired me, after all.

For some reason, though, I kept the envelope. And after I heard he'd died, I couldn't stop thinking about it for a long while. To the point where I regularly rooted it out and re-read it.

I comforted myself with the vague idea that, theoretically, I could still, one day, find out what it meant: if, by some miracle, I ever found myself in Tubbercurry again.

Well, that miracle happened. About five years ago, I was invited to my niece's wedding in Ballymote. That part of the family lives round there. They were going to hold the reception in a big marquee in Tubbercurry.

I was in two minds about going at first. But Barry appeared to me in a dream. He was dressed all in white: white polyester trousers, white Oxford shirt open at the neck. He was extending a brown A4 envelope with a pleading look on his face. "For God's sake help me find rest!" he said, through his tears.

I woke up knowing I had to go. Not primarily for the wedding. Oh, I'd pop my head round the Church door, go through the motions of congratulating the happy couple, add my gift-wrapped John Lewis toaster to the pile of presents, wolf my *salmon en croûte*, guzzle my free pint of Kilkenny, dance the conga with some berk laughing and tearing at the vents of my suit in an effort to stay upright. Oh yes, I suppose I'd have do all that. But it wasn't my primary motivation.

A full twenty-five years had passed since Barry's death, and it took me three days to find the envelope with the message on, even though I live in a very small house. It was at the bottom of a wicker-basket full of bric-a-brac I'd assembled when I moved here, ten or twelve years ago. As often happens, I'd already been through that basket three times.

I don't like planes, so I took the ferry, and, would you believe it, I got the envelope out of my pocket – I can't even remember the reason – and it blew out of my hand and landed in the Irish Sea.

For a moment, I could have cried. But then I got to thinking: maybe Barry did that. To teach me a lesson. It didn't matter either way, because I'd memorised the message. 'I'd like to see you mash tyres with a pair of six-inch sprouts' was engraved on my heart, so it wasn't anything like a complete loss.

That night, I expected to dream about Barry again – either a reassurance or a sacking – but I didn't. In the morning, I got dressed and went to the wedding.

To cut a long story short, another miracle: Barry's friend, Tommy Healey, was actually *at* the reception. Or someone with that name, and about the right age. Small world, small locality: probably everyone in the locality knew everyone. The marquee was as big as a warehouse and there must have been a hundred people present, all having a whale of a time.

'Tommy Healey' was an old man. He wore a crumpled black suit and shiny loafers, and he sat at the bar eating prawn cocktails. Soon as he finished one, he'd call the waitress and demand another. I must have watched him get through about twelve. He had a pint of stout to one side.

I only found out it was him because people kept coming up and exclaiming, "Tommy Healey!" then shaking his hand and slapping his arm, like he was their oldest friend. A few moments later, they'd make a polite excuse, and he'd move on to his next prawn cocktail. Eventually, one of his friends opened his arms wide for a hug and exclaimed, *"Tom-my Hea-ley!"*, pronouncing each syllable like it was a word on its own.

But of course, he might not be *the* Tommy Healey.

I gathered my courage and approached him. "Tommy Healey?"

He looked up expressionlessly with his mouth full. "Yeah?" he said.

"Do you remember a Barry Timms? A long time ago it'd be now, but he used to work in haulage."

His eyebrows came down. He grimaced. It took him a full minute and a half to search his memory-banks, then he said: "Small feller? Bald? From Liverpool? Superintendent of a lorry-yard?"

"That's the one, yes."

"So what about him? Is he here?"

I hadn't foreseen how awkward this was going to be. "He's dead. He died over twenty-five years ago." I was blushing now, I could feel it. "But before he died, he asked me to pass on a message. To you. He said – I mean, this might sound mad, but I'm just following instructions – he said: 'I'd like to see you mash tyres with a pair of six-inch sprouts'."

There was another long silence. Tommy seemed to withdraw into himself in search of a key, then he started to giggle.

I was about to ask him what it meant when, God help me, he started to choke.

I don't remember the details of what happened next. It later turned out he'd taken a king prawn into his windpipe. There was an almighty commotion as everyone gradually realised what was happening. Four men took turns slapping him on the back, then walked him outside the tent with me in pursuit, and they finally managed to get him to cough the prawn up. But then he had a heart attack.

There were people all around him now, kneeling in the mud and shouting confusedly at each other. Tommy Healey jabbed his finger at me and croaked something. He retched. Then he sighed and closed his eyes.

A doctor pushed through the crowd, checked Tommy Healey's pulse, administered the kiss of life, checked his pulse again, then sat up miserably on his haunches and pronounced him dead. About ten minutes afterwards, the ambulance arrived.

When I got back in the marquee there were ten pints of beer standing on the bar. Everyone was looking at me. You could have cut the silence with a knife.

One of the women who'd been kneeling with him during his last moments was the first to speak.

"He said to get you these," she announced, through her tears.

"Thanks, but I don't particularly - "

"It was his last wish."

I spent the rest of that afternoon drinking and trying to explain what had passed between us. But no one had the faintest idea what 'I'd like to see you mash tyres with a pair of six-inch sprouts' meant - or *might* mean. Worse: I'm pretty sure no one even believed me.

And the thing is, I don't know whether those ten pints were a reward or a punishment. I mean, it's pretty difficult to drink ten pints in one sitting. If you're forced, it's the sort of thing that might poison you.

That night, I dreamt about Barry again.

"You bloody idiot," he said.

ENGLISH RIFLES

Fortieth birthday two months ago. Didn't think then I wouldn't ever be *having* another birthday. Shit, lots of things never hit me that day. Like, that I'd be here on death row, in some country no one had even heard of before I got here, just an hour to live.

Look at me, huh? The mighty fallen. Locked up somewhere just big enough to stand up in, patch of sunlight crossing the room every day through a grille. Night freezing, no blanket. Ain't seen my reflection for a month, not since I was … captured. Muscles all shrivelled. Could fight my way out of anywhere once, me versus ten. That strong. Couldn't now: bits of knotted string where my biceps were. And I ain't washed since I arrived. Fucking amazing I haven't caught nothing. I don't even know about the scars, what they look like. There must *be* scars. I had the shit kicked out of me in the 'debrief', as they called it.

Funny, it's not that I'm about to die I mind. Dying's, like, an occupational hazard in my line. No, it's the dying *under a cloud* that gets me … Because believe it or not I really didn't know.

I'm shivering now. Cold - or fear?

Wonder if anyone'll ever try to clear my name.

Shouldn't think so, no. No, shit, not now. Too much fucking crap under the bridge.

I'm innocent actually. In my … 'heart'. That's what counts isn't it? Yeah, I'm innocent. Really.

… Yeah wow, that's right. Thought we were fighting *rebels*, see. Technically, we were. And you know, 'rebels' is that sort of word: seems to have an inbuilt guilty sound, yeah? 'Specially if, like me, you think the rebels are killing innocent civilians.

Yeah, I was being paid too. A lot. Active service in six countries before I arrived here so I didn't come cheap. Dog of War, one of those; one of them professional rebel-fighters you hear about. Just point me at 'em, that was my motto.

Never considered ethics, no. Ethics, politics: no can do. You've not got the luxury of right and wrong when you're in my game. Never get anything done if you start thinking about all that shit. Their war not mine, that's what I always tell myself. I'm just a hired hand. Mind my own business. Glad to.

The big shots were pleased to see me, course they were. Someone of my calibre? You bet. Day I arrived I was put in a BMW with two little flags on the bonnet and driven straight to the President. Absolutely what I wasn't expecting. *So* not the usual: bussed straight to some jerry-built warehouse-cum-barracks, tossed a gun and helmet and told to get cracking. No, looked like my CV had gone before me for a change.

Stepped out at the Presidential Palace. Frisked, saluted, and taken to meet El Supremo himself. Six foot two, white tunic with gilt epaulettes, couple of rows of decorations, square shoulders. Thought he'd be a right snotty bastard, but not a bit. Put me on the spot though. 'Are you really the man who killed Roberto Mgwese last year?', 'Did you really ambush and destroy an entire military convoy with just six fighters under your command?', 'How many men would you say you've killed in all?' Guess he must have known the answers: they're in the public domain. Except the last one, of course. Don't even know the answer to that one myself! 'You kind of lose count after the first couple of hundred,' I told him. We had a good laugh. Wasn't actually joking, though. Think he knew that too.

That night he threw a massive shindig in my honour. Planned long before I got here apparently, soon as he knew I was coming. 'This is Simon and he's going to save our country!' he said. Must have been over a thousand people there, all big players. And so OTT, coming up like, 'Thank Christ you're here, now we'll all be safe'. And the women. And the gifts, the promises of houses and cars and swimming pools and gold this, and diamond that. I'm telling you, man, I really, really wanted to squash those rebels. God help me, I even thought I'd settle down here afterwards. Okay yeah, I'd heard the President had his dark side, but I thought I could handle that. I've known lots of guys with 'dark sides'. Never stopped me getting on with them before. *Au contraire*, as the Frogs say.

Next day they took me to meet my 'regiment'. The usual bunch: one half locals just out of diapers - didn't know one end of a gun from the other - the other, seasoned pros, men after my own heart. Expected I'd have my work cut out keeping them off each other's throats. Can get that way sometimes, especially when things aren't going well.

Luckily, they *did* go well. Right from the word go, fighting those rebels was like cutting butter with a hot knife. Useless sods didn't even give half as good as they got.

Took me about six weeks before I realised that ... well, that it was almost, like ... *too* easy.

Strange thing is, the easier it got, the more pathetic they looked. Like they just seemed to be *lying down asking for it*, know what I mean? Like blind vermin, bit like that. Made us ten times more brutal. Wasn't just me: we egged each other on. You won't *get* this unless you've been there yourself: fact is, it's quite hard to kill women and kids unless your friends are enjoying doing the same.

'For the long-term good of the country', that's what we told ourselves. If they couldn't breed, they couldn't make a comeback, yeah? That's why this civil war had dragged on so long, everyone said that. Grudges passed down the generations. We were being bold – but imaginative. For the long-term good. 'You can't make an omelette without breaking all the eggs,' the President told me the night of the party. 'Every *single* egg,' he said, looking me right in the eye.

... Didn't know the United Nations had stepped in, no. Never listened to the news. Even if I had, I wouldn't ever have believed it. I didn't know about the international shit, the outrage. Hell, I swear to God it didn't feel like genocide. It was bold, that's all; for the long-term good.

Anyway, one day I just stepped out of my HQ – my tent – and there I was, surrounded by ten or twenty blokes in blue helmets pointing rifles at me. Nowhere to hide, no way out. Sudden as that.

They wanted to fly me to The Hague, try me for war crimes. Couldn't get my head round that. Shit, this was *me*. Never thought I'd hear my name, 'genocide' and 'war criminal' in the same sentence. Don't suppose anyone does, though. A laugh, when you put it like that, yeah? You almost laugh, yeah? - The thing is though

I really didn't know what I was doing. Like I said, it didn't feel like genocide.

After that, things went fast. Top speed. They decided to keep me here. Sign of faith in the new order maybe, I don't know.

The UN insisted on a 'fair trial' so I had to be represented. Lawyer and me parted ways quite early on, though. I wanted to plead not guilty. Fine by him, but he wasn't happy with my 'line of defence'.

Luckily, see, I knew who'd been supplying a lot of the guns I'd been using. 'Made in England'. That's right: 'under licence from the Foreign Office' we'd been doing business with the President for decades. Without those weapons, I couldn't have done the killing. Not on the scale I did.

So, my defence became, Why did my own government provide me with guns and bombs? Answer: because they didn't think it was *their* war. They didn't want to ask questions about the rights and wrongs of someone else's mega-screw up, oh no. Their job was to make sure English businesses stayed nicely in the black, no questions asked. So, if *I* was going to be tried for war crimes, *they* ought to be tried for supplying me. Like drugs: quids in if you can nab the user, but if you can nab the supplier too, you're laughing. Shit, we weren't that different.

Wasn't much of a defence, even I could see that. Problem being, it involved me admitting things. And of course, there's no chance – ever – that someone's going to call HM government to book for flogging guns to mass murderers. Rot's too deep. You'd have to turn the entire world upside down to get that sort of result. Best hope, a few liberal do-gooders tut-tut, admit maybe I'd got a point - then forget all about it.

Guns don't shoot people, people shoot people. Yeah, I knew the old saying, who doesn't? It's shite obviously. Should read: *guns don't shoot people and people don't shoot people, people-with-guns shoot people.* Doesn't trip off the tongue in quite the same way, though, does it?

The trial: from their point of view, something to be got over as quickly and quietly as poss. Especially since I was going to be doing my own defence. Anyhow, I decided not to point the finger at the British government after all. Non-bloody-starter. No, I decided to go with the truth.

A fancy foreign guy, a philosopher, once said, 'a willing error is not an error'. Sounds pretty la-di-dah, huh? What it means is if you knew what you were doing was wrong, you wouldn't do it. People only do wrong out of not knowing stuff.

The best thing being that, in my case, it was true. I really *didn't* know those rebels were innocent. Child-soldiers, as they call them, are ten a penny in this corner of the world. Women soldiers too. Here, no one's innocent. Everyone's guilty until proven otherwise.

Course, it was all one big piss in the wind. Hundreds of people in the public gallery all looking at me like ... like I don't know. The verdict's a foregone conclusion. The prosecutor - about the President's age, podgy, full of himself - was an old hand. He was willing to concede, just for the sake of argument, he said, that I *didn't* know. On the other hand, he was fully convinced that I *should have known*, that I was in *a position to know,* and that my *wilful self-deception* was tantamount to *criminal negligence*. Given *the scale of the atrocities,* etcetera, etcetera, yawn, yawn.

There on, my defence went tits-up. How the fuck was I to know what I *should have known* but didn't know? Talk about pseudo-intellectual bullshit.

... So here I am. An hour to live.

Funny, but almost the last feeling I've got left is ... How to put it? ... A kind of patriotic feeling? Proud to be English. Because I know this sounds a bit off the wall, but to be frank, well, those English rifles were really good.

There's this one image I just can't get out of my head, see. Me, looking through a telescopic sight; this woman, maybe twenty, twenty-five, running away across a cornfield, kid in one arm and tugging this wizened old guy behind her - granddad maybe, I don't know. And there's this tree in front of them, yeah? Quite a trunk on it. *Bang,* one shot. Straight through the old man, straight through the girl, straight through the kid, and – when I looked later – straight through the tree.

Three generations and a tree.

Bloody frigging *genius*, yeah?

NOT OUR REAL NAMES

'George':

A clear sky and a full moon. The three of us came up from the valley through a birch wood along a broad, muddy path so scoured by the rain it had left knee-deep hollows in places. In the far west, a meteorite flared and fell. As we ascended, 'Lucy' and I somehow managed to pull ahead. We knew it wouldn't take long for 'Jack' to catch up, though, because we could see the underside of his swimma glowing through the trees, some way back. We stopped to wait for him, but he never arrived.

*

'Jack':

Five hundred revolutions, then for some reason an extra one – a five hundred and first. No explanation I can imagine. Five hundred programmed in, then it just … does one more.

Let me be clear, because you're probably thinking, maybe it progressed under its existing momentum. Perhaps there was some kinetic energy left in the system. A bit like a pendulum winding down. That's your idea. Am I right?

But it doesn't explain the really *odd* thing here, which is that the unanticipated revolution went through exactly three hundred and sixty degrees then stopped dead.

I can be even more precise about how weird we're talking. I don't know how much you know about geometry – I didn't know much myself till the aftermath – but degrees can be subdivided into 'minutes', and those can be further cut down into 'seconds'. Sixty minutes in a degree and the same number of seconds the level below that. So, a second's got to be pretty small, yes? Invisible to the naked eye probably. Maybe you'll appreciate the strangeness then, of an unforeseen full cycle consisting of three hundred and sixty degrees and *no minutes and no seconds*.

Let me state what I'm describing here, in case you haven't guessed already. It's the wheel of a swimma. Maybe you've seen one, maybe not, depending on what section of the universe you inhabit. I don't know whether there are equivalent things on Earth, the 'big reference planet' as it's laughably called. Or anything much at all about Earth, to be honest. It's got like one long paper side without a top or bottom, and a single circle, also paper, attached to the front by a metal spindle. The spindle isn't important. It can be as flimsy as you like. But every so often, the 'wheel' – which is what we usually call it – goes through exactly five hundred revolutions, and that's what gets us from place to place. Naturally, there's a bit of glowing underneath, of course there is. Sometimes the circle curls in on itself a bit, depending on temperature or humidity. That's also irrelevant.

Now I know lots of people with swimmas. It's always five hundred or nothing. In all recorded history, no variation. So obviously no one believes me about the extra one. But two days later I did the test in my *morhaus*, so I know there was an exception. The problem is, with time only going one way here, once you've done anything once, you can never do it again. It's not like I can repeat my investigation in public – or at all. I know, and I *know* I know, but that's as far as it's possible to get. I'm utterly alone with my realisation.

Now I accept I'm making a fuss about it. You're probably wondering what the consequences were. Must have been pretty dire, for me to be blabbing on so much, right? Answer: well, not really. Yes, I lost contact with 'George' and 'Lucy', but that sort of thing happens all the time where I am. (Incidentally, I don't mean I lost them in the sense that I might ever find them again. Rather, they're probably long dead by now.) But I'd probably have lost them anyway. They were offered the chance of swimmas, yet they chose not to have them. They were both always "on the way out", as they say. I wasn't particularly attached to either of them. Maybe to 'Lucy', because of her eyes. I'm not ashamed to admit that.

No, it's not the consequences that bother me. It's what it *means*. Because it must signify something. Let's imagine it had been three hundred and sixty-seven degrees, twelve minutes and six seconds – not even *that's* meaningless, because it shouldn't carry on at all. But to go on for exactly three hundred and sixty *period*, that's too much of a coincidence. Like all two hundred suns on Varans turning green at exactly the same moment. You'd have to think there was something behind it. Some*one*.

"But three hundred and sixty's just a number!" Well, dear reader, if that's how you're thinking, good gracious, you've already missed the point. True, any number's arbitrary. Obviously, a circle can be divided into any number of slices, halves, quarters, eighths, three-sixtieths, thousandths. But it makes no difference to the thing in itself. It's the circle that's the point. The fact that it carried on for *one full circle*, no more, no less!

Put it another way. Say you were just standing there and a perfect sphere appeared in the air right in front of you. And you knew you weren't hallucinating: it was objective reality. And it had never happened before, to anyone, just you. And thanks to its presence you lost contact forever with your friends. I don't think you'd just write that experience off, put it down to chance. Spheres and circles aren't random phenomena. Despite appearances, they don't occur anywhere in nature, as someone from the 'big reference planet' – Plato, I think it was – conclusively showed, only last year.

No, it's my firm conviction that there was someone behind it. Obviously, I'm not thinking of a person in anything like the sense that you or I, or 'George' or 'Lucy' are - or in their case, *were* - persons. It would have to be someone with immense power, with inscrutable purposes and whose intentions aren't unquestionably benign. Not necessarily a god, if that term has the remotest meaning nowadays, but certainly a highly advanced being.

I've talked about this a little bit to others. The discussion always comes back to the same thing, though. Granted, the circle is the queen of geometric shapes, but in our world it's always attached to a swimma, and the swimma moves by mystic manipulation of the number five hundred. True, it's that number as applied to a circle, but look at it any way you like, 'ten times fifty' (as it used to be called) isn't intrinsically significant. It's a glaringly banal member of the numeric pantheon.

What people usually want to tell me, in other words, is that it was a coincidence. Perfection can't attach to imperfection. Even if we accept it was a full circle I experienced, it's only a five hundred and first specimen. As such, it effectively trumpets its own negation.

But obviously, if someone outside this world – say, beyond reality in the sense that we know it – wanted to communicate with me, then he or she would have to abide the imperfection. In my world, he or she could only ever show a perfect circle against the relatively contemptible backdrop of a swimma.

No, no, no, I hear you cry, let's not get too carried away. It's a mistake to imagine the swimma's inimical to perfection. It just isn't perfect itself. That's an important distinction, such as only a crass person would overlook.

Anyway, what it boils down to is this: *I* believe it had meaning, yet I'm alone in that. Others sometimes sympathise, but that's their limit. I can't let it bother me. Why? Because I've got to concentrate all my energies on discovering what the meaning *is*.

Apropos of that, almost the first thing I stumbled upon, once I decided there was a meaning and I had to unlock it, was this little parcel of horror …

> ~~A clear sky and a full moon. The three of us came up from the valley through a birch wood along a broad, muddy path so scoured by the rain it had left knee-deep hollows in places. In the far west, a meteorite flared and fell. As we ascended, 'Lucy' and I somehow managed to pull ahead. We knew it wouldn't take long for 'Jack' to catch up, though, because we could see the underside of his swimma glowing through the trees, some way back. We stopped to wait for him, but he never arrived.~~

… on the top shelf of an unused reading room on the sixty-third floor of Garnol's Imperial Library. Almost indecipherable, yes, but it contains my name, and Lucy's, and describes an event at which I was allegedly present, but wasn't. Unsurprisingly – and I have this on the authority of the Chief Imperial Curator herself - nothing in the narrative is to be understood literally.

For a while, I thought I was making progress with it. It's a metaphorical wheel. A symbolic story in which I lose my friends – Lucy above all – and to whom I return, full circle, by means of an unsettling discovery in the Imperial Library. I lose them within the story; I'm later reunited with them, but somehow externalised: outside the story.

But deeper reflection persuaded me that couldn't be right, because then it wouldn't be a wheel, it would be a spiral. Because who's to say there's not some further stage where I'm 're-united' with Lucy by means of a text that depicts me reading the original text, and so on, *ad infinitum*?

Of course, there'd still be hope even then. You probably don't know much about spirals – I myself didn't until this – but of the many different types, one's the end of hope, the other isn't. The Archimedean spiral takes one further and further from the centre. But in the logarithmic version, there's a limit. The curve decreases until everything's enclosed in a circle and there's a path back to the hub.

It looked like I'd reached an impasse – reliable deductions, perhaps, yet impossibly abstract - when I began having these vivid dreams every time I got in the swimma.

Now obviously, everyone dreams in a swimma; that's not what I mean. These were *intense*. Dreams of Lucy. Except she always had these huge, round eyes, so big they left no room for anything you might call a face. Just watching me, without expression.

It took me a while to piece together what it meant, because she seemed to be trying to tell me something. Then one day, I realised. She was reading – *this*; these words I'm writing now! Just as I'd picked up the text about the ascent of that wooded hill in the Imperial Library, somehow she'd found a story about me and set about reading it. And she was trying to extricate me.

Anyway, I thought feverishly about how I might help her. There had to be some means, however cryptic.

In search of a 'key', I spent six weeks 'divining' in the deserts of Larnatal; I dived in Mantinark; I even went to one of those moons of Glauser for a 'consultation' … and you don't do that unless you're pretty much fixated. And all the time, every second: the feeling of those eyes, those big *eyes*, just watching me.

Then one day, the feeling just … disappeared. Maybe not so surprising, in retrospect. It was the time of year when all the swimmas go to sleep, and the sea and the sky susurrate and turn golden. Time stops.

*

"Lucy?" I whisper.

*

"Yes?"
Two voices. George. She's with George.

*

A clear sky and a full moon. The three of us come up from the valley through a birch wood along a broad, muddy path. In the far west, a meteorite flares and falls. As we ascend, Lucy and I pull ahead. But we know it won't take long for George to catch up. We stop to wait for him.

THE BALLAD OF SALLY L. HARVEY & MARTIN S. TAYLOR

Sally L. Harvey was lovely, he knew that, didn't everyone, but she'd said a bad thing. An unforgivable thing - if she'd actually said it. Something he'd never get over. Yes, yes, she might *not* have said it. Oh, she probably had, though. *Stop it! you're being a freak!* he told himself. But how *dare* he! How dare he call himself a freak when she probably *had* said it! Suddenly, he was almost crying. He didn't like himself sometimes, the way he talked to himself. He licked his thumb and carefully smoothed his eyebrows down.

Martin S. Taylor was sitting alone at a corner table in the Lancaster Arms with a half-empty pint of *Bishop's Finger* in front of him. Sally L. Harvey was due in ten minutes. His left hand was turning a beer-mat like a turbine powering an indignation even he could see was morbid. Someone unkind might have said he just wanted to see Sally L. Harvey again, that's why he'd supposedly 'taken umbrage' last night. Admittedly, with her radiant face, perfect teeth, spectacular black glasses, soft downy nasal hair, bony neck, and big hands, she was definitely worth seeing. But that … *thing* she'd said. No, it wasn't to be sniffed at, not in a month of Sundays. *If* she'd said it. She *had* said it!

Martin S. Taylor's newly-washed long hair, smart velvet jacket and ironed-with-a-crease chinos were all undermined by the things he couldn't change: his forward-facing ears, lopsided beard and deep-set eyes. He looked – his room-mate said before he went out - like a gorilla dressed up for blending in. But it didn't matter. At forty-four, he was about to stand up for his right not to be the butt of any more snide remarks. And that was an important matter. More important than 'blending in'. Much more.

Across the lounge, the fireplace looked his way with the expression of a shocked mouth. It was surrounded, in an accentuating circle, by antique brasses of different sizes and topped with a poster advertising today's gay pride march, due any time now along the seafront, two streets away (the Landlord had hoisted a 'Homosexuals Very Welcome' banner outside in the hope of drumming up extra custom). The carpet was dark and thin, the walls cream, the lighting subdued. Over at the bar, two men guarded a pair of lagers and a newspaper. A smell of frying onions came from the kitchen, presumably in readiness for lunchtime in about half an hour. One of the spotlights above the bar flickered.

Yet surely, they couldn't have been her words. The whole sentence was just too complicated. Four parts to it: '*Just about anyone you can think of*' - that was one; '*is better than you*' another; '*at just about anything*', and, finally, '*you'd choose to put your hand to*'. Four. She'd been talking fairly quickly, and they'd all been drinking. How likely was it she'd have been able to frame such a complicated sentence in one go, and he'd have understood it in one go? He must have reconfigured it somewhere along the line. He must have. And yet - what *had* she said?

The terrible thing was she had a whole three years on him. At forty-seven, she was bound to know which buttons to push to make a man wince and, more importantly, how to convincingly play the innocent afterwards. Yes, of course she was.

Two laughing young women, dressed as frogs, burst through the saloon doors, with a pair of amphibian heads hanging on the backs of their costumes like hoods. Their feet were webbed, forcing them to lift their strides as they walked, and their faces were green. The taller wore a pair of wrap-around sunglasses and a pink Alice band. The shorter one's bob shone in the style of conditioner adverts. The funereal atmosphere in the pub seemed to hit them like a wave of low pressure, and they stopped in their tracks and dropped their laughter on the floor where it was munched up by the worn carpet.

"I'll get the drinks," the taller one said, removing her sunglasses. "What are you having?"

"But he couldn't have meant what I thought he meant," the other replied. "Apple Spritzer, *s'il vous plait*. That would have been stupid."

"He *is* stupid. Apple Spritzer, yes? That's what you've got to take into account, Heather: he *is* stupid."

"I guess so, yes. No, I'll just have a lemonade on second thoughts," Heather said, reaching into her costume for a scratch. *"Une limonade!"* she exclaimed with a giggle, as if the whole of the French language was an opportunity for humour, no more.

"I think you deserve better."

"I know, Rosie, I know. He wasn't even at the march. I didn't see him, anyway. But then, he's big friends with that bitch Sally."

Martin S. Taylor sat up. *Sally!*

"How about a vodka, then?"

Heather laughed in surprise. "When you said, 'I think you deserve better', I thought you meant: better than Martin!"

Martin! Suddenly, he and the fireplace were bound in camaraderie, both dumbfounded. An over-reaction, for sure … but still! *But still!*

Rosie and Heather changed their minds about *une limonade* and decided to go to the Ladies instead. For one mad moment, he felt the urge to intercept them: to ask, what *about* Martin and Sally?

But then Sally L. Harvey herself came in, dangling her car keys on her thumb like someone not intending to stay. Her hair was drawn back in a ponytail that left her timid-looking expression and pale complexion quite bare. The black buttons of her red shirt were fastened all the way to her neck; her blue floral-print skirt was just long enough to sweep the floor; the shoelace of her left tennis shoe was broken.

Martin S. Taylor stood up. "Hello, Sally L. Harvey, how are you?"

"Fine," she replied tersely. "Look, I'm not staying. I know what this is about. No, I won't have a drink, no. I know what Alice M. Chambers has been telling you. She's trying to get us together, yes? Well, it won't work. I like you, Martin S. Taylor, of course I do, doesn't everyone, but it could never, ever succeed, not in a million, zillion years. It's not just that there's no spark, oh no, it's more than that. The truth is," she went on, swinging her hips like someone unsure whether to make this particular confession, "I don't really feel attracted to men, full stop. Full stop. I've just been outside, marching along with the gays, maybe that's why. Yes, you're quite a good catch. Or I suppose you would be, that is, if I liked that sort of thing. But I don't. *Full stop.* And that's all there is to it. There, I've said it. I've poured my heart out. Full stop." She let this news sink in. To break the silence, she whispered, "Full stop."

"Er, sorry I didn't know anything about that," Martin S. Taylor said eventually.

"What?"

"I didn't know anything about Alice M. Chambers trying to get us together."

"Hell. Oh, hell. Bloody hell."

"*Is* she?"

"Okay, just forget everything I said, okay? Yes, I know it's going to be a bit difficult, now it's all in the open. God, I'm a fool. Okay, take five, Sally L. Harvey, take five, don't be too hard on yourself, there's a sensible girl, it's not your fault, nothing is." She flapped her hands six centimetres before her face, as if the indignity of spontaneous human combustion might still be avoided. "Okay, okay, yes, it was a bit of a bombshell, maybe it was, I know, me standing in the middle of a pub, telling you I'm" – she used her fingers to make scare quotes - "'not attracted to men', and so on and so forth, but the thing is, and I'm absolutely convinced - "

"So *is* Alice M. Chambers trying to get us together? Are you sure?"

"Don't tell me you didn't at least suspect?"

"I *didn't* suspect! It wasn't about that, anyway."

"Well, what the hell was – *is* it about? Look, Martin S. Taylor, I'm busy. I thought this was about Alice M. Chambers trying to get us together. If it's about anything other than that, it must be about something less important. I haven't time for games. Spit it out on the carpet. Let's be having it, whatever it is. I'm busy."

The frogs suddenly came back from the toilet and sat down two tables away behind Sally L. Harvey's back, each with *une limonade*. Martin S. Taylor could hear them continuing their conversation about other-Martin and other-Sally.

"I wanted to ask you whether you said ..." he began – he could feel himself beginning to blush – "... I mean, did you say, last night ..."

"Did I say what?"

"Oh, it doesn't matter."

"Tell me, Martin S. Taylor," she demanded. "I want to know."

The blush had reached the tips of his beard-hair. "Well, since you insist. Did you say: 'Just about anyone you can think of, is better than you at just about anything you'd choose to put your hand to'?"

"What?"

"'Just about anyone you can think of, is better than you at just about anything you'd choose to put your hand to'," he repeated super-quickly.

"I don't even know what that means. Say it again ... slow-ly."

'Just about anyone you can think of..."

"Yes?"

"Is better than you ..."

"Mm-hm?"

"At just about anything ... you'd choose to put your hand to."

She pinched her chin. "Is that it?"

He nodded.

She sighed and flapped her hands at her face again. "Well, no, I didn't say that, actually, Martin S. Taylor. No, I certainly didn't. So, I've just had a wasted journey, haven't I? Do you know how much petrol costs, nowadays, Martin S. Taylor? Do you? *Do* you? *One pound bloody ninety-one a bloody gallon, that's how much!* And you make me come out here - *why?* So you can ask me if I said, 'Just about everyone anyone thinks of is better than anyone everyone thinks of'? Are you *insane?* No, I didn't say that! *Why would I? Bloody hell, Martin S. Taylor!*"

"Sorry."

"Sorry isn't good enough!"

Martin S. Taylor reached in his pocket and took out a handful of change. He fished out a pound coin, a fifty, two twenties and a penny, and put them, one item at a time, on the table. "Sorry," he repeated.

"That's better," she said, calming down as quickly as she'd flared up. She scraped the money into her palm and put it in her pocket.

"Would you like a drink?" he asked.

"Providing I don't have to talk to you. I might as well get *something* out of today."

"What are you having?"

"I'm driving. It'll have to be a lemonade."

He switched his eyebrows to 'sophisticated + urbane' and smiled. *"Une limonade?"*

"Shut up. Just get me the drink."

He went to the bar and leaned in a puddle of lager. Behind him, he could hear the frogs laughing and hooting, obviously having a really good time. He looked surreptitiously at Sally L. Harvey. A rain cloud had gathered over her and she was looking disconsolately at her feet. Maybe she was working out how to do something about her broken shoelace.

"Dave! Customer!" shouted one of the two men at the bar. "Seventeen across," he murmured to his friend. "Eleventh century inventor of the first geared clock. Three, six, two, six. Second letter's a 'b'."

"Ibn Khalaf al-Muradi," his friend said.

The landlord appeared from the dark nether-land behind the bar. His polo shirt and black beltless trousers had obviously been selected to complement the carpet. He walked with a limp and smelt of frying onions and sesame oil. He dried his hands languidly on a tea towel.

"What can I get you for, squire?" he said.

"Two lemonades, please," Martin S. Taylor replied, doing his best to be equally cheery.

The landlord took two bottles of Schweppes and a pair of glasses from beneath the counter. He half-filled each glass and set the bottles beside them. "Ice and lemon with that?"

The question caught Martin S. Taylor unawares. "I, er – yes – yes, I will," he said, knowing there wasn't sufficient time to think about it. He was among men now. He had to be decisive.

But what if Sally L. Harvey didn't like ice and lemon? That would be disastrous. She'd go mad.

Yet it was too late now. "One-seventy," the landlord said.

"Is it possible to – um – have a hankie with it?" he asked.

"A … *hankie?*" The landlord paused. He looked up, as if peering inside his own head for confirmation. "You mean *a handkerchief?*"

"I was just thinking: my friend … might not like ice and lemon, after all, and, if not … she could fish it out, and put it on the handkerchief. Maybe."

The landlord looked like the fireplace.

"I mean, she probably *will*," Martin S. Taylor said. "Like it, I mean. It *is* nice. *I* like it, obviously."

"She could put it in the ashtray if she doesn't like it," one of the two men behind him said.

"We don't have ashtrays anymore," the landlord said bitterly. "It's all no bloody smoking now." He sighed and something inside him seemed to collapse. "Look, I'll get you a fingerbowl from out the back. Wait there."

Listening to the two frogs laughing again, Martin S. Taylor began to feel depressed. It was as if he was stuck in a turgid little pool of deep seriousness, and over there, where the frogs were, was a sparkling little pool of happy frivolity. Grey, sticky, tired dejection, versus carefree delight: the very essence of The Good Life personified by two middle-class frogs with *limonades*.

Ideally, he'd have liked to join them, but he didn't know how to go about it. Offer to buy them another drink, maybe? He knew from past experience that wouldn't work. They were dressed as frogs. He'd get it wrong. He'd probably ask if he could buy them a fly. No, he was better off sticking with Sally L. Harvey.

The landlord returned with a fingerbowl on a tray. Next to it stood a Whittard's tea infuser: two little wire mesh hemispheres clasped together by a spring-operated handle. "I thought she could use that to get the ice and lemon out," he said.

One of the two men with the crossword looked across and shook his head. "I would have thought a slotted spoon might be better. What on earth's that?"

"How the hell are you going to fit a slotted spoon in a glass that size?" the landlord replied. "You'd never get it past the rim."

"Ice and lemon float. You'd just have to skim the surface."

The landlord turned on Martin S. Taylor. "Which one would *you* prefer then?"

"I don't mind," Martin S. Taylor said. "Whatever's best."

"I'd go for the slotted spoon," the man at the bar said.

Martin S. Taylor shrugged. "I'll take the slotted spoon, please."

The landlord swore under his breath. He picked up the tea infuser and limped back into the kitchen.

"Eleven down," said the man at the bar. "A device for showing moving pictures. Stands in the corner of most living rooms, only not so much in the developing world. Two letters. Begins with a 't' … if we've got six across right."

The landlord returned with a slotted spoon and banged it down on the tray. "One-sodding-seventy."

Martin S. Taylor reached into his pocket and pulled out a handful of change. He picked out a pound coin and four twenties, and put them on the bar one by one.

He should really thank the landlord for going beyond the call of duty. "Keep the change," he said.

He picked up the tray and went back to Sally L. Harvey. But she wasn't there. Which probably meant she'd gone home in her car. On the plus side, though, he now had two lemonades to himself. He sat down.

But after he'd been sitting there no more than ten seconds, he heard a 'Pssst!', like air being let out of a tyre.

He ignored it.

But then it happened again.

He tried to ignore it again.

Then it happened a third time.

Whatever it was, it seemed to be coming from behind the concrete pillar on the other side of the pub. Was someone trying to attract his attention, perhaps? It seemed unlikely. He didn't know anyone here.

None the less, he should probably investigate, just to be on the safe side.

But what if someone stole his lemonade while he was investigating? What if that's what it was? A trick? To make matters worse: what if Sally L. Harvey hadn't gone home at all? What if she'd just gone to the toilet? And what if she came back from the toilet, after the lemonades had been stolen, and went, *Where's my drink, Martin S. Taylor? You promised me a lemonade. Where is it?* What would he say?

There was another 'Pssst!'

The situation was becoming unbearable now. He could feel himself becoming upset. Another few minutes and he'd be welling up.

Just as it seemed things couldn't get any worse, he had an idea. He could walk over to the pillar backwards. That way he could keep an eye on the lemonades. If anyone did steal them, he could describe them to the police.

It took him exactly forty seconds, but when he reached the pillar and looked behind it, there, amazingly, was Sally L. Harvey. She sat on the floor hugging her knees to her face and shivering. She'd taken her glasses off. Her eyes were bloodshot and wet, and her cheeks were shiny where tears had obviously run down and she'd wiped them away. She sniffed. When she saw him, her eyes opened wide, and she grabbed him and pulled him down. He almost fell on top of her.

"What's the matter?" he asked.

She opened her mouth to speak, but nothing came out. She tried again.

"I'll go and get our lemonades," he said.

Before she could stop him, he'd gone back, picked up the tray and returned. She grabbed her lemonade and raised it, shaking, to her mouth. It seemed to revive her slightly.

"What's this?" she whispered, indicating the fingerbowl and the slotted spoon.

"I thought you might not like ice and lemon. I thought you could take them out if you didn't."

For a moment, she looked even more emotional than she had when he'd first come over. *"Thank you!"* she said, as if she couldn't imagine anyone else treating her with more consideration. She seized the slotted spoon and began frantically skimming off the ice and lemon and transferring it to the fingerbowl. Then she took another sip, squirting the lemonade into her cheeks with her tongue, then into her mouth again with her cheeks, then back into her cheeks with her tongue, and so on, until it was thoroughly warmed up and flat, and she could swallow it without fear of catching a cold or burping.

"So, what's the matter, Sally L. Harvey?" he asked, tasting his own lemonade.

Her eyes glazed over.

"I won't tell anyone," he promised.

"We're both going to - *die!*" She tried to say it collectedly, but on the word 'die', her voice cracked and she began to sob again, silently. Martin S. Taylor put his arm round her and put his own lemonade to her lips. She drank, swilled and swallowed, drank swilled and swallowed, gradually calming down as this new batch of lemonade worked its way into her system. "Those two - *things!*" she said, at last. She was jabbing her finger in their direction.

"The frogs?"

She looked at him in amazement. "*Frogs?* Martin S. Taylor, they're not *frogs!* Why would you say that? Frogs are about *this big!*" She made a 'U' with her thumb and index finger and held it four centimetres in front of his eyes. "And frogs are wet, and they go 'croak, croak' – maybe not like that: that was a frog from a children's storybook: more like this: 'Ark, ark' – a bit more glottal, I don't know. And they crawl about on their stomachs and live in ponds. They don't come into pubs and talk about – and talk about - "

"Maybe they're people dressed as frogs. That was my thinking."

"Oh, right," she said. "Oh, right. Oh, of course. Yes, right. *That's* likely, of course it is. Why didn't I think of that? Oh, what a fool I've been. They're not *people*, Martin S. Taylor!"

"What are they, then?"

"If you can't work it out for yourself, I'm certainly not going to tell you."

"Please."

"No. We've got to get out of here. Is there a back way?"

"I should think so."

"We've got to get to my car."

"Why?"

"*Because!* Listen, I heard them talking. They were talking about *us!*"

"Yes, I know. But I thought they were talking about another Sally and another Martin."

"You *knew?*"

"Yes, but I thought it was about another Sally and another Martin."

"My God."

"What did they say?"

She swallowed, hard. "Listen, Martin S. Taylor, before I tell you. All that stuff I said earlier about not being attracted to men, and how we could never get together in a million, zillion years: it was all lies. I love you, Martin S. Taylor. I always have, I always will. It's no use fighting it any more. If we ever get out of this alive, I want us to get married and have four children, two of each. I wasn't marching along with the gays earlier. I don't even know what a gay looks like. I just said that to throw you off the scent."

Martin S. Taylor lit up. "I've also been fighting an unsuccessful battle against our fate, for what it's worth. In fact, if it hadn't been *you* that said, 'Just about everyone anyone thinks of is better than anyone everyone thinks of', I don't think I'd have been remotely upset."

"But we established I *didn't* say it."

"Hypothetically, I meant. Wow, is Alice M. Chambers going to be pleased!"

"Is that a yes?"

"It completely is!"

"Good. To business, then."

"What did they say?"

"They said, *I'm going to kill Sally when I see her. I mean it, I'm not joking. And as for Martin, you don't even want to know what I'm going to do to him.* That's word-for-word what they said!"

Martin S. Taylor felt the blood drain from his face. "Bloody hell."

"Exactly. We've got to get to my car."

"And go where?"

"Anywhere. Abroad. How much money have you got?"

"Four pounds sixty-seven."

"One pound ninety-one into four pounds sixty-seven," she said. "That's two-point-four-four-five-zero gallons. But wait! I've also got the one pound ninety-one you gave me earlier, plus three pounds twenty-four I picked up before I left home this morning. And I'm sure there's a two pence piece in the glove compartment. That means we've got nine pounds eighty-four altogether. So we can afford … hang on … five-point-one-five-one gallons. Although I don't know offhand how many petrol stations round here have pumps with that sort of accuracy."

"We'll cross that bridge when we come to it. How many miles to the gallon does your car do?"

"Good question. Thirty-six-point-one. So, thirty-six-point-one multiplied by five-point-one-five-one. That's one hundred and eighty-five-point-nine-eight-one miles. How far is it to Dover?"

"From here? I don't know. I could ask at the bar if they've got an atlas."

"Are you mad? It's a miracle the - *things* haven't spotted you already!"

"If it's more than a hundred and eighty-five-point-nine-eight-one miles, we could walk the rest of the way."

"I don't want to leave my car, Martin S. Taylor. I love it."

"What sort of a car is it?"

"A yellow one. We could go to Roxforth Manor, in Surrey." She spoke with the quiet determination of someone forcing her words out. "I really don't want to, though. It would have to be a last resort. We could, say, go up to the house, and maybe have a look through the windows at night, and see if Mummy's actually … *changed* yet." She went purple and retched. "Sorry, sorry. Daddy keeps writing to me, begging me to go back. But he's probably been infected as well by now. But if we look through the windows … we might …" She retched again.

"Okay. Stay there. I'll go and see if there's a back way out of the pub."

"Don't leave me, Martin S. Taylor. I'm frightened."

"Okay, let's go together." He grabbed her hand and pulled her to her feet, being careful to hug the pillar so the Things wouldn't see them. "Let's go through there," he said, pointing to a mysterious black door directly before them.

A moment later, they found themselves in a large, empty kitchen with several white stoves against the wall – each with a frying pan of steaming onions - a washing machine with its door open, and a large stainless-steel sink and drainer full of dirty plates. Above the sink there was a large frosted window. Martin S. Taylor hastily unlatched it and helped Sally L. Harvey up onto the sink. She was nearly outside when the landlord came in.

"What the - bloody *hell?*" he exclaimed. He stopped in his tracks.

"We were just looking for an atlas," Martin S. Taylor lied.

"*Come on!*" Sally L. Harvey shouted. She was through now.

Conveniently, the landlord turned and hurried back the way he'd come. Martin S. Taylor climbed onto the sink and calmly slotted himself through the window-frame. A moment later, they were sitting side by side in Sally L Harvey's yellow car.

"Check the glove compartment!" she said.

The two-pence piece was still there. Martin S. Taylor took it out and held it up for her to see. It glinted magically in the sun.

"I love you, Martin S. Taylor," she said.

He noticed she'd never looked so beautiful before. Her teeth gleamed in the sunshine, her skin was as smooth and shiny as a six-centimetre section of bath enamel, her hair was like a scallop shell, and even her clothes looked newly ironed.

They kissed, and their entire future flashed before their eyes. How they'd marry & be blissfully happy & she'd be eternally beautiful & he'd be forever 'the handsome one' & they'd live in a Georgian mansion on the far side of Brighton with four children & a Wheaten Terrier called Tony Feather & how they'd become international figureheads in the fight against globalisation & objectification & alien invasion & not even the Second Coming would be able to faze them because as long as their love lasted - and it would last forever! - they simply couldn't be fazed, full stop. *Full stop!*

As they pulled out of the car park, they looked back at the pub. In the quaint lead-latticed window, they could see the thwarted, ugly faces of the two Things, like medieval gargoyles everlastingly crushed by St. Michael and his angels.

Martin S. Taylor wound down the window and let out a 'Yippee!' as the wind caught in his lopsided beard. Sally L. Harvey threw her head back modishly and began to laugh. They looked exultantly at each other, unable to believe their luck.

Then she tightened her grip on the steering wheel, parp-parped the horn and put her foot down on the accelerator.

BOOKS BY JAMES WARD

General Fiction
The House of Charles Swinter
The Weird Problem of Good
The Bright Fish
*Hannah and Soraya's Fully Magic Generation-Y *Snowflake* Road Trip across America*

The Original Tales of MI7
Our Woman in Jamaica
The Kramski Case
The Girl from Kandahar
The Vengeance of San Gennaro

The John Mordred Tales of MI7 books
The Eastern Ukraine Question
The Social Magus
Encounter with ISIS
World War O
The New Europeans
Libya Story
Little War in London
The Square Mile Murder
The Ultimate Londoner
Death in a Half Foreign Country
The BBC Hunters
The Seductive Scent of Empire
Humankind 2.0
Ruby Parker's Last Orders

Poetry
The Latest Noel
Metals of the Future

Short Stories
An Evening at the Beach
Wadhurst Ghost Stories

Philosophy
21st Century Philosophy
A New Theory of Justice and Other Essays

Lightning Source UK Ltd.
Milton Keynes UK
UKHW011958160921
390713UK00008B/485/J